"You think the death squad will risk an attack in the forest?"

"Oh, they'll be coming," Mack Bolan replied. "Your people are an obstacle, and worse than that, you kicked their butt last night. There's payback coming, and I'd say sooner rather than later."

"You're right," Reese said. "We'd better prepare."

There was no doubt in the Executioner's mind that the death squad was coming. He knew the men they'd be facing—not their names or faces, but the way they thought, their need to punish even minimal resistance with a crushing show of force. They would be eager to avenge their fallen comrades, reaffirm their own machismo with a ruthless massacre.

He knew the type, and he was ready, long before he heard the helicopters coming from the east.

DON PENDLETON's
MACK BOLAN®
JUNGLE LAW

A GOLD EAGLE BOOK FROM
WORLDWIDE®

TORONTO • NEW YORK • LONDON
AMSTERDAM • PARIS • SYDNEY • HAMBURG
STOCKHOLM • ATHENS • TOKYO • MILAN
MADRID • WARSAW • BUDAPEST • AUCKLAND

First edition April 1996

ISBN 0-373-61447-0

Special thanks and acknowledgment to
Mike Newton for his contribution to this work.

JUNGLE LAW

Printed in U.S.A.

Greed is a bottomless pit which exhausts the person in an endless effort to satisfy the need without ever reaching satisfaction.

—Erich Fromm

Greed has no limit, but there comes a time when someone has to stand and say "Enough!" The time is now, the place is here, and God help anyone who doesn't get the word.

—Mack Bolan

It was a miracle of sorts that anyone survived the crash. The Embraer EMB-120 had been cruising at an altitude of fifteen thousand feet when the explosion ripped through its cargo hold and brought the sleek bird down. Unfortunately for the man who built the bomb, the dynamite he'd used was old and unreliable. Three of the seven sticks were total duds, and so the aircraft with its twenty-seven passengers wasn't destroyed outright.

Still, it was bad enough.

The blast killed three and maimed two others who would surely die. Explosive decompression rendered several more unconscious as the plane nosed over in a steep dive toward the earth below. The tail assembly was a write-off—no more elevators, no more rudder—but the pilot saved them with a Herculean effort, hauling backward on the yoke until he thought the wings would be ripped off, flaps sluggish in response but getting there at last. The plane had dropped eleven thousand feet before it leveled off, and there was still no way to keep it airborne in the long run, even with the Pratt & Whitney turboprops at full rev, sucking fuel like there was no tomorrow.

Which, Lorenzo Alegrete told himself, was more or less the truth.

In moments they had dropped to treetop level, still two hundred feet or so above the ground but falling rapidly. It was impossible to stay aloft, so the pilot started looking for a place to crash-land, any kind of open space at all. There was none to be found, however, and he lost control in the trees, three minutes after the explosion.

It was the treetop crash that saved their lives. The trees acted as a cushion when the aircraft hit, and the Embraer hung up in the branches of one forest giant after clipping several others. A dive straight in would certainly have finished everyone on board, but lurching, while far from pleasant, was at least a gentler ride.

Alegrete was unscathed, and therein lay delicious irony, for he was certain he had been the bomber's target. It was always possible that someone else aboard the plane had homicidal enemies, of course, but he was no believer in coincidence. His mission, and the haste in which he had departed Rio de Janeiro, would have been enough to make his adversaries reckless, drive them to extremes.

As if the bastards needed an excuse.

Three dead and two more on the way, because of him. It left a sour taste in Alegrete's mouth, but he refused to shoulder the responsibility for someone else's crime. His mission was designed to stop them, after all, prevent more killing and restore some measure of humanity to modern-day Brazil. It was a testimony to the times they lived in, Alegrete thought, that men of wealth and influence would vote to kill two dozen perfect strangers simply to ensure his silence.

And his enemies had failed, at that.

He stood back from the twisted wreckage of the plane and knew it could have been much worse. A fire would probably have killed them all before they reached the forest floor, but it had rained since they came down, and he had no more fear in that regard. They could do little for the injured where they were, but once again the bad news had a bright side: only half a dozen of the passengers and crew had suffered injuries severe enough to stop their walking out in search of help. The dead would have to wait, and they could always leave someone behind to watch the bodies, keep the forest scavengers at bay until help arrived.

The jungle was a problem, certainly, but once again he reckoned they were fortunate. Bahia Province had its share of wilderness, and he was looking at some now, but it was nothing to the obstacles they would have faced in Amazonas or the Mato Grosso. Here a man who kept his wits about him, watching out for snakes and such, could reach the highway linking Salvador with Jacobina and Juàzeiro, to the north. With any luck at all, they might flag down a ride before the unofficial search began.

For Alegrete knew that someone would be coming after him. They had to verify the kill, make sure he was forever silent and retrieve the documents he carried with him. The pilot would have beamed a Mayday signal once he got the aircraft leveled off to some extent, and those who wanted Alegrete dead would have no trouble learning the coordinates. A few *cruzeiros* in the right hands, and a hit team could be on its way while the police were trying to recruit a pilot for the search.

How long? He checked his wristwatch, calculating it had been three-quarters of an hour since they fell to earth. His head still ached from banging on the seat in front of him, but headaches were a part of life. He wasn't dizzy, had no double vision, and his limbs were sound. If necessary, he would walk all night and all day tomorrow to prevent his enemies from winning.

The others seemed inclined to take their time recuperating, several nursing injuries that would have seemed inconsequential under different circumstances. That was shock, he realized, and the proximity of sudden death. Survivors frequently reported feeling guilty in a situation such as this, ashamed of the relief that came with living through a near-catastrophe. Some compensated by exaggerating minor aches and pains, as if to share the suffering of those with major injuries and thus assuage their guilt. Whatever the explanation, Alegrete knew it could be hours yet before the rest of them were ready to hike out. And as the day wore on, the threat of nightfall in the jungle would discourage most from trying it at all before the following day.

He couldn't afford to wait.

How could he warn the others, make them understand the danger they were facing through inaction? Would they take his word that he had been the target of the bomb—and if they did, what then? For all he knew, they might react with violence, gleefully avenge themselves on one who held himself responsible for their predicament. In that case, he would be no better off than if he sat and waited for the hunters to arrive.

He had to try, in any case.

"Please listen."

Parched and weary, he could barely hear himself. He cleared his throat to try again.

"Please listen to me."

Slowly, grudgingly the others broke off conversations, turning toward the sound of Alegrete's voice. A few looked curious, a few resentful. Most were simply waiting, maybe hopeful that he would have some idea for hastening their nightmare to a close.

"We shouldn't stay here," Alegrete told them when he had their full attention. "We can walk out to the highway, find some help."

"You know which way to go?" an older, balding man inquired.

"I do," said Alegrete, pointing. "That way."

"Why?" A woman asked the question, curious and vaguely hostile all at once.

"The highway should be east of us," he answered. "It is past noon, and the sun is moving westward. If we walk due east—"

"What sun?" a young man interrupted. "All these trees around, don't tell me you can see the sun."

He had a point, but Alegrete couldn't let it go. "It doesn't have to be precise," he said. "The highway runs from Salvador up to Juàzeiro, right across the province, north and south. Keep moving westward, and a blind man couldn't miss it."

"Not if he was going west, perhaps," the young man said, "but surely if he turned himself around somehow, he would be lost."

"Why can't we just wait here?" An older woman posed the question, dabbing with a tissue at a cut along her hairline. "They'll be looking for us, won't they?"

"They may not come."

"Not come!" The young man who had challenged him before was fairly sneering now. "Why not?"

"Suppose they didn't hear the pilot's signal," Alegrete said, "or the coordinates were garbled in transmission. They could start the search a thousand miles from here. It could be days before they find us."

"They'll be looking for the plane, though, won't they?" a young brunette asked. "I mean, they won't expect a lot of people wandering around the jungle."

"I think—"

"Let's ask the pilot," said the young man with the attitude. "He's still in charge, according to the law."

The pilot wasn't talking, though; his lower face was distorted, swollen and discolored like a freakish eggplant. He made a show of listening before another wave of pain kicked in and left him moaning incoherently. The copilot, for his part, was unconscious at the moment, and the young man's effort to revive him was a waste of time.

"We ought to light a fire," a woman declared. "When they come looking for us, they will see the smoke."

"She's right," somebody else put in. "A signal fire."

"But," Alegrete said, "the longer we stay here—"

"The better chance we have of being rescued," the young man said, interrupting him once more. "Somebody help me build a fire. Who has a lighter? Matches?"

Alegrete gave it up. He recognized that he wouldn't be able to convince them now, and he would have to go alone if he was going. When he thought about it in that light, himself alone against the forest, he had less enthusiasm for the project. He had nothing in the way of weapons, no way to produce a fire when darkness fell. He would be helpless, at the mercy of the forest predators.

A boy of eight or nine, the only child among them, had begun to gather kindling when he stopped and asked the group at large, "What if the smoke brings Indians?"

"There are no Indians in Bahia," a man of middle years replied. "The government got rid of them."

Their minds at ease on that score, the survivors set about collecting firewood with a vengeance. It was something they could do, instead of sitting idly by and hoping for a rescue that might never come. If nothing else, it occupied their hands and minds, a kind of therapy.

Within ten minutes they had gathered enough wood to build a bonfire five or six feet high, most of it laid aside while some of them got busy with the kindling. They had trouble lighting it at first, since there was no such thing as dry wood in the forest, but they got it started after several anxious moments, with some crumpled newspaper one of them found inside the plane.

The damp wood gave them smoke, all right, but it kept shifting with the restless breeze, so the campers dabbed teary eyes and moved frequently to seek clean air. A couple of the men were cursing now each time the acrid smoke came back to find them, and it brought a smile to Alegrete's lips. So much for "roughing it," when most of them had never spent a night away from indoor plumbing and electricity in their lives.

It didn't seem that any of the smoke would reach the treetops, much less summon help from miles away, but Alegrete worried all the same. His enemies wouldn't rely on smoke signals if they had the pilot's last coordinates, but any little thing could help them find the crash site, make it easier for them to track him down.

"I hear an airplane!" the boy declared.

In fact, Alegrete thought when his ears picked up the distant sound, it was a helicopter, flying low, inbound from the southeast. One aircraft, by the sound of it, but one would be enough. If his suspicions were correct, they had no need of room for extra passengers.

"We're saved!" one of the older women said before they even glimpsed the helicopter. Most of them were on their feet now, capering about or slapping backs and shaking hands as if some effort of their own had brought the miracle about.

Alegrete also rose and picked up his briefcase, but instead of moving toward the plane, he edged a little farther from the campfire, seeking out the forest shadows. If it was a rescue ship, all well and good. If not...

The chopping sound of rotors was directly overhead now. Alegrete couldn't see the helicopter and doubted whether any of them could, but they were waving, calling out as if the chopper's crew could hear them over all that engine noise two hundred feet away.

Relief washed over Alegrete as the helicopter gunned its engines and kept on going in a general northerly direction. Several of his fellow passengers were shouting curses now, two of the women weeping openly.

"They left us," the boy said. "Why would they leave?"

"Don't worry," the young man replied, continuing his role as self-appointed spokesman for the group. "They'll soon come back."

"They couldn't land here, anyway," one of the women said. "They have to find a clearing for the rescue team."

Alegrete worried that she could be right. Suppose his enemies *were* in the helicopter and they *had* made out the wreckage down below. The hit team would re-

quire a landing field, somewhere close by. Hike back
from there and finish it.

He tried to tell himself that he was being paranoid,
but he couldn't escape the nagging sense of dread that
settled on him like a clinging shroud. If he was wrong,
so much the better. He would start again from Salvador and pray for better luck. He had a passport waiting for him in São Luis, and from there his way was
clear to Puerto Rico, on to the United States.

Alegrete trusted the Americans—some of them,
anyway. When they had seen his evidence, they would
be forced to act, at least through diplomatic channels. With Brazil's strong dependence on American
markets and foreign aid, a little pressure from Washington could go a long way toward putting things
right.

Another forty minutes ticked away, and Alegrete
had almost convinced himself that they were safe,
when once again the boy's sharp ears picked up a
sound the rest of them had missed.

"They're coming back!" he said excitedly.

Lorenzo strained his ears for any sound of helicopter engines, but the sky was silent overhead. He
glanced back at the boy and found him pointing toward the forest, north and east, beyond the crumpled
wreckage of their plane. Another moment, and they
all heard voices, several men who took no pains to
camouflage their progress.

Unobserved by his companions, Alegrete rose and
slipped into the shadows, tried to make himself invisible. Unless they had the camp surrounded, which he

deemed improbable, the new arrivals would be visible to him before they had a chance to count heads in the makeshift camp, much less select one passenger from the assembly. If they came in peace, as rescuers, there would be ample time for Alegrete to reveal himself. But if his darkest fears were realized . . .

He waited, sweating through his ruined sport shirt, clinging to the briefcase with a grip of steel. Behind him he had marked a narrow game trail through the trees. It wasn't much, but if he had to run, at least it offered something in the nature of a chance.

The arrogant young man was moving forward, one arm raised to greet the new arrivals, calling out a welcome. Alegrete had a glimpse of figures moving through the shadows, well beyond the plane, but he couldn't make out their faces or the clothes they wore. One of them called back to the young man, sounding cheery, and Alegrete felt himself beginning to relax.

The shooting started seconds later, with a short burst from some kind of automatic weapon. He could see the muzzle-flash from where he stood, and watched the young man stagger, going over backward like a cardboard cutout in the breeze. He fell without a sound, twitched once, then lay still.

The other crash survivors froze for one long moment, gaping at the body, then the raiders opened fire in unison and everybody scattered, seeking cover. Alegrete left them to their own devices, turned and ran like hell to save himself.

The sound of gunfire seemed to last forever, but he understood that only moments passed between the first shots and the last. He hesitated for a heartbeat in the sudden, ringing silence, but his fear came back at once, propelling him onward through the shadows.

They were bound to have a photograph or a description of their target, orders to retrieve the evidence he carried. Still, it would take time for them to count the bodies, check each face and realize their man wasn't among the dead. With that decision made, they would be stalking him again.

How long before they found him in the forest? Were they jungle trackers or the standard urban gunmen of the death squads? With the latter, Alegrete thought, he just might have a chance, however slim. But if they had real hunters on his trail, he was as good as dead.

He could only do his best, and that meant running until his heart exploded in his chest, resisting if they overtook him. He wouldn't surrender now, when he had come this far and left so many souls depending on him as their last real hope.

And there was Juliana.

If he failed, what would become of her? How could his enemies allow her to survive?

He found new energy in fear and fury, running like a man whose life depended on it. Nothing mattered but survival and the success of Alegrete's mission to America. His focus narrowed to a single point on the horizon, and determination drove him on.

Behind him, less than fifteen minutes later, the assassins found his trail and started double-timing after him, due west.

CHAPTER ONE

Cinelândia, the giant public square in downtown Rio de Janeiro, is a major draw for tourists in the daytime, when its myriad shops are open, selling everything from emeralds to "native" art. Mosaic sidewalks, smiling merchants and the climate that makes Rio famous lure shoppers from around the world and empty their wallets with a modicum of style.

It is a different story after dark, however, when the metal shutters fall on doors and windows, locking out the night. Shop owners make for home, and tourists who are wise will follow their example, seek diversion elsewhere.

For those who never seem to get the word, however—and for those who seek a special kind of entertainment in the city—Cinelândia is capable of dishing up surprises after dark. A lonely visitor with cash in hand can buy companionship—male, female, even children, if the price is right. Drugs are available in quantity and in varieties that would embarrass the police, if they weren't already paid to look the other way.

Nocturnal browsers take their chances on the streets of Cinelândia. They are as likely to be raped, robbed, beaten, even killed as to enjoy themselves with secret vices. Some of those who prey on nighttime visitors to Cinelândia are certainly adults, with years of prison time behind them, but increasingly the predators are children, working by themselves or running in voracious packs that scandalize—and sometimes terrorize—the neighborhood.

They are *meniños de rua,* literally "children of the street," and while such waifs have been familiar sights in most Brazilian cities for the best part of a century, their character—and the response evoked—has changed in recent years. Once regarded merely as a nuisance, pests equivalent to rats and roaches, the Brazilian street kids lately have been blamed for rising crime rates in the cities, targeted by civic leaders and police for street sweeps, beatings, even vigilante action by the death squads that have scourged Brazil since World War II.

Living on the street was not Jeremy Huxford's idea of a good time, and he certainly didn't fit the general mold of Brazilian street kids. For starters, he wasn't Brazilian, but rather the son of a deputy cultural attaché at the American Embassy in Rio. Running away from home—or what passed for home these days— had been a last resort, what his counselor in D.C. would have called a "cry for help." He didn't know about the psychobabble, but the move had been designed to get attention, and in that regard it was successful to a fault.

He was getting all kinds of attention these days, and the irony was that it might get him killed.

The custody battle between his parents had dragged on for the year and a half since they'd split. His father had the edge, with his connections in the government, access to high-priced lawyers who had decades of experience in laying down a smoke screen. When his mother caught a break in court, the next step was a transfer out of country, to Brazil, in fact, where distance complicated everything.

It wasn't that he hated living with his dad exactly, but for Jeremy the foreign posting meant a life of fending for himself and passing more or less unnoticed ... unless he did something wrong. There was a staff to clean up after him around the embassy, of course; it wasn't as if he had to cook and clean or anything like that, but there was definitely something missing from his life. The bitterness between his parents tainted every conversation with his father, ruined everything, and when he spoke of going back to the United States, the old man pitched a fit.

So he had run away and hung out with friends he had acquired in Cinelândia when the old man and his watchdogs weren't looking. Jeremy had money for a while, but he had shared it with his friends, and in a few days it was gone. The stealing didn't bother him so much; he told himself the shops and markets gouged their customers in any case, and they were certainly insured. It was a kick at first, though he had definitely missed his bed when it was time to curl up on the sidewalk, using cardboard or a piece of moldy rubber as a sleeping pallet.

Still, sleeping out was one thing; being hunted down like an animal was something else.

He had expected something in the way of hassles from the cops, a roust from time to time, but they were killing people on the streets of Cinelândia these days. It wasn't an official policy, as far as Huxford could tell—why would they dress in black, with ski masks, if they had no fear of retribution?—but he didn't see the government expending any energy to stop the death squads, either. Every morning brought some new report of street kids beaten, terrorized, gunned down by roving gangs of adults that appeared wherever homeless children congregated, leaving bodies in their wake.

He had been lucky so far, missing all the heavy action, though a couple of his friends weren't so fortunate. Arturo had been clubbed and slashed with razors two weeks earlier, but his attackers let him live for reasons none of the street kids could understand. A few days later Dulcinea had been raped and shot by three men old enough to be her father. And just two nights before, a gang of masked men in a jeep had opened up with automatic weapons on a group of sleeping children: three were dead or dying when the smoke cleared, half a dozen others badly wounded.

Jeremy was scared—no doubt about it. He considered giving up and going home at least a hundred times a day, but he wasn't that desperate yet. Most children are invulnerable in their own minds, far too quick and clever for their enemies.

This night, a Thursday, he was crashing with a dozen others in an alley on the north side of the square, between a bakery and a jewelry store. The smell of baking bread would wake him in the morning, and they had a chance of begging breakfast from the baker's wife if they looked pitiful enough.

No problem there. He didn't like to think about how long he had been forced to go without a bath, or what he smelled like in his grubby clothes. That was a problem for another day.

Right now he had to concentrate on getting through the night alive.

He heard the jeep before he saw it, engine revving, driving with the lights off to secure a measure of surprise. The squealing brakes were like a fire alarm to his companions. Children were on their feet and scattering on instinct, some of them still half-asleep.

At first he thought the pricks were throwing fireworks as a joke to get the street kids running, but a second later he heard bullets snapping overhead, a harsh, insectile sound that set his teeth on edge.

He focused all his energy on forward motion, sprinting through the littered alley, well aware that he was running for his life.

MACK BOLAN HAD the walkie-talkie in his hand before the jeep completed half a circuit of the square. It could be nothing, but he didn't like the odds. A carload of gorillas running dark in Cinelândia meant trouble of the killing kind, and he didn't appreciate the new twist in his plan.

In fact the timing sucked.

Ideally Bolan would have liked to make the lift without armed opposition, drop the youngster off and go about his business, but it wouldn't be that easy now. The embassy and Orson Huxford had some competition from a wild card that had turned up in the game.

He thumbed the red Send button and said, "We've got a problem."

"I'm on top of it," a male voice told him, speaking from across the square. "Just say the word."

"I'm getting there," another voice added. "Let's not be hasty, people."

"You need a roadblock, let me know," a third voice said.

The men of Able Team were standing by, their presence helping Bolan face the prospect of the set unraveling before his eyes. It should have been no chore to lift the boy, with three men helping him, but now...

He heard the squeal of brakes, was moving as the jeep stopped dead some eighty yards due west of his position. In the darkness Bolan saw the passengers unloading, hooded men in black, with weapons in their hands. He drew the sleek Beretta 93-R automatic as he ran, its fire-selector switch already set for 3-round bursts.

The last thing Bolan wanted was a running firefight on the square, with children in the cross fire. It wasn't his choice, however, and he had to cope with situations as they came. If this was what it seemed to be, another hit-and-run excursion for the death squads, he would have to intervene by any means available.

And that meant deadly force.

The sound of gunfire banished any doubts as Bolan sprinted toward the jeep. A streetlight threw his shadow out in front of him, and so the driver saw him coming. He poked a stubby weapon out his window and unleashed a burst of fire that struck sparks on the pavement off to Bolan's right.

Bolan dodged toward cover in the doorway of a small boutique, expensive costumes on the window mannequins. A second burst from his assailant brought the plate glass raining to the ground and toppled dummies to the sidewalk, plaster heads and limbs detaching on impact.

The angle wasn't great, but Bolan risked a shot and was rewarded with the sound of bullets striking metal somewhere on the body of the jeep. The driver started leaning on his horn to call the others back and get the hell away from there, still pinning Bolan down. At some point he would have to stop and reload, but in the meantime he had the Executioner covered, halting his advance.

"I'm pinned," he said into the compact radio. "Can anybody nail that guy?"

"I'm on it," a familiar voice assured him.

Leave it to the Ironman, Bolan thought.

Just don't leave it too long.

CARL LYONS GOT his nickname from the nerves of iron that he displayed when he was one of L.A.'s finest, in the bad old days before he met Mack Bolan and his life was changed. The nickname stuck because he still attacked each problem with the same tenacity and vigor he had shown while taking pushers, pimps and killers off the mean streets of Los Angeles.

All things considered, Lyons didn't mind the interruption of their plan, except that children were at risk. It was inevitable that his path would cross the death squad's, and it might as well be sooner instead of later. Still, their job this evening was to pick up a specific child, return him to his father at the embassy and go from there. A killing situation wasn't on the menu, but the first thing he had learned about police work—reinforced when he'd signed on with Able Team to join Mack Bolan's war—was that the unexpected had a way of turning up at inconvenient times.

Like now.

He had the big Colt Python in his hand before he finished speaking on the walkie-talkie. Clipping the small transceiver to his belt, he bolted from the shadows on the south side of the square. Guns were going off inside the alley, and he could picture children running, then falling as the bullets ripped their flesh.

It angered him, and Carl Lyons in a rage was every bad guy's nightmare.

At forty yards and closing, Lyons pegged his first shot at the jeep. The big .357 Magnum bucked and boomed, its echo rolling back and forth across the empty square. The hit car was a ragtop with plastic windows, but he heard the bullet strike, like someone slapping canvas.

Close but no cigar.

The driver swiveled in his seat, ignoring Bolan for the moment, squeezing off a burst toward Lyons. They had him in a cross fire now, but he wasn't about to give it up while he had ammunition left and friends nearby.

The Python's second round struck metal, probably the gas can mounted on the tailgate of the jeep. It didn't set the gasoline on fire, like in the movies, but there was potential there if Lyons could get close enough to strike a spark.

The other goons were coming back, responding to their wheelman's signal with the horn. It had to be confusing, in the middle of an easy strike on unarmed children, to discover they were flanked and coming under fire.

And the grin on Lyons's face wouldn't have put his enemies at ease.

One of them had him spotted from a distance, leveling some kind of submachine gun, laying down a screen of cover fire while his companions piled into the jeep. A swarm of angry hornets made Lyons duck, then pitch forward, skinning palms and knees on contact with the pavement.

His third shot, from a prone position, came within an inch or two of taking out the hit car's left rear tire. No prize for coming close, and they were rolling by the time he tried again. Another hit on canvas with the hollowpoint, and he could only hope that it went on to find some flesh inside.

He scrambled to his feet and palmed the walkie-talkie as the jeep sped out of range. "They're running, Gadgets! Hurry up!"

"Coming!"

On the far side of the square, bright headlights winked to life, and a dark sedan erupted from cover in the shadow of a shop that specialized in skimpy lingerie. It raced around the square and skidded to a halt six feet from Lyons, waiting while he climbed into the shotgun seat.

"Where's Striker?" asked the man behind the wheel.

"The jeweler's on your right, a half block down."

"Okay, hang on."

"Just do it, man."

Their targets had a lead, and there was still no way of telling whether Rosario Blancanales had found the boy or if he was in time. It was amazing, Lyons thought, how such a simple gig could go to hell in nothing flat.

Still, they would have to try to salvage something, even if it meant a running battle in the streets. The very least the death squad owed him was a chance to even up the score, and Lyons always played to win.

Right now it was the only game in town.

IN VIETNAM, a lifetime earlier, Rosario Blancanales had been dubbed "the Politician" for his skill at winning hearts and minds, negotiating settlements without resorting to bloodshed. He could handle blood sports, too, when it was called for, and his role on Sergeant Mack Bolan's Pen Team Able hadn't been confined to talking peace, by any means.

This night, it seemed, there would be little opportunity for him to talk at all.

His part of the arrangement, once they had the street kids spotted, was to work his way around behind their flop and come in from the blind side, close the exit hatch while Bolan made a more direct approach. He had a photo of their subject memorized, allowing for the changes that a month of living on the street was bound to bring about, and Blancanales reckoned he would know the youngster when they met, dark night or otherwise.

How many thirteen-year-old Anglos could there be among the street kids of Cinelândia?

The pickup was supposed to be a quick, nononsense kind of operation, take it easy on the other kids but get it done and run their charge back to the embassy by dawn. The shooters turned it into something else, a game of life or death, and Blancanales feared they might have ruined everything.

He had the alley covered, moving in, when Striker's warning crackled from the radio. *"We've got a problem."* Pol had barely registered the words before he heard a squeal of brakes and boots slapping on the pavement, and a spray of automatic-weapons' fire came sweeping down the alley like a rain squall, driving him to ground.

The kids were up and running by that time, alerted by the first sounds of the approaching jeep. Blancanales had to give them credit; they were used to waking at the slightest hint of trouble, running for their lives.

The trouble with a stampede, other than the flying bullets, was that Blancanales would have difficulty telling one child from another as they rushed him in the dark. He couldn't use his side arm with the slender, dodging shapes obscuring his line of fire. He left the Model 92 Beretta in its shoulder holster, crouching like a wrestler as the children scampered toward him. Some of them had spotted him already and were dodging left and right like ferrets. They would take him for a member of the hit team, maybe strike at him with fists and feet as they went by. He would be lucky if he didn't take a blade between the ribs, Pol thought, and still he had to spot one child among the ten or fifteen rushing him.

In fact young Jeremy made it easy, calling out in English to a boy immediately on his left. Pol lunged and caught an arm, hung on and closed his eyes as Jeremy wheeled back around and punched him in the face. The kid was strong—Blancanales had to give him that—but desperation didn't make up for technique. He swung without direction, like a wild man, losing some of the potential force on glancing blows.

Pol wrapped both arms around him, twisted the boy to one side in his grip, thus blocking any straight kicks to the groin, and pulled him down into a crouch. The gunners at the far end of the alley were still unloading with their submachine guns, bullets chipping brick on either side, some clanging into garbage Dumpsters. Blancanales saw one of the youthful runners stumble, sprawl facedown and stay there, twitching on the pavement.

The boy was biting him and snarling like an animal.

"For Christ's sake, take it easy, kid! I'm on your side."

The words, addressed in English, seemed to do the trick. He gave up gnawing on the Politician's arm and let himself be carried from the alley in a dodging, weaving rush. The shooting stopped before they reached their destination, but you couldn't trust a lull in combat; the enemy might simply be reloading, making ready for another fusillade.

"Who are you?" Jeremy demanded after several heartbeats, when the hostile fire didn't resume.

"Let's say I'm from the embassy and let it go at that."

"My father called the spooks?"

More firing from the square, but this was different. There was no mistaking the report of Lyons's Magnum, twice as loud as anything the goons were carrying.

"You're going home," Pol told the boy. "Don't give me any shit, okay?"

"And if I run away again?"

"I'd say that's up to you. Right now I've got friends risking everything they have to save your skinny butt. I'd like to think you're worth the effort."

Moving toward the second car with Jeremy in tow, Blancanales thought about the others and wished he could be with them for the mopping up. Another gun could make the difference when the odds were close, but he had orders. Grab the boy, make sure he was secure. Deliver him at any cost.

Done.

He would keep his fingers crossed for Bolan and the other men of Able Team. If anything went wrong, he would be pleased to teach the other side why paybacks were a bitch.

CHAPTER TWO

The jeep sped west from Cinelândia, oblivious to traffic in the early-morning hours. Its driver left the lights off, shooting frequent glances toward his rear-view mirror. Even with the Ingram MAC-10 submachine gun in his lap and three armed friends to keep him company, he still looked worried, ill at ease.

Beside him, twisted halfway in his seat to stare out through the back, Gregorio Aznar was plainly shaken by the firefight they had just survived. A former sergeant of police in Rio, fired two years earlier for an accumulation of brutality complaints, including armed assault upon a leftist judge, Aznar had been a stalwart member of the death squad well before he lost his job. He made no effort to count bodies anymore, although he still kept clippings now and then on cases that possessed some special interest. Never once, in all that time, had he been forced to run off like a coward with his tail between his legs.

Until this night.

"Who were those bastards?" Cesaro asked, from the back seat.

"How in hell should I know?" Aznar snapped. "They didn't introduce themselves."

The other back-seat gunner, Naldo, cursed and said, "It was an ambush. They were waiting for us."

"Maybe not," Aznar replied. "It could have been coincidence."

"Damn!" Pirro blurted out, his hands white knuckled on the steering wheel. "Behind us! Someone following!"

"Be ready," Aznar commanded. "Pirro, lose them if you can."

Almost before he finished speaking, Pirro whipped the jeep hard left into a side street, cursing as a drunk pedestrian lurched out in front of them and nearly wound up as a trophy on their bumper. They were past him in a heartbeat, running north now, with Aznar watching out behind.

The headlights followed, swerving through the turn but staying on the pavement, rapidly accelerating once they found the way.

"That's some coincidence," Naldo said, mocking him.

"Shut up! All you have to do is stop them."

Naldo shot a killer glare in his direction and replied, "Don't fret, Gregorio. I won't let anybody hurt you."

Under different circumstances, Aznar would have taken up the challenge instantly, lashed out at Naldo with his fist or gun, but they had all the problems they could handle at the moment. He was trying to remember what had happened back at Cinelândia, the details. He had counted two men firing on the jeep, but now they had a car. Did that mean others? Would they all be armed? Who were they?

The police had never given Aznar any trouble on his little outings with the death squad. Some of them were members, after all, and most could sympathize with the results achieved: removing criminals and Communists from circulation where the courts had failed to do the job. Investigations into death-squad killings were perfunctory at best, and he couldn't imagine homicide detectives setting up an ambush on the street that way, risking a confrontation with their own.

But who, then?

At the moment Aznar's first priority was shaking off the tail, or killing his tormentors if he could. They had a lesson coming, and the bodies could be useful, maybe clear up their identity and motives.

"The next street up ahead," he snapped at Pirro. "Turn left, drive for half a block, then stop."

"Right in the middle of the street?"

"If you have time to park against the curb, then be my guest."

"Naldo, Cesaro. You be ready when we stop. I want to give these bastards a reception they won't soon forget."

"No problem," Naldo answered. "I was tired of running, anyway."

"You'll get your chance to prove it," Aznar told him, concentrating on the Uzi submachine gun in his lap. He changed the magazine, made sure there was a live round in the firing chamber as he waited, one hand braced against the dash as Pirro took them through another screeching turn.

Another moment now, and he would give these faceless attackers ample reason to regret their meddling in his business. It was their hard luck that they wouldn't survive to profit from the lesson. Still, you had to take such risks for granted when you trifled with the best.

The jeep slid to a halt, and he was on the pavement seconds later, scuttling toward the curb as headlights blazed behind them, making the street as bright as day.

THE CHASE WAS SHORT and sweet. The jeep ran five blocks west, three north, then made another sharp turn west into a side street where there were no lights to speak of. Bolan had sufficient time to verify that Blancanales had the boy, then he got busy with his hardware, trading the Beretta for a Heckler & Koch MP-5 K, one of the shorter, more reliable submachine guns in a market that was big on compact killing tools.

In front of him, Schwarz had the wheel, Carl Lyons in the shotgun seat. The Able Team warriors didn't waste time talking, satisfied with monosyllables as they kept track of their absconding quarry on the late-night streets of Rio.

"Turning!" Lyons snapped, and pointed as the jeep swung left.

"I noticed that," Schwarz told him, just a hint of acid in the driver's tone. "Hang on!"

They made the turn on two wheels, headlights burrowing an incandescent tunnel in the night. In front of them, the jeep had stopped dead in the middle of the street, its passengers unloading in a scramble, breaking off to either side. A couple of them were already firing by the time Schwarz hit the brakes.

It would be each man for himself, no time for strategy or orders. Bolan trusted his companions, battle-hardened experts that they were, and concentrated on his own piece of the action as he bailed from the sedan. A ten-yard sprint took him to cover on his right, with bullets snapping at his heels, and then he slid behind a squat Volkswagen parked against the curb.

It looked like four men in the hit team, with the driver, and he had to figure all of them were armed, proficient when it came to killing. The Brazilian death squads had no place for pacifists or hangers-on; the typical initiation was an execution in cold blood, and applicants who failed to make the grade wound up as victims, branded as informers and subversives when they died.

Four seasoned killers, then, and those were fairly decent odds. If there was money riding on the outcome, Bolan would have backed his two companions all the way.

He edged around the Bug to scout his field of fire, but ducked back again as bullets stuttered past him, chipping concrete from the sidewalk. He had a clear fix on the muzzle flash, assuming his selected target held the same position, but he had to find a better angle of attack.

Across the sidewalk, six or seven strides, a recessed doorway beckoned him. The brick wall offered cover, while the new position would let Bolan bring his adversary under fire. His only option, at the moment, was to hide behind the Bug and waste his ammunition firing blind, without a hope of scoring.

He came out firing from the hip to pin his target down and give himself some stretch. The gunner had his share of nerve, responding with a long burst even under fire, but Bolan made it to the doorway in one piece. He calculated half a dozen rounds or so expended from his magazine, which left him twenty-odd to play with. Now the trick was lining up a shot that wouldn't waste what he had left.

It was a risky play, but Bolan seemed to have no options at the moment. Dropping to a crouch, from there to hands and knees, he braced himself in preparation for the move. Once he committed, it was all or nothing, do or die.

He lunged from cover, sliding prone across the sidewalk, suddenly exposed to hostile fire. Downrange his adversary saw the golden opportunity and came up firing, giving it his best. To get the perfect angle, though, he had to show himself, step out from where he had crouched behind a gray sedan.

And that was all the edge Mack Bolan needed.

Firing for effect, he stitched the gunner with a rising burst from groin to throat, the parabellum shockers lifting his adversary completely off his feet before they dumped him backward on the sidewalk. Bolan watched him twitching for a moment, verified that he wasn't about to rise again, then pushed off from the pavement, sprinting toward the vehicle that moments earlier had served as cover for his enemy.

He made it as another burst of automatic fire rushed overhead, with inches left to spare. Beside him one dead man was stretched out on the ground, and that left three. A couple of them were across the street, exchanging fire with Schwarz and Lyons, while the third had never really left the jeep. He crouched in front of it, no more than twenty feet away, with ample room to cover Bolan's latest vantage point.

So much for progress.

He would have to root out the second gunner, and soon, before the locals got around to summoning police. It was a neighborhood of shops, but some of them would have apartments on the upper floors. The hour was late, but gunfire in the street would rouse at least a few of the tenants, and someone would inevitably telephone the police.

Which meant that he was running out of time.

Bolan checked the MP-5 K's load and braced himself, prepared to make the rush that would be all or nothing. For one of them, at least, the end was near.

HERMANN SCHWARZ HAD a couple of the shooters spotted as he broke from the driver's side of the sedan and heard bullets strike the open door behind him. They would have to ditch it now, whatever happened, to avoid a confrontation with police, but that was looking down the road. Right now his full attention focused on the gunmen who were firing at him from the cover of a storefront and minivan parked up against the curb.

He triggered two quick rounds from his Beretta, wishing he had something heavier to even out the odds, but that was what he got for driving. They had extra hardware in the trunk, but somehow Gadgets didn't think his adversaries would agree to wait while he went back and made his choice of weapons.

If he had an edge, it was the fact that these death-squad commandos were a cocky bunch, accustomed to a free ride anywhere they cast their net. Police ignored them for the most part, and the daily papers that protested their activities were often targeted for midnight vandalism, bombs or arson. Meeting solid opposition on the street would be a shock, which was reflected in their shooting as they sprayed the street like madmen, wasting precious rounds.

Schwarz risked a peek around the corner from his chosen doorway, and caught one of the shooters stepping out to give himself a better field of fire. It was the opening he needed. Sighting down the Beretta's slide, he squeezed off three rounds in rapid fire. He saw the gunman stagger, lurch to his right and bump solidly against the plate-glass window of a music store. It held his weight, and Gadgets watched the guy slump to his knees, face pressed against the glass, before he toppled onto his back.

Before he had a chance to gloat, another burst of automatic fire erupted from behind the minivan. Schwarz ducked back as chips of masonry spun past his face. Not bad, he thought, but they were trimming down the odds. If he could just get close enough—

Lyons seemed to come from nowhere, charging past him, blasting with the big Colt Python as he ran. Schwarz hit the deck and stuck his head out, tracking his teammate as he sprinted toward the minivan. A six-gun, Jesus! If the shooter didn't tag him, he was bound to come up short on ammo when it counted most.

Schwarz took advantage of the opportunity his friend had given him. He broke from cover with the Beretta leading in a firm two-handed grip. If Lyons could keep the gunner's head down, maybe they could finish him together, wrap it as a kind of double play.

In fact the shooter lost his nerve. It was a fatal error in the circumstances, bolting from his sanctuary like a scalded cat, as if the open sidewalk was a better place to hide. He came out shooting, did his best, but it was nowhere close to good enough. The long burst from his SMG went high and wide, smashing windows somewhere off to Schwarz's left, before the Python and Beretta opened up in unison to cut him down.

"You like to push it," Gadgets told his friend as they crouched together in the shadow of the minivan.

"Hell, it's the only way I know."

"He could have tagged your ass."

Lyons flashed a boyish grin. "With you to back me up? The bastard wouldn't dare."

"Did he know that?"

An easy shrug from Lyons. "You can ask him, if you've got a Ouija board."

"Some other time."

"Okay. What say we wrap this up and see if we can make it to the embassy in time for breakfast? They're supposed to have a great buffet."

THE SHOOTER CROUCHED behind the jeep was milking short bursts from his SMG, conserving ammunition at the same time he kept Bolan pinned. It had the makings of a standoff, the Executioner wishing he could weigh in with a frag grenade, some smoke, whatever, to distract the gunman while he made his move. They would be running out of time, and he could feel frustration gnawing at him. Each moment wasted in a stalemate put his friends in greater jeopardy and risked their mission in Brazil.

They hadn't traveled all the way from the United States to drop four gunners in the street and let it go at that. Pol had the boy, of course, and that was something, but their search for Jeremy Huxford had only been a handle on the larger game, a way inside the labyrinth. If they got hung up now, it would have been for nothing, wasted time and effort while the death squads held their grip on Rio and the countryside.

The MP-5 K's magazine was almost empty now. Bolan switched it for another, then braced the little SMG against his knee. He needed a diversion, and the Able Team warriors had their hands full on the far side of the street.

Bolan had it now, if he could pull it off. The jeep was built for rugged service, but his SMG was packing hot loads, full-metal jacket, and he had a decent chance to reach the fuel tank.

Bolan crawled back along the length of the sedan that gave him cover, edged around the rear to get another angle. He could see the jeep from there, a clear diagonal, and estimated where the gas tank would be situated, underneath the rear deck, just above the axle. Half a dozen rounds ought to do the job.

The soldier saw his chance and took it, holding down the MP-5 K's trigger, watching holes sprout on the flank and fender of the jeep. His adversary didn't bother to return the fire, as he had no clear view of his target from the wrong end of the vehicle. Another moment passed, then Bolan heard the steady drip of gasoline escaping from the ruptured tank.

The next bit was the tricky part. If Bolan missed the proper angle, he could fire all night and never strike a spark to light the dripping fuel. With any luck, though, if he got it right, he could transform the jeep into a flaming hulk and flush his target into view, finish the job before police arrived to ring the curtain down.

He took a moment, aiming, calculating angles, then squeezed off. Four rounds, and Bolan caught the break he needed. Bright flames took hold beneath the jeep and spread to the gas tank, followed seconds later by a blast that nearly flipped the jeep end over end.

The shock wave punched his target backward, singeing hair and eyebrows, rolling him across the pavement like a rag doll. Even so, the gunner kept a firm grip on his weapon, came up ready to defend himself in spite of his disorientation.

Bolan went in through the smoke and flames, heat baking him on one side as he sprinted past the jeep. His adversary glimpsed a shape approaching and responded with a burst of automatic fire that missed the mark by inches. The soldier dodged and rolled, a second burst caroming off the pavement to his left and spraying him with crumbled bits of asphalt.

He was up and firing in a heartbeat, catching his opponent with a long burst from the SMG, the parabellum shockers drilling, lifting and spinning him. The gunman skittered through a jerky little dance, his weapon clattering on the pavement, and he went down on his face as Bolan lifted off the trigger.

The Executioner was scanning left and right for other targets when he saw his comrades moving closer in the firelight. There was no more hostile fire, no enemies to challenge them. The game was over, and not a moment too soon. In the distance Bolan heard a siren wailing, others joining in like stray coyotes baying at the tropic moon.

"We're getting short," Lyons said.

Bolan nodded. "How's the car?"

"It needs some bodywork," Schwarz replied, "but it should get us to the embassy."

"That's all we need," Bolan said, moving back toward the sedan.

They had a date with Orson Huxford at the consulate, to talk about his son—and other things. The man from Washington had information that would help them carry out the next phase of their mission, and they had the necessary ticket now.

Mack Bolan meant to be there when the trade went down.

CHAPTER THREE

Ironically the U.S. Embassy was less than half a mile from Cinelândia, but in the opposite direction. Military guards and tree-lined avenues appeared to be the rule in that exalted neighborhood, where few of Rio's quarter-million unemployed and hungry ever had a chance to glimpse the way the rich folks lived. Pol's car was waiting for them on the street when they arrived, with Blancanales at the wheel, a smaller figure beside him. Underneath the streetlights, Jeremy Huxford looked grubby, somewhat shaken by the killing he had seen up close and personal, but otherwise unharmed.

The gate guards were Marines, all business. Bolan spoke a name and waited while they checked in with the sergeant of the guard.

A moment later they were cleared to pass, with no pat-down by the guards. Another pair of uniforms were waiting for them at the entrance, glancing curiously at the boy and trying not to be too obvious about it.

Orson Huxford was a tall man in his early forties, who had kept himself in decent shape despite the hours that he had to have put in behind a desk. He had a politician's ready smile, firm handshake and the kind of voice one normally associated with radio announcers. Bolan pegged him as an actor who would play the role required of him in any given circumstance. At the moment he was cast as Father, putting on a demonstration of relief. Not strictly bogus, Bolan thought, but neither was it totally sincere. He wondered briefly what was going on behind the scenes in this domestic play, then let it go.

The boy, once lifted out of Cinelândia, wasn't their problem. Orson Huxford had requested help, a plea that somehow made its way to Stony Man Farm, and in return he offered information that would put them fully in the picture for their current mission. It was simple give and take, no room for Bolan to start worrying about a youngster he had barely met.

"How are you, son?" Huxford asked.

"I'm okay," the boy replied.

"You had us worried."

And to that, no answer. Jeremy avoided looking at his father, his dark eyes shifting here and there around the book-lined room where they had been assigned to wait.

"You need some rest," Huxford said, taking charge. "A shower wouldn't hurt you, either. Run along, now. We'll discuss this later."

"I can hardly wait."

When Jeremy had left them, Huxford faced the others, giving each of them in turn a penetrating stare. It was the kind of look you could interpret half a dozen different ways, from curiosity to gratitude to thinly veiled contempt. The guy was a career diplomat, clearly used to mingling with others like himself, stuffed shirts who talked for hours without saying anything of substance, covering their private thoughts and hidden motives with the sugar-coated language of diplomacy.

"I want to thank you for my son," he said at last. "You can't imagine...well, that's neither here nor there. You found him and he's safe. That's all that matters."

"There was trouble," Bolan told him, driven by a sudden urge to crack the diplomat's facade, remind him that another world existed outside embassies and lavish drawing rooms.

"Oh, yes?" He sounded curious but not concerned.

"Another shooting with the street kids," Lyons told him from the sidelines. "You can read about it in tomorrow's paper if you have the time."

"That's dreadful. Were there...injuries?"

"Both sides," Bolan said. "No count on the children, but you've got four shooters dead. Don't be surprised if they turn out to be policemen."

"I assume there's nothing that would link this to the embassy?"

"Not yet," Lyons answered, staring holes through Huxford's skull.

"Well, then...we had a bargain, I believe. You need some information, yes?"

"That's right."

"Please understand, as cultural attaché I don't deal with things like this myself. Still, one hears things, meets people."

"I suppose one would."

If Huxford caught the sarcasm, he chose to let it pass. "The person you should talk to lives in São João de Meriti." Huxford smiled indulgently. "That's north of Rio, on the Rodo Presidente Dutra."

"I imagine we can find it," Bolan said.

"Of course." The smile winked off, as if someone had thrown a switch. "Her name is Juliana Alegrete. She's an activist on human rights and the environment, persona non grata with the powers that be. Her brother was the founder of a local group that agitates for government reform—improved democracy, what have you."

"Was?" The question came from Schwarz.

"He's dead. About two months ago, I think it was. A plane crash, up in Bahia. Some kind of charter flight went down with all hands in the middle of the jungle. Tragic."

"I can see you're broken up about it," Lyons said.

"There's no need—"

"Juliana Alegrete," Bolan interrupted him. "Is she expecting us?"

"She is. I spoke to her not half an hour ago. She'll meet you at the Jardim Zoologico at half-past ten. The monkey house. She's wearing red. Try not to be conspicuous, for her sake."

"We'll do our best," Bolan said.

"In that case, I suppose our business is concluded."

"One more thing before we go."

"Yes?"

"About your boy."

"I really don't—"

"Your average twelve- or thirteen-year-old won't take up sleeping on the street and risking murder every night unless there's something wrong at home. You might consider that before you fall back on the status quo."

"I'll keep that fact in mind," the diplomat replied. His tone was stiff, resentful.

"Food for thought," Bolan suggested. "Next time, when you pick him up, you might be talking to the coroner."

Outside, Carl Lyons shook his head. "The guy's a stiff. They shouldn't let a dick like that have children."

Bolan shrugged. "Take it up with Congress," he said. "Meanwhile, let's catch some breakfast, then we have to meet a lady at the zoo."

THE MEETING PLACE WAS a deliberate choice on Juliana Alegrete's part. She didn't want the Yankees coming to her house, for fear that she was being watched, and meeting at the zoo could also help to make a point about the cause that had already cost her family so much. She had no way of knowing if the strangers would be sensitive to such concerns, but it was worth the effort. They had traveled all this way to do a job, and Alegrete thought it might be helpful if they knew what they were fighting for.

She thought about her brother while she showered and dressed. Nine weeks had passed since Lorenzo's flight had gone down in the jungle, north of Morro do Chapéu, and while his body hadn't been among the passengers recovered from the wreckage, Alegrete knew that he was dead. Why else would the investigation of the crash have been so hasty and perfunctory, sealed caskets for the other victims to conceal their wounds. She hoped Lorenzo hadn't suffered in his final moments, but the fight went on in any case. If his assassination was supposed to put her off, somehow defeat the cause, her enemies were very much mistaken in their estimate of her character.

Alegrete finished, made a final survey of her image in the full-length mirror and prepared to leave. She had been up for hours, since the phone call from the embassy, preparing mentally for any questions the Americans might ask. It made no sense that they would travel all this way to turn her down, but you could never say for sure with foreigners, especially with diplomats and "spooks." She wondered idly if these men would represent the CIA or some clandestine agency that she had never heard of, hidden from the world by cover names, disinformation, secret budgets.

Would Lorenzo have approved her action, turning to the Yanks for help? It was a fact that he was bound for the United States when he was killed, but Juliana understood that he was seeking diplomatic aid, the kind that manifested itself in verbal warnings, economic sanctions and the like. What would he think of her impulsive move to escalate the struggle, bringing force to bear?

Already she had seen results, before she even met with the Americans. The early news reports were filled with details of a shooting in the predawn hours on the streets of Cinelândia. Three homeless children had been killed, five others wounded, and while that wasn't unusual these days, the rest of the report was nothing short of startling. Someone had been waiting for the death squad this time, and the hired assassins had themselves been killed. Their names weren't available as yet, but all of them were said to have "apparent links" to the police.

Alegrete knew what that meant. It was common knowledge in Brazil that members of the death squads were recruited largely from the ranks of past and present soldiers or policemen. Where else could the murder teams find men who weren't only trained in use of weapons, prone to sudden violence, but indoctrinated with the ultra-right-wing sentiments they needed to conduct a vigilante war against suspected "traitors" in the populace at large? More to the point, it was no secret that police and military leaders often covered for the death squads—buried evidence, intimidated witnesses and otherwise diverted justice from its goal. If they weren't directly implicated in the executions, the brass were at least satisfied with the results and spared no effort to allow the murderers free rein.

Alegrete knew she was a likely target, following Lorenzo's death, but she refused to let herself be paralyzed by fear. If she surrendered her beliefs and principles, it meant her brother would have died in vain. More to the point, she couldn't face herself if she turned tail and ran with other lives, the very future of her homeland, hanging in the balance. She wasn't a heroine by any means, but Juliana had been cursed— or blessed—with stubbornness that barred her from retreating when she knew her choice was right and just. If she was killed, her death would serve as an example to the others, motivate them as Lorenzo's execution motivated her to greater effort.

She took the usual precautions when she left her house. A drive around the block to check for watchers, see if anyone was tailing her, and then she drove a winding course through residential streets where a pursuer would be obvious. There was a possibility they could have bugged her car, some kind of tracking signal, but she didn't have the time or tools to check for homers at the moment. Alegrete reckoned she would have to take her chances, risk the meeting at the zoo and trust her contacts to take care of the security arrangements.

Driving south toward Rio, Alegrete kept a sharp eye on her rearview mirror, finally satisfied before she reached the zoo that she hadn't been followed. There were other possibilities, of course: a leak or wiretap at the U.S. Embassy would let the watchers set their trap without an inconvenient highway tail. She thought about it and shrugged off the notion, deciding she was on the verge of turning paranoid.

It was another victory for those who ran the death squads, when Brazilian citizens refrained from speaking out because of what *might* happen as a proximate result. Ideally, then, the butchers wouldn't have to lift a finger once the terror permeated every level of society.

The parking lot outside the Jardim Zoologico was filling up when Alegrete arrived at 10:05. She bought a ticket, passed the turnstile and began to make her way in the direction of the monkey house. Alegrete didn't care for zoos but she wanted the Americans to have a brief glimpse of Brazilian wildlife, and a meeting in the jungle had been totally impractical. This way, at least, if they had any sensitivity, the Yanks might understand what was at risk, some measure of the loss Brazil was suffering each day.

She took her time, not rushing it. If the Americans were late, she didn't want to make herself too obvious. Her red dress was the recognition signal, nothing in the way of cryptic passwords that they used in all the James Bond stories. Alegrete trusted her ability to spot a foreigner when he approached her, and a code would make no difference if her phone line or the embassy's was tapped.

The monkey house was pandemonium, with agile figures darting through the trees above and scuttling busily along the ground in search of food. A few sat still and groomed one another, watching Alegrete through the wire mesh of their spacious home until she almost felt that *she* was on display, the primates dropping by to study her. It was a new sensation, but it didn't mitigate the sorrow she felt each time she looked at creatures in a cage.

The man appeared beside her like a shadow, silent on his feet. One moment Alegrete was alone, and the next he lounged against the railing on her left and spoke her name.

"Ms. Alegrete?"

Clearly an American. There was no faking the complexion or the accent. If the death squad sent a ringer, Alegrete was convinced that she could spot him at a glance.

"And you are?"

"Mike Belasko." It was almost certainly a lie, but she didn't care about his name. "Why don't we take a walk?"

"ARE YOU ALONE?" The question came out sounding casual, but Bolan had the lady pegged as someone who watched out for details, taking care of business all the way.

"We're covered," he informed her. "You were clean when you arrived, as far as I can tell."

"To business, then. Was that your work in Cinelândia this morning?" She cut to the chase without a break.

"We had a minor disagreement with some trained gorillas on the homeless question."

Alegrete laughed at that, then caught herself, as if recalling that their business hinged on life and death. "You must excuse me if I don't grieve for their loss."

"No reason why you should." He hesitated for a moment, then went on: "I know about your brother."

"Ah. What is it that you think you know?"

"A plane crash. I'm assuming you don't think it was an accident."

"I *know* it wasn't. The police refused to let an independent expert see the wreckage. Relatives weren't allowed to view the bodies of their loved ones. Too much damage from the crash, they were advised. Lorenzo wasn't found at all, I'm told. Officially he wandered from the crash site in a daze and never made it to the highway. Sad, but what can I expect with so much ground to cover? There are snakes, wild dogs and jaguars, rivers, quicksand.... Well, you see the problem, surely."

There was bitterness in the woman's tone, and Bolan couldn't blame her. "He was on his way to Puerto Rico, as I understand, to meet with someone from the States."

"That's right. He had a briefcase filled with evidence he hoped to lay before your State Department, maybe the United Nations—anyone who had the power to help."

"With what, exactly?"

"You've already met the death squads. I assume you realize their work isn't confined to homeless children on the streets."

"I know their spokesmen talk about preserving law and order," Bolan said. "Some of their targets are political, religious, gays, whoever doesn't measure up."

"You've heard a portion of the story, then. There's more. You know about what's happening in Pará, Amazonas, all the inland provinces?"

He took a long shot. "You're referring to deforestation?"

"In a word. It sounds so tidy, yes? Like pulling weeds out of your garden. What it means in practice is the destruction of the largest rain forest on earth. For almost twenty years now, ranchers, timber cutters, speculators in petroleum and such have been allowed to purchase giant blocks of forest—some the size of Holland. It is theirs to do with as they wish. Cut down the trees for lumber, burn them if they have some other plan in mind. Of course, they never give a second thought to animals, the ozone layer—or people."

"Indians?"

"My country has a long, dishonorable record when it comes to dealing with the native population. Not unlike your own, in fact, except that we—the army, I should say—still use tactics that went out in the United States a hundred years ago. Forced relocation. So-called education at a level that prepares them for a janitorial position or a great job shining shoes. For those who won't be moved, air drops of poisoned food and clothes infected with disease. If all else fails, machine guns seem to do the trick."

"The death squads?"

"More and more the army tries to keep its hands clean. When the military ran the government outright, from 1964 to 1985, there was no problem killing anyone they wanted to. The press was censored. Anyone who raised a fuss about it could be jailed on treason charges, as a 'Communist.' These days it takes a little more finesse, but money talks. The bloody work gets done."

"Your brother had the evidence?"

"*Some* evidence, at least. He spent two years investigating links between the death squads and the government, collecting names, addresses, tracing phone calls, photographing private meetings from a distance when he could. It isn't just the army and police, of course. They're stooges taking orders. Someone else supplies the money and the bright ideas."

"And I suppose your brother traced the money men?"

Alegrete smiled. "It's quite a list," she said, "but one concerned him more than any other. Have you heard the name of Daniel Nazare?"

Bolan frowned and shook his head. "Can't say I have."

"He's a Brazilian transplant, if you will, to the United States. His parents made the move, I think, when he was still a child. Today he's an American on paper, but he lives in Rio. Something in the tax laws, I suspect, and managing an empire needs his personal attention."

"What's his business?"

"Cattle, for the most part, though he also has some interest in petroleum, I think. Lorenzo didn't give me all the details. Friend Nazare owns about one-third of Pará Province at the moment, but he won't be satisfied until he has it all. Imagine a half-million square miles of forest, all leveled for grazing land and oil fields.''

Bolan thought about it, and he didn't like the picture that it conjured in his mind. How many billion trees and animals would that be up in smoke? How many aborigines uprooted, if they even had the chance to run, before a hit team cut them down?

"He isn't doing all that on his own."

"Not quite. His stooge is an assistant minister of the interior, one Manolo Uribe, from Brasília. It would be his job to make sure bribes are passed along, arrange the necessary permits, grease the wheels when there is killing to be done. Of course, I have no evidence. The documents—"

"It won't be necessary," Bolan told her.

"No?"

"I'm not a lawyer, and I don't work for the State Department. If your information checks, there may be something I can do outside official channels."

"Like this morning, with the children?"

"Circumstances alter tactics," Bolan said. "The less you know, the better off you'll be."

"Of course, I understand." She hesitated, smiling wistfully. "You know, my brother was committed to nonviolence. He believed that any use of force, except in self-defense, was morally unjustified."

"That's one view. I guess it all depends on what you're calling self-defense."

"Sometimes, these days, I simply want revenge." Her comment had the tone of a confession.

"Well," he said, "there's something to be said for payback, too."

"And does it work?"

He smiled. "You'd be surprised."

CHAPTER FOUR

Juliana Alegrete's evidence of a conspiracy in Rio may have vanished with her brother, but she still had names, addresses and contacts filed away. The list she gave to Bolan when they parted at the zoo was typed out, single-spaced, two pages long. She had apologized, admitting it was incomplete. With fifteen death squads operating in Rio alone, some competing for targets or sniping at one another when they ran short of "subversives" to butcher, compiling a definitive list was impossible.

Bolan thanked her with a smile and told her it would get him started, anyway.

His first stop on the hit parade was a storefront office in Rio Comprido. On paper the tenant was a fraternal order calling itself the Guardian Society, composed of past and present cops who—theoretically, at least—hung out together as a kind of social club. In fact, he knew, the Guardian Society was no more than the flimsy cover for a right-wing death machine that killed ex-convicts, street kids, gays and "liberals" without distinction. In their eighteen months of operation, it was estimated that the Guardians had executed some two hundred fifty citizens in Rio de Janeiro and Minas Gerais. Of those, fifteen were fugitives from justice on outstanding charges at the time they died, but spokesmen for the Guardian Society—while careful to deny all links with vigilante action—hailed the work of "unknown patriots" in making Rio "safe for decent families." Authorities, predictably, could find no evidence on which to hang a murder charge.

And that would be the major stumbling block, as far as Bolan was concerned.

From day one of his private war against the Mafia, on through his stint with Stony Man, one of his ironclad rules had been that he would never kill a cop. No matter how corrupt or brutal, whether paid off by the Mob or acting on some dark, malignant impulse of his own, each officer was still, in Bolan's sight, a "soldier of the same side." Some lost their way, or maybe even took the job in hopes the badge would double as a hunting license, and he was the first one to admit that some cops should be locked away for good. When it came down to *killing* them, however, he would leave that to the mechanism of the state, if they were tried, convicted and condemned. He didn't force his view on others when the chips were down or criticize his fellow Stony Man warriors if they dropped the hammer on a dirty cop, but Bolan's hands had never snuffed a lawman's life and never would.

The previous night had been a gamble, squaring off against a hit team from the death squad, knowing some of them were active-duty officers, but he had run on instinct, thinking of the children first, and early news reports had served to put his mind at ease. The dead from Cinelândia included one *ex*-cop and three

Brazilian army rejects who were cashiered in disgrace for running private arms deals on the side.

So far so good, but he would have to watch his step around the Guardian Society. Its public membership included several dozen active-duty officers, and while he had no doubt that some of them deserved a cold hole in the ground, the Executioner didn't intend to take that task upon himself.

Still, there were ways and ways. A private scruple when it came to killing cops didn't mean Bolan had to leave them totally unscathed.

He made a drive-by of the Guardian Society's headquarters and drove around back. They didn't bother posting guards, presumably relying on connections and their reputation as a hard-ass outfit to discourage their potential enemies. Most times, Bolan thought, one or both protective screens would be enough to do the trick, but he wasn't the average social activist.

He parked in a small lot down the alley, locked his rental car and walked back to the office. The Guardian Society had found its niche between a low-rent nightclub and a laundry. Bolan didn't bother seeking symbolism in the choice, but focused on his target as he reached the unmarked door at the back.

And found it locked.

He listened briefly, checked both ways along the alley and applied his lock pick with an extra measure of dexterity and care. The last thing Bolan needed at the moment was a lot of noise to warn his enemies of an intruder. The advantage of surprise might see him through, combined with nerve and skill, but he couldn't afford a blunder at the starting gate.

He beat the lock in twenty seconds flat, exchanged the pick for his Beretta 93-R with the custom silencer attached and slipped across the threshold. He left the door ajar behind him as an exit hatch and to avoid unnecessary sound. The back room of the office was a catchall storage space, with everything from stationery, coffee filters and the like to half a dozen automatic rifles in a wall rack on his left. There were no empty spaces in the gun rack, but he knew that didn't mean the tenants of the office were unarmed.

He followed voices through a narrow hallway until he reached the office proper. There were only three men in the place, as far as he could see, all grouped around the farthest desk of three from where he entered. Call it fifteen feet, and any shots he had to make from there would have to be precise, nonlethal hits.

He took it as a challenge, more or less.

The three guys had their backs to Bolan as he entered, bending over what appeared to be a map spread on the desktop. Only one of them was obviously carrying, a semiauto pistol on his hip. The Executioner announced his presence with a shot that took out the fluorescent light above their heads and showered them with broken glass.

He had their full attention now, three pairs of eyes trained on his face like weapons. He could see the *pistolero* sizing up his chances, wondering if he could pull it off. Instead of waiting for the guy to jump and risk a moving target, Bolan went with the initiative and slammed a parabellum round into his shoulder, pitching him over backward, out of sight behind the desk.

"Do either one of you speak English?"

"I know some," the man on his right admitted.

"Okay. First thing, get your amigo to a doctor, then I think you'd better call the fire department."

"Fire?" The goon was either having problems with translation, or his mind was still locked on the image of his fallen friend.

"Did I forget to mention that I'm burning down your office?"

Bolan brought the thermite canister from underneath his jacket as he spoke. The two men tried to back away from him at sight of the grenade, but came up short against the desk.

"I'll give you thirty seconds," he informed the English-speaker. "Starting now."

The guy on Bolan's right said something to his friend in Portuguese before the pair of them made haste to lift their fallen comrade, hoisting him between them as they made tracks for the street. The Executioner kept them covered all the way, in case one of them tried to use the wounded gunner's pistol, but they plainly didn't care to press their luck.

When they were clear and out of sight, he pulled the pin on the incendiary bomb and dropped it on the floor between two metal filing cabinets. He reached the alley exit and cleared the threshold by the time it detonated, spewing white-hot coals of phosphorous around the room.

It would require an expert team to douse that blaze, and little would remain of the Guardian Society's headquarters when the smoke cleared.

It was starting small, he realized, but they had time, and he wasn't alone on this one. By dividing up his hit list with the men of Able Team, they could accomplish more within an hour's time than Bolan could in three or four if he was on his own.

The death squads were about to take a beating, but they didn't know it yet.

THE SUBURB KNOWN as Bonsucesso lay six miles northwest of downtown Rio de Janeiro. It wasn't the most affluent neighborhood, despite its cheery name, but neither did it qualify as poor by normal standards in Brazil. If there was such a thing in Rio as a haven for the middle class, then one such area was Bonsucesso.

Middle-class or not, in any city Rio's size, most neighborhoods were plagued by crime, and this was no exception. Burglaries were commonplace, and daylight robberies weren't unknown. The rape and homicide statistics didn't rival Rio's slums, by any means, but they were high enough to keep the residents on edge, encourage them to look the other way if certain civic-minded souls resorted to vigilante methods in defense of life and property.

The death squads had their hooks in Bonsucesso, as in every other neighborhood of Rio. They had started out with targets who were obvious and indefensible: perhaps a child molester, or a flagrant thief who skated through the courts time after time without real punishment. From there it was an easy step to charting misdemeanors, keeping watch on neighbors who were prone to speak out on behalf of civil liberties or cast their ballots for a left-wing candidate. Almost before the locals knew it, they were looking at a reign of terror by a team of covert thought police who seemed to know their every move. Somehow, for all the deaths and disappearances of so-called "criminals," the neighborhood was never really safe.

Carl Lyons knew the pattern, recognized the way things worked in countries where democracy was still a relatively new idea. Old habits were a long time dying, if they ever died at all, and there was always a potential strongman waiting in the wings to "save" his country from the threat of progress. Lyons had no patience with the strong-arm types who used the corpses of their countrymen as stepping-stones to power, and it pleased him any time he got the chance to take them down a peg or two.

Like now.

His first of several targets in the suburb was a drinking club that catered to police and their *compadres* on the fascist fringe. There was a world of difference, in the Able Team leader's view, between a cop who bent the rules sometimes to do his job, and those who made the rules up as they went along, preferring a police state to the free expression of ideas. His years behind the shield left him with nothing but contempt for cops who sold out their badges for cash or half-baked ideology, and unlike Bolan, he had no compunction when it came to dealing harshly with the men who sullied law enforcement's name.

The club was barely open when he got there, but it still had something like a dozen customers—split between the bar and two small tables on his right—as he went in. The Uzi Lyons carried had two magazines clipped end-on, in an L-shape for convenience, sixty-four rounds altogether, with a few spares weighing down the inside pockets of his sport coat.

He went in shooting, one burst for the ceiling, so that anyone who felt like ducking out the back would have a chance. No takers, as it happened, and his second burst mowed down a pair of shooters at the bar, stopped cold before they had a chance to reach the pistols on their belts.

He held down the Uzi's trigger and swept the full length of the bar, saw liquor bottles detonate and the ornate mirror come down in pieces. Number three was quick enough to draw his weapon, even got a shot off as the parabellum manglers drilled his chest, brought crimson gushers spurting into view.

The last guy at the bar was breaking for the kitchen, almost made it to the swing doors before a short burst from the Uzi hammered home between his shoulder blades. Momentum carried him the extra six or seven steps and dropped him on the threshold, wedging the doors open with his bulk.

The gunners seated at two tables on his right were scrambling for their lives as Lyons swung around to face them, tracking with the Uzi, laying down another deadly stream of fire. He caught the first guy with his feet tangled in his chair and blew him over backward in a tumbling sprawl. Beside him, number two was groping for his pistol, cursing in Portuguese, when Lyons took his face off with a 4-round burst and dropped him out of sight behind the table.

Most of the others had their guns drawn now, and Lyons made a dive for cover, flipped the nearest table on its side and threw himself behind it as the bullets started coming in.

He reached beneath his jacket, to the back, and found the frag grenade that he had clipped onto his belt as life insurance, for a situation such as this. In nothing flat he yanked the pin, released the safety spoon and lobbed the high-explosive egg well clear of his position, toward the major source of hostile fire.

His adversaries either failed to see it coming, or they didn't recognize the object as it wobbled toward them, struck one of the tabletops and bounced onto the floor. A heartbeat later, when it detonated, screams of anguish filled the room, competing with the sound of thunder ringing in Lyons's ears.

He didn't rise immediately, but rather slid to his left and peered cautiously around the table, checking out the status of his enemies. Another three men down that he could see, and two of those still on their feet were plainly wounded, bleeding freely from the scars of shrapnel that had torn their flesh. One stood apart from his companions, dazed but otherwise unharmed, and Lyons nailed him with a rising burst that made him dance for several jerky steps before he fell.

The cleanup took another thirty seconds. Switching magazines before he rose, Lyons finished off the mortally wounded gunners where they sat or sprawled in creeping pools of blood. A final survey of the killground and he was out of there, retreating toward his car while curious pedestrians came flocking to investigate the sounds of battle.

The ghouls would get their money's worth this afternoon, Lyons thought, and he wasn't nearly finished yet.

In fact he was only getting started.

CAPTAIN EMILIO BARBOSA'S day had started badly, with the early call from Cinelândia, and it had gone downhill from there. At first he had been almost willing to believe that Aznar's team had run afoul of rebels, or that some of the street children had armed themselves in self-defense, but neither theory fit the facts as they were now unfolding. New attacks upon the death squads had been made in Rio Comprido and Bonsucesso, twelve dead in the latter event, and there was simply no explaining it within the captain's normal frame of reference.

One clash could be dismissed as a coincidence, perhaps a group of criminals who got the better of their stalkers for a change, but *three* raids, maybe more by now, meant some kind of well-organized campaign was under way.

The very notion shocked Barbosa. In his nineteen years as a policeman, nine of those before the junta fell and ten more since the advent of "democracy," there had been no occasion when the death squads suffered such a blow to their prestige. There was a show trial now and then, of course, to satisfy the Yankee press; occasional convictions were arranged, with the sentence typically suspended, but resistance on this scale was totally unprecedented.

Someone clearly meant to turn the tables on the death squads for a change. It was Barbosa's job to find out who and why, make sure their efforts came to nothing in the end.

It was a fact of life in Rio de Janeiro, and throughout Brazil, that certain ranking members of the government, the military and police regarded vigilante death squads as a necessary adjunct to the justice system. Courts were sometimes lenient when they should be strict, and some offenses weren't even classified as crimes these days, with all the talk of "human rights" and universal suffrage.

Barbosa wished he could turn back the clock, reverse the so-called "progress" made since 1985, when military rule was scrapped in favor of a representative democracy. Respect for law and order had been mandatory in those good old days, when vocal dissidents were swept up off the streets like so much garbage and treated to a session on the parrot's perch or dragon's chair. Some disappeared entirely, and the world was better off without their kind, subversives who were more concerned with equal rights for Communists and the like than economic progress for the state.

The death squads, to Barbosa's way of thinking, were democracy in action, strongmen standing up to

save their country in her darkest hour, beating back
the rabble, traitors, mongrels, parasites and scavengers through force of arms. There might be statutes on
the books that called for him to intervene, prevent the
squads from operating, but Barbosa recognized a
higher law.

But all that was in jeopardy today. Unless he could
identify the men responsible for these attacks, arrest
them or provide the death squads with sufficient information for their men to do the dirty work, the system as he knew it could be torn apart.

Where would it end?

The jangling telephone derailed Barbosa's train of
thought, cut through apocalyptic visions of society
gone mad, without restraints. He lifted the receiver,
fearing more bad tidings.

"Yes?"

"Emilio, how can this happen?" Nothing in the way
of salutations from Luis Obidos, who cut directly to
the chase. Barbosa grimaced, knowing the commander of the largest single death squad in the city
would expect hard answers, which were so far un-
available.

"We're picking up some rebels," Barbosa said.
"They'll be questioned. Otherwise, the only thing we
know for sure is that the gunman in Rio Comprido
spoke English."

"An American, Emilio?"

"Don't jump to conclusions, Luis. Our witnesses
don't say he was American."

"And if he was, what then?"

"You know as well as I do how we stand with Washington," Barbosa answered. "Liberals in Congress talk about the death squads at election time, but they still vote for foreign aid. They don't want Castro's revolution spreading out from Cuba while they're trying to persuade the world that communism is extinct outside of Asia."

"Even so, who can say what they will do?"

Barbosa thought about it, frowning. "Maybe you should ask Nazare, or his friend Manolo. You can reach them, Luis. They have no time for a lowly captain of police."

Obidos pondered the suggestion for a moment; you could almost see him nodding at the far end of the line as he made up his mind.

"I will," he said at last. "Someone should get in touch with Washington and make sure we don't have a larger problem."

"Carefully, Luis. Our friends must be discreet. It won't sit well with anyone if they start asking favors for the death squads."

"Don't be foolish," Obidos chided. "Manolo has a talent for these things. He is a statesman, after all."

"I hope so, Luis. What we don't need at the moment is a brand-new problem."

"I'll take care of it. Just do *your* job and track down these bastards before I lose another dozen men."

The phone went dead before he could respond. Barbosa cradled the receiver with more force than necessary, taking out his anger on the silent instrument. Obidos made him furious sometimes—such arrogance—but that was just another part of life. At heart he knew they were the same, with common goals, the same commitment to maintaining order in Brazil.

Obidos was right in that respect. It was Barbosa's job to find the men responsible for the attacks and bring them in. The law demanded it. And if he had to kill them in the process, well, it was a risky business, taking shots at the police.

With any luck, he still might have the riddle solved by sundown. Otherwise, the captain knew, he could be looking forward to a long and sleepless night.

IN NITERÓI, across the Bay of Guanabara, a veteran death-squad ally named Bartolo Carlomagno ran a weekly newspaper, the *Call to Arms,* which went beyond the usual approach to coverage of vigilante action. Where most other papers in Brazil were satisfied to duck the issue or refer to death-squad executions as acts committed by "persons unknown," the *Call to Arms* ran front-page lists of victims, with a summary of their suspected crimes against society. Carlomagno's editorials were long on vitriol and short on facts, but he avoided lawsuits for the most part, since potential litigants were more afraid of being gunned down on the street than slandered in the press.

Rosario Blancanales had a week-old issue of the newspaper beside him, on the front seat of his rental car, when he parked across the street from Carlomagno's office. Checking out the street, he saw no evidence of guards around the place, though any number could be hidden in the upstairs windows of adjacent buildings.

Never mind. The opportunity was there in front of him, and he wasn't about to let it pass.

He took the paper with him, rolled up in his hand, and dropped it in a trash can at the curb. His lightweight jacket was unzipped, granting clear access to the Browning double-action pistol that he carried in a shoulder rig, along with the incendiary sticks that filled his pockets.

It was party time.

He breezed in from the street and flashed his most endearing smile at the receptionist, a young, petite brunette whose outfit might have been a minidress or double layer of spray paint. Under different circumstances, Blancanales would have gladly passed the afternoon right there, just staring at her, but he still had work to do.

His Portuguese was rusty, but a brushup on the flight down from the States had left him functional. "I need to speak with Mr. Carlomagno," he informed the young brunette.

"And you are . . . ?"

"Mr. Browning."

The brunette paged through her date book, putting on a luscious frown. "I'm sorry, but you don't have—"

"An appointment? No, but it's an urgent matter. Mr. Carlomagno will be glad he took the time to see me."

That was stretching it, and no mistake, but he was hoping to avoid a show of force with the brunette if possible.

"Forgive me, sir, but I have strict instructions to admit no one without a prior appointment."

"I understand, of course." He kept the smile in place and watched hers fade as he produced the pistol. "As it happens, I'm afraid we'll have to bend the rules this time."

"Please, sir—" There was a note of panic in her voice.

"The best thing you can do," Blancanales interrupted, "is leave right now. You have a car?"

"Outside."

"Pick up your bag and go. Don't bother looking for a telephone. Police can't help your boss today."

Blancanales figured she would make the call regardless, but he didn't need much time. He saw the lady out, then made his way around her desk toward Carlomagno's inner sanctum. The place was small and strangely silent for a newspaper office, circumstances the Able Team warrior ascribed to the fact that Carlomagno received most of his copy direct from the death squads themselves. Any competent wordsmith could touch up the grammar and make a few calls to confirm basic facts. The printing would be done at some commercial plant, perhaps in Rio, while the editor-in-chief held down the other staff positions on his own.

It was essentially a one-man show, and Blancanales had come to shut it down.

Carlomagno was changing ribbon cartridges on his electric typewriter when Blancanales barged into his office. The death-squad apologist was one of those rare men who looked like his name: tall and broad in the chest, with massive shoulders that supported a square-cut head and a bull neck. His graying hair was crew cut, thin enough on top to show his sunburned scalp. The one concession to his journalistic guise would be the half lens reading glasses perched precariously on his big hooked nose.

"And who are—?"

Carlomagno saw the pistol halfway through the angry question, and the sight of it dried up his voice. The big man cleared his throat, flushed crimson with embarrassment at being tongue-tied, but the Politician hadn't come to hear him speak.

His single shot, muffled by the custom silencer, drilled into Carlomagno's forehead and punched him backward, rolling freely in his high-backed swivel chair.

Done.

The rest was busywork, distributing the fire sticks so that nothing would escape the blaze. Pol opened Carlomagno's filing cabinets, heaped photographs and papers on the floor and dropped a slim incendiary in the middle of it all.

Hot news today, but it wouldn't be covered in the *Call to Arms*.

Pol hit the street before the first incendiary flashed and sputtered, smoky tendrils giving way to white-hot flames. He had the car in motion, northbound, by the time the smoke detectors started shrilling for a lifeless audience in Carlomagno's office.

Ashes to ashes.

There was still a list of targets waiting for him back in Rio, where the others were at work on missions of their own. Blancanales hoped to join them soon, when they were done with the preliminaries, and get on with setting up the main event.

The death squads had a taste of bitter medicine in store, but it should taste familiar going down. Sometimes, the Politician thought, it really *was* more fun to give than to receive. It all depended on the gift and the recipient.

In this case, death for some would be a gift of life to others. It was funny how the game played out sometimes, and he was in it for the long haul.

CHAPTER FIVE

Three days a week Juliana Alegrete worked with homeless children in the streets of Rio de Janeiro. She had followed this routine for close to eighteen months, and saw no reason why she ought to stop because of the Americans and their campaign against the death squads. The street kids were dying every day—from illness, from neglect, an average four per day from homicide—and trying to pretend that they didn't exist would only make the problem worse.

Despite its great leap toward democracy in 1985, Brazil had next to nothing in the way of social programs for the poor, the homeless, the disabled and diseased. Whatever help the street kids found outside of predatory gangs had mostly come from private individuals or local churches. Homeless children numbered in the tens of thousands all across Brazil, while private shelters offered sanctuary for a tiny fraction of that number. The Brazilian government had pledged one billion dollars for a new child-literacy campaign back in 1993, but so far little of the cash had reached its destination. Graft and waste diverted most of it to useless, dead-end programs or the pockets of a chosen few in government.

The grim statistics told a story of their own. Despite the richest economy in Latin America, Brazil, with 152 million citizens, had thirty-two million children living in families with incomes below thirty dollars per person per month. The top twenty percent of Brazil's population earned twenty-six times as much as the bottom twenty percent. In the United States, by contrast, with its Rockefellers and teeming ghettos, Alegrete knew the disparity was closer to nine percent.

Street kids left home for many different reasons. Some were physically abandoned by their parents; others fled from dingy, overcrowded institutions operated by the state; some ran from households where the press of bodies strained the budget and the food supply beyond endurance; others were encouraged to leave home and thereby give the family a little extra breathing room. Abusive parents, dead or missing parents, almost anything could put a child out on the street. Some thought the life would be adventurous, a chance to spread their wings and play at being adults. By the time they learned the truth, it was too late to change their minds.

Juliana Alegrete and her brother had been fortunate in that regard. They "came from money," as the saying went, and both were educated at the finest universities before their parents died together, in a plane crash, while en route to visit natives on the upper reaches of the Amazon. Juliana's father, a physician, was himself the son of wealthy parents, but he broke the mold by nurturing a social conscience, often put his money where his mouth was, and his children learned to do the same. Juliana knew that she would never want for money, barring some Homeric spending spree, and when Lorenzo's will cleared probate, she would have more ready cash than any one person truly needed.

Part of it would go to help the children of the streets.

Alegrete didn't fool herself into believing she could change the basic facts of life in Rio, much less for the nation as a whole. It was impossible for her to locate all the street kids in Brazil, much less make any lasting difference in their lives. But she could help a few, from day to day, and helping didn't always mean a gift of cash.

She volunteered two afternoons a week at a shelter run by the São Martinho Aid Society, not far from Cinelândia. She offered classes to the children, taught them how to read and write, do simple math and, sometimes, how to stay away from trouble with the law. She also helped out in the shelter's kitchen, the infirmary, wherever there was work to do and willing hands in short supply. On other days she prowled the streets and got to know the children on her own time, spoke to them in private, steered a few toward jobs or trade schools, sometimes helping them with the tuition and expenses. She also worked with prisoners, donated time and cash to Amnesty International and several native groups that were active in opposition to political violence, death squads and the rape of the environment.

All this had marked her as someone whom the power structure would be pleased to crush if she

stepped too far out of line. Lorenzo had been such a
threat, with his persistent digging into public records,
dogging the police and money men who kept the death
squads operational throughout Brazil. The evidence he
gathered had been too revealing, too potentially explosive, and it cost his life. His enemies had won, to
the extent that he was silenced and his evidence erased,
but Juliana wouldn't let it rest at that.

Belasko and the others were her instrument of vengeance.

She felt guilty somehow, when she put it in those
terms, but what was wrong with hitting back when you
had been unjustly wounded? Brazilian law would
never punish those who killed her brother, so she took
a stab at justice on her own. And if there was a price
to pay for that come judgment day, she was prepared
to take her medicine.

The São Martinho shelter was an old brick building
on a corner lot, three stories tall, with murals painted
by the children on its outer walls. Inside there was a
kitchen, dining room, infirmary and common room
with television, all on the ground floor. Upstairs the
space had been divided into sleeping rooms for sixty
children, though an occupancy double that wasn't
unusual. At that, the shelter housed no more than one
percent of Rio's homeless children on a given night,
and few of those were constant tenants, most remaining for a day or two, perhaps a week, before they disappeared into the streets again.

Alegrete showed up early for her shift that Friday
afternoon, spent time among the children in the com-

mon room before reporting to the kitchen. She would help with serving lunch and cleaning up, before her reading class convened at two o'clock. As always, she was curious to see who would remain from last week, which new faces would appear.

The midday meal was stew, prepared with meat and vegetables donated by a grocer in the neighborhood. No tax deductions were allowed for gifts to charity, but some Brazilian Christians lived their faith instead of merely offering the Lord their hymns and prayers on Sunday. More than once, Alegrete had gone out to purchase groceries for the shelter, but today's meal was on the house.

She didn't see the strangers enter, but heard the children crying out before she glanced up from her work to track the source of the commotion. Fights weren't uncommon at the shelter, and she was prepared to intervene if no one else was handy. This was something else, though, and her blood froze as she heard the sound of gunshots in the common room.

TAJO LOPEZ WAS DETERMINED not to make the same mistake his friend Gregorio had made in Cinelândia last night. When he was sent to do a job, the job got done, and there were no excuses, no loose ends. It didn't matter if a gang of leftist rebels was at large, or if the street waifs had machine guns. Lopez had a reputation to protect, and he wasn't about to be humiliated in the eyes of his superiors.

At that, the job was relatively simple, even for a daylight operation. Lopez and his flying squad of gunmen were to raid the São Martinho shelter and raise whatever hell they could among the nuns and children there before they grabbed a certain woman who was working as a part-time volunteer. It would have been much easier to simply kill her, but Lopez's orders were specific. His superiors had questions they desired to ask before she died, and it was his job to bring her in. With any luck, perhaps he would be able to participate in the interrogation. From the photo he was shown to help him spot the target, Lopez knew he would enjoy some time alone with this one if he got the chance.

And if he didn't, killing her would still be fun.

The five-man team included Lopez's driver and three backup gunners for the hit. They carried Uru submachine guns, standard issue for Brazilian military and police. The simple weapons had only seventeen moving parts, and they could lay down a screen of 9 mm parabellum fire at 750 rounds per minute. Lopez's denim jacket came equipped with special hidden pockets to accommodate spare magazines, and if he still ran short, the Browning semiautomatic pistol slung beneath his left arm would be adequate to cope with any challenges the nuns and homeless children might provide.

When they were two blocks from the shelter, he took a ski mask from the paper bag between his feet and passed the others to his soldiers in the back. The woolen mask was hot and scratchy on his skin, but he wouldn't attempt a raid on São Martinho without covering his face. There were bound to be survivors, and you never knew, these days, when someone in the neighborhood would have a minicam on hand to film the action for posterity. Their car was stolen, and the license plates were lifted from a second vehicle, but none of that would matter if the gunners wound up on TV with their bare faces hanging out.

The shelter's placement, on a corner, made it easy for their driver. He would keep the engine running, with a loaded shotgun ready just in case. Lopez wasn't afraid of the police, but you could never tell when some pathetic would-be hero might appear from nowhere, and he had to think about the unknown gunmen who had killed a number of his friends within the past twelve hours.

He hit the pavement running, heard the others close behind him as he crossed the sidewalk, scattering a group of children on the front steps of the shelter. There was no point shooting them when it would only serve to warn the ones inside, perhaps allow the woman time enough to get away.

The common room was something else, though. They were well inside the shelter now; the wretched urchins were watching television just like normal human beings, several of them glancing up in time to see the guns before a hail of bullets swept their ranks. It felt good, firing into them, the bodies tumbling, sprawling, but Lopez didn't forget the main point of his mission. They could always kill street kids in Cinelândia, but he had sworn to find the woman. He mentally kept her face in front of him as he moved on, the others following.

They neared the kitchen, and a nun came out to meet them, walking stiffly with a dazed expression on her face. Lopez was raised a Catholic, but he was also wise enough to know that certain nuns and priests were socialists or worse, no less than traitors to the government and to God. Without a second thought, he fired a short burst from his Uru, dropped the holy woman in her tracks and stepped across her body as he kept on moving toward the kitchen.

Chaos reigned there, with wretched children diving under tables, searching for an exit, any way at all to save themselves. His soldiers opened up and dropped a few, but Lopez's eyes were focused on the woman, standing there behind a serving table, with a steaming ladle in her hand.

It would have been so easy: raise the submachine gun, squeeze the trigger and the woman was history. His orders were to bring her back alive, however, and it would go badly for him if he failed. With that in mind, Lopez approached the serving table, smiling through the scratchy fabric of his ski mask as he spoke.

"Mrs. Alegrete, you will come with me at once."

"It's 'miss,'" she informed him coldly in the lull that followed gunfire. And without a moment's hesitation, she swung the ladle toward his face.

Lopez recoiled, his left arm rising to deflect the blow, but he wasn't quite fast enough. The stew she had been serving splashed his cheek, soaked through the woolen mask and burned on contact with his skin.

He cursed, was just about to rip the mask off when he realized the consequence of such an action.

And by that time she was running out the back way, down a corridor where several children had been shot, their slender bodies scattered on the floor like piles of cast-off clothing. Lopez sprinted after her, called out for his commandos to be quick about it, stop her before she could escape.

She almost made the door, but Lopez caught her with a yard to spare, his free hand reaching out to snag the collar of her blouse. She wriggled in his grip, cloth shredding, buttons popping, giving him a glimpse of lacy bra and soft, round breasts before he swung the submachine gun at her head.

And that was all.

She went down in a heap at his feet. He wasted precious seconds waiting for his pulse to stabilize, the fury ebbing now that she was at his mercy. There would be no more resistance. He had won.

It was an hour's drive to the delivery point, but he wasn't concerned about the trip. First thing, when they had cleared the neighborhood, they would discard the stolen car and move their hostage to another. The police would find their vehicle and make the usual announcement of persons unknown, with investigation ongoing.

Two blocks from the shelter, Lopez pulled off his ski mask and felt the raw skin of his face. Already there were blisters forming where the stew had scalded him. He swiveled in his seat and peered down at the woman, lying trussed up on the floor behind him.

He would definitely have to ask for time alone with this one, he thought. She owed him that much for his trouble, and the little bitch would have some blisters of her own when he was done.

It's "miss," she had told him. Still unmarried, then. Could she still be a virgin at her age?

The mental image of their private time together was enough to keep him smiling as they carried Juliana Alegrete on a one-way ride to meet her nemesis.

THE RADIO WAS TUNED to let Pol Blancanales keep up with the latest news while he was driving from one target to another. Most of it was boring stuff, the normal run of politics and petty crime, but there were bulletins from time to time that helped him track the other members of his team. He knew their targets, just as they knew his, and he could chart their movements by reports of clashes on the street. The headquarters of the Guardian Society was up in smoke. A certain bar had been attacked, with heavy casualties. There were reports of sniper fire from Piedade, where a pair of ex-policemen had been killed, a serving captain wounded in the groin.

The all-news station had another shooting to report, this time from downtown Rio de Janeiro. Several men in ski masks, armed with automatic weapons, had attacked the São Martinho children's shelter. The police hadn't released a final body count, but it was known that children had been killed, together with at least one member of the staff, a nun called Sister Seina. Such attacks weren't unusual in Rio, though a daylight raid against the shelter and a nun's death made the outing noteworthy. More to the point, survivors indicated that the gunmen had abducted someone from the shelter: an adult who volunteered her free time to the children several days a week.

The missing woman was identified by staffers at the mission as one Juliana Alegrete. Listeners might be expected to recall that Juliana's brother had been killed two months ago, while flying—

Blancanales switched off the broadcast and started looking for a telephone. He didn't know if Striker would be close enough to catch a signal on the two-way radio, and Pol wasn't inclined to beam this message out across the town, in any case. A land line would be adequate, ring up the big guy's pager, stand by for the callback.

He could only wonder now if Juliana's kidnapping was linked to their campaign in Rio, or if members of the death squad would have grabbed her anyway to finish what they started with her brother two months earlier. It could go either way, but there was one thing Blancanales had no doubts about: the Executioner's reaction when he heard the news.

There would be hell to pay for someone, whether Juliana Alegrete was alive or dead. If grabbing her had been a ploy to ease the heat, somebody's brainstorm was about to backfire.

Everything that went before that moment had been practice, simply warming up. Now someone had seen fit to raise the stakes, and Blancanales knew exactly what that meant. He had been witness to the Executioner in vengeance mode on more than one occasion. It was something he could never quite forget.

He spied a phone booth on the corner, one block down, and signaled for a lane change, slowing into the approach. A part of him was apprehensive, dreading the delivery of bad news, but there was no alternative. And when he thought about it, the inevitable escalation of their blitz in Rio should reduce the length of the campaign.

Unless, perhaps, the whole thing went to hell.

"Hang on," the Politician muttered to himself as he prepared to park his car. "It's going to be a bumpy ride."

THE CALL CAUGHT Bolan coming off his third strike of the afternoon. He had surprised three members of the death squad, all in uniform, as they came out the back door of a brothel. They were collecting their protection payments for the week, and from their smiles, he guessed that some of it was taken out in trade. Whatever, any thoughts of pleasure were immediately banished as the Executioner appeared before them with an Uzi in his hands.

He could have killed them where they stood, but these were cops, albeit of the kind who tarnished any badge they wore. Instead of gutting them with parabellum manglers, Bolan held the Uzi's muzzle low and cut their legs from under them, the trio going down in blood and sobbing cries of pain. He didn't bother going through their pockets for the payoff money, figuring the cash would make a start toward reconstructive surgery on shattered knees.

He wore a silent pager, with no risk of a careless tone betraying Bolan at a crucial moment. The vibration on his hip meant there was someone on the line, and while he didn't recognize the number on the LED display, that much was standard. Any member of the Able Team force who tried to reach him on a land line would be using a public telephone.

He found a booth, returned the call and listened silently, his stomach roiling, to Pol's recap of the news report from Cinelândia. His thoughts were racing as he ordered Pol to reach out for the others, bring them all together for a meeting. They would use the zoo again, since it had served them well before. The parking lot, this time. Say fifty minutes, to allow for driving time.

It was a good sign, Bolan tried to tell himself, that Juliana had been kidnapped from the shelter. If the gunmen simply meant to kill her, there was no point dragging her away when they had murdered others on the spot. In theory, that meant someone wanted her alive...and that was where the happy train of thought broke down.

Abduction by the death squads never ended well for any target. In Bolan's recollection, there were rare accounts of victims who survived, but they could hardly be described as fortunate. Without exception, they had suffered grievous torture, sometimes crippling injury or mutilation. Those who lived were left deliberately, as an example, object lessons to the petty criminals and "undesirables" who were a staple of the death squad's hit list.

Juliana was among the savages, and she wouldn't be rescued by polite negotiation. Something else was called for, Bolan realized, and his comrades from Able Team would know exactly what he had in mind as soon as they received the news from Pol.

When dealing with a terrorist, the Executioner had learned to speak his adversary's language. Not that Bolan was a linguist, even though his travels had exposed him to a wide range of dialects. But he was fluent in the tongue of violence, one method of communication every terrorist and savage understood by heart.

When life and death were riding on the line, sometimes you had to spell your message out in blood, with letters three feet high. The Executioner was short on brushes at the moment, but he had enough equipment to get by.

And what the hell, it never hurt to improvise.

CHAPTER SIX

It was a relatively simple plan: the team would tackle each and every target on their list, emphasizing the expensive targets, anything to hit their adversaries where it hurt the most. Leave messages along the way, whenever possible, to make it clear their enemies could stop the carnage any time they wanted to by setting Juliana free. There was an element of risk involved, a chance the death squad's leaders might go crazy in their fury, kill the woman by way of payback, but it was a chance they had to take.

Without the effort, Bolan knew, she was as good as dead.

And if his guess about the snatch team's motive was mistaken, or if Bolan's message reached the brass too late to save her life, well, then, the Executioner could *really* settle down to cleaning house.

His first mark was an arms dump on the waterfront at Ponta do Catalão. The target was a few miles from the Galeao Airport, on Ilha do Governador, and its private dock gave unlimited access by sea, through the Bay of Guanabara. Arms shipments from the States, from Argentina, Eastern Europe and the Middle East could pass unnoticed through the shabby-looking warehouse, thereby ensuring the death squads never came up short of ammo in the crunch. Police and customs men were either paid to look the other way, or else ignored the traffic out of loyalty to the death squad's "law and order" hype.

It was the kind of place that rated guards, and Bolan scanned them from a distance, through binoculars, before he made his move. They had the look of common thugs about them, which didn't rule out Brazilian cops by any means, but from their ages, haircuts and the fact that all of them had free time on their hands while leaves were being canceled for police, he reckoned none of them was active duty at the moment.

Fair enough. He had a bit more latitude this time around.

He drove in closer, parked a block out from the target and took the Uzi with him when he left the car. His army-surplus jacket was a bit warm for the season, but its ample pockets let him carry extra magazines for both the SMG and his Beretta, as well as a couple of incendiary canisters. Unless they had an army tucked away inside the warehouse, Bolan thought his preparations would be adequate.

The four guards he had spotted were divided up between the loading dock and pier to cover both approaches. Bolan kept the Uzi out of sight, beneath his jacket, as he went for the direct approach, across the smallish parking lot and toward the loading dock.

One of the shooters saw him coming, pointed Bolan out to his companion, and they both stood ready as he closed the gap between them, standing there with weapons braced against their hips—an automatic rifle on the left, a riot shotgun on his right. At that range either one could put him down, and he couldn't afford to give them any edge at all.

One of the gunners challenged Bolan, calling out to him in Portuguese when he had closed to thirty paces. Twenty would have been more like it for an easy tag, but he would take what he could get. Instead of answering—which he couldn't have done, in any case— he whipped out the Uzi and sprayed the loading dock with parabellum rounds from left to right.

The rifleman took half a dozen hits before he toppled over backward, dying as he fell. His weapon clattered on the concrete but didn't discharge. Beside him, trying hard to save himself, the lookout with the shotgun almost had his weapon leveled when a line of blowholes opened in his chest and filled the air with crimson spray. He went down gasping, lost his shotgun when he hit the deck and lay there twitching for a moment before the movement subsided.

The others would be coming from the pier, and Bolan waited for them, marked their progress by the sound of startled voices as they ran around the north side of the warehouse. He was ready with the Uzi, had the sights lined up and waiting, when his targets blundered into range. Bolan fired a dozen rounds and watched the gunners stagger, reeling, going down together in an awkward sprawl, limbs tangled.

He pulled the nearly empty magazine and replaced it with a fresh one as he crossed the loading dock, stepped over prostrate bodies on his way to reach the nearest door. It opened at his touch, and Bolan edged his way inside the warehouse, half expecting shots from the interior. Instead, the only sound he heard was something close to sobbing coming from the general direction of a glassed-in office just ahead.

He didn't bother knocking on the door, which stood ajar as he approached. The sole survivor of the warehouse crew was kneeling with his back to Bolan, struggling with the combination of a bulky safe. It was impossible to tell if he was bent on putting something in or taking something out, and Bolan didn't care.

"Hello, there," he said, covering the guy as he turned back to face the sound of Bolan's voice.

His eyes locked on the Uzi, staring into death. He muttered something Bolan couldn't understand, perhaps a plea for mercy.

It was worth a try. "Do you speak English?"

"Yes. A little."

"Well enough to take a message to your boss?"

"A message?"

"To your boss."

"I'll try."

"Your life depends on it."

He understood that, anyway, and responded with a hasty nod. His round face glistened with the sweat of fear.

"I'm looking for a woman. Juliana Alegrete is her name. Repeat it."

"Juliana Alegrete, yes."

"Your boss knows where she is, or he can find her. If she comes to any harm, he's dead. The best thing he can do to help himself is let her go."

The kneeling man gave back a slightly garbled version, close enough to pass. He had the name right, and the gist of Bolan's message. It seemed foolproof, if he didn't lose his voice completely after Bolan cut him loose.

"Remember, if you run without delivering the message, I'll hunt you down. Believe that I can do it, when you see your friends outside."

Another jerky nod, and Bolan stepped aside, his Uzi waggling toward the open doorway.

"Go, then."

Bolan didn't have to tell the man twice. Almost before he finished speaking, Mr. X was up and out the door, shoes slapping concrete as he ran. The outer door slammed shut behind him, but it didn't mask his cry of panic when he saw the bodies on the loading dock.

It was a short stroll back into the warehouse proper, where stacks of wooden crates and cardboard boxes were carefully arranged with space enough between the rows to let a forklift pass. He palmed the first incendiary can and dropped its safety pin, released it in an easy sidearm pitch that carried thirty feet or so, with touchdown in between two rows of merchandise. The second canister went off to Bolan's left and came to rest against a bulky wooden crate.

He didn't know exactly what was in those boxes, and it made no difference for Bolan's purposes. His message would get back to the survivor's boss, presumably Luis Obidos or a trusted underling, with the destruction of the warehouse and its contents serving as a kind of exclamation point. It was a start, but he wasn't about to let it go at that.

IT WAS A SMALL WORLD after all, Hermann Schwarz thought. Four thousand miles from home, and there were still reminders everywhere. What was São Paulo, after all, except a Hispanic version of St. Paul, where Able Team had once maintained a storefront office? If he needed any further proof, the situation of his target said it all. What were the odds of flying all this way and winding up in a Brazilian suburb called Indianapolis?

Forget about the quirky circumstance and focus on the job.

So far so good.

It had been Striker's choice to split the team, sending Schwarz and his companions on a field trip to São Paulo. They could spread the grief around that way, put more heat on their enemies than if they all hung out in Rio, smoking members of the death squad there. It made good sense, but Gadgets didn't like the thought of leaving Bolan on his own, two hundred miles away, while every cop and right-wing hooligan in Rio de Janeiro scoured the streets to bring him down.

Still, there had been no point in arguing, and here he was in Indy, more or less, about to bust a gambling club "protected" by the death squad in return for twenty-five percent of any profits. It felt like old times, moving down the sidewalk with the hardware heavy underneath his jacket, spare mags dragging down his pockets. In and out, a relatively simple job, except that Gadgets had to try to leave a message, which would mean survivors and an added risk.

He put the doubts on hold and nodded to the doorman. Gadgets grimaced when the guy addressed him like a native, rapid-fire Portuguese going over his head in a flash. As the human roadblock stood there waiting for an answer, he brought out the stubby MP-5 K submachine gun and stuck it in the bouncer's face.

It was a miracle, the way technology could bridge the gap between two different cultures.

As Gadgets marched his captive through the leather-padded doors, soft music reached out to wrap itself around them as they entered. He was ready when the doorman made his move, some kind of bogus kung fu thing that might have worked if they were in the movies. As it was, Schwarz took a quick step backward, shot his adversary in the chest and stepped across the twitching body on his way to the casino proper.

It was early yet, before the real crowds started turning out, but Gadgets spotted twenty-five or thirty people at the tables, mostly following roulette and baccarat. A slinky hostess was about to greet him when she saw the weapon in his hand and lost it with a breathless squeal, just loud enough to bring the floor boss over from his place beside the roulette table. Gadgets had him covered all the way, and since the guy didn't appear to have a weapon, he was smart enough to play it cool.

"Do you speak English?" Gadgets asked him when the guy was close enough to hear him, and was answered with a jerky nod in the affirmative.

"Okay, so here's the plan. I'm shutting down your little operation here." The floor boss's eyes went wide at that, but he didn't reply. "I give a free pass to the players, if they're smart enough to take it, but the club will need some renovations when I'm done. You've got the good part, though. First thing, you get to choose if you will live or die."

The floor boss thought about it for a moment, acting macho for the woman's benefit, before he said, "I choose to live."

"That's good. We've got a special on survival, one time only. For the prize, you have to take a message to your boss."

"What message?"

"It's an easy one. I've been looking for a woman. Juliana Alegrete is her name. That won't mean anything to you, but someone higher up will recognize it. Here's the message—if she comes to any harm, your boss goes down with everything he owns. The smart thing is for him to cut her loose while he's got something left to save. You get all that?"

The guy repeated it, almost verbatim. He would have to dress it up a little when he went before his master, but the major theme would still shine through.

"Okay, you pass," Schwarz said. "Why don't you take the lady here and hit the bricks. I'd join you, but I've still got some remodeling to do."

The floor boss hesitated for another moment, finally nodding to the hostess, and they left the club together. Schwarz heard the woman gasp at the sight of the unlucky doorman, then they reached the street and he had other things to think about.

Like bringing down the house.

First thing, he had to lose the party crowd. For that, he aimed his submachine gun at the ceiling and triggered off a burst of six or seven rounds that captured everybody's full attention in a flash. A couple of the women screamed, but no one bolted. They were busy watching, waiting.

Gadgets had no way of knowing which ones in the group spoke English—maybe none of them—but he would have to do his best with what he had.

"Get out!" he ordered them. "The club is closed now. Move!"

For emphasis he fired a short burst toward the bar, exploding liquor bottles, scarring polished wood. That got them moving in a miniature stampede, a couple of them going down, then struggling to their feet again and moving on.

He almost missed the gunners slipping from the back room, under cover of the exodus, and might have come to grief if one of them wasn't the hasty kind. A wild round from the heavy pistol hissed by Schwarz's face, with something like a foot to spare, and he was turning back to meet the threat before the others had their target framed.

There were three shooters, two with side arms, one with what appeared to be a 12-gauge shotgun. Gadgets neutralized the long gun first, squeezing off a rising burst that ripped the gunman from his inner thigh up to his breastbone, spinning him around before he dropped onto his face.

And that left two.

The others had their range now, firing for effect, but Schwarz was quicker, dropping out of sight behind a roulette table. It was bolted to the floor—no hope of tipping it for better cover—but at least the setup let him watch his adversaries as they jockeyed for position, moving closer, yard by yard. He had a rat's-eye view of legs and feet as they prepared to rush him in a hasty pincer movement, one approaching from his right, the other from his left.

Schwarz took the left-hand gunner first, because he was the closer of the two. A short burst took his knees at thirty feet, legs folding in a crimson blur, and Schwarz was ready when the soldier fell across his line of fire, loosing another burst to pin him down and keep him there.

He swiveled toward the sole surviving shooter and found his enemy had cut the gap by half, unloading as he ran. Schwarz raised the MP-5 K, squeezed the trigger and heard the firing mechanism snap against an empty chamber.

Damn it!

There was no time to reload, and Gadgets dropped the SMG, already reaching for his holstered side arm. The Beretta 93-R with its custom silencer was set for 3-round bursts, the safety off, and Gadgets stroked the trigger twice before he had a solid chance to verify his mark.

Six rounds were away in something like a second and a half. Some of them found the charging gunner, three or four by Schwarz's estimate. His target reeled, spouting crimson as he fell to hands and knees.

The guy was staring at him when he finished it, no pleading in the eyes. Another 3-round burst from fifteen feet, and it was done.

Schwarz stowed his side arm and fed the SMG another magazine while he was scrambling to his feet. The club was empty now, unless they had somebody hiding in the back, and that wasn't his problem at the moment. He had come to trash the joint, and he was swiftly running out of time.

The two incendiary canisters looked small in Schwarz's hands, but they would do the job. He pulled the first one's pin and lobbed it toward the bar, where it could feed on polished wood and alcohol. He rolled the second one across the floor and watched it come to rest beneath the roulette table that had seen its final play that afternoon.

And it was time to leave.

Nobody was waiting for him on the sidewalk when he got there, and it was an easy walk back to his car. He had more visits to make before returning to Rio.

CALVINO BIENVENIDO LIT a fresh cheroot, shook the match out and dropped it on the gravel at his feet. The automatic rifle tucked beneath his arm was getting heavy after four long hours on the job, and he was wondering if it was all a waste of time.

There had been trouble in the city—he knew that much for a start. And while he wasn't on the privileged list of those entitled to a detailed briefing, he could watch TV and listen to a radio as well as anyone. He knew that someone had been sniping members of the death squad since the previous night, in Rio and the suburbs, choosing targets randomly... or so it seemed.

The brass hats obviously thought there was some kind of conspiracy involved. A group of Communists, perhaps, the Fidelistas who kept popping up from time to time and causing problems in the countryside. It was unusual for them to operate in urban settings, but their idol's health and influence were fading, so Bienvenido guessed they might be getting desperate.

He hoped so, anyway. It would be interesting to see some solid action for a change, instead of chasing street kids through the littered alleyways of Cinelândia.

Bienvenido was assigned to guard a safehouse in Tijuca, south of downtown Rio de Janeiro. Despite its label, members of the death squad rarely used the house to hide in, since the law was rarely motivated to pursue them. Rather, it was utilized for keeping hostages secure, sometimes for questioning a subject prior to execution. Vacant at the moment, it was still a valued piece of property, complete with soundproof rooms and all the tools required for wringing answers out of tight-lipped prisoners. Three guards besides Bienvenido were assigned to watch the house, and he was in charge.

He didn't argue when the brass was giving orders, but the detail still impressed him as a waste of time and energy. With three men under him, he could have taken to the streets, grilled suspects by the dozen until someone spilled the information he required. Start with the Communists and socialists, work through the so-called liberals if necessary, maybe wind up with the "greens" who spent their time protesting "rape of the environment." Somewhere along the line, he had no doubt, the names of those responsible for recent crimes against the public peace would be revealed.

Bienvenido didn't view himself or his associates as criminals. Of course, they broke the law from time to time, but it was necessary in a setting where the very fabric of society was under siege. When members of the death squad were compelled to strike out in defense of common decency, because the legal system failed to deal with the subversives and degenerates who made a mockery of law and order, why should he feel guilty at the end results? They did only what courts and prosecutors should be doing in the first place— taking care of business, cleaning up the streets.

This standing watch, though, was the kind of thing that grated on Bienvenido's nerves. It took him back to when he was a soldier, in the days before a young lieutenant caught him with a woman at his post and he was cashiered out of service. It was pitiful, the way the little bitch had lied and said he forced her, took advantage of her "innocence" and roughed her up when she refused to let him have his way. He would have liked to punish her once he joined the death squad, but Bienvenido couldn't honestly recall her face, much less her name.

And now he was on sentry duty once again, the same old tedium of pacing back and forth, examining the shadows for imaginary enemies. At least this time he had a little rank, some weight to throw around. The others knew he was in charge, and if he chose to take a break before much longer, they wouldn't complain.

In fact Bienvenido felt like breaking for a while right now. He could go back inside the house, pretend that he was checking out the doors and windows. See if there was anything to drink, perhaps some beer or wine.

He took the walkie-talkie from its belt sheath, raised it to his lips and thumbed down the transmitter button. It was easier to use the radio than walk around and see the others one by one.

"Fernando, this is Number One. I'm going in to check the house. Acknowledge."

There was only static when he lifted off the button, waiting. Nothing, when he should have had an answer back in seconds flat.

"Fernando! Answer me!"

More silence.

Worried now, Bienvenido tried the others. No response from Rafael or Yago, either. What was going on? One man might leave his radio switched off by accident, but not all three. Now he would have to go around and check on each of them in turn, forget about that drink until he found out why they weren't responding on the radio.

But wait. If there was something seriously wrong, what could he do about it now, one man alone? Bienvenido caught himself before the fear took hold, remembered who he was, the grave responsibility with which he had been honored. Any show of cowardice would finish him with his superiors, while a display of courage must inevitably lead to recognition, maybe to promotion.

He had wished for action; now it seemed his wish might just be granted, and Bienvenido wasn't sure exactly how that made him feel.

He spit out the cheroot and checked his rifle, making sure he had a live round in the chamber and that the safety was off. Fernando was his second-in-command, assigned to watch the west side of the property, and he was now Bienvenido's first concern. He would be the first to have his ass raked over red-hot coals if he was dozing on the job.

He never got the chance to chastise his subordinates, however. He had taken no more than a dozen steps when the safehouse exploded, flames and blackened shards of lumber leaping skyward, while the shock wave knocked him down. Bienvenido lost his rifle when he fell, too groggy from the blast to realize that he had been disarmed until he saw a tall man walking toward him through the drifting pall of smoke.

He missed his weapon then, but he wasn't without
resources. Even in his muddled state, he still had sense
enough to reach back for the pistol on his hip, defend
himself against this man in black whom he had never
seen before.

He saw the muzzle-flash, some kind of automatic
weapon leveled from the stranger's waist, and then it
felt as if Bienvenido's gun arm had been ripped out of
its socket. He had never felt such pain, was certain that
he had to be dying. Still, his eyes were clear. He focused on the stranger as he stepped up close, bent
down and spoke in English.

"Can you understand me? Nod or blink your eyes
for yes."

Bienvenido tried to blink his eyes and apparently
succeeded.

"So, you want to live?"

More blinking, rapidly, as if his eyelids had a mind
of their own.

"I have a message for the men who gave you this
assignment. Can you handle that?"

He blinked again, without enthusiasm this time.

"Juliana Alegrete. Say the name."

Bienvenido did his best, his lips struggling with the
syllables. His enemy seemed satisfied.

"Okay. Your people have her, and I want her back.
The heat stays on until she's safe and sound. You understand?"

Bienvenido nodded, blinking wearily.

"You'll pass the word along?"

Blink, blink.

"So live."

The stranger turned away and left him there, heat from the fire baking Bienvenido on one side, while the other felt a creeping chill. It seemed like hours, maybe days, before the sound of fast-approaching sirens gave him reason to believe he might survive.

CHAPTER SEVEN

Bolan's next stop in suburban Guadalupe, off Avenida Brasil. One of the local death squad's ranking officers, a thug named Ciro Calderone, maintained a high-rise office there, from which he sold insurance to prospective targets. He often took out a second policy that named himself or members of his family as beneficiary, in case it proved more profitable to dispose of the subject than keep him alive. It was a variation on the old Black Hand extortion racket, made more odious by the pretense that it was practiced in the name of God and country.

The Executioner had a notion it was time to shut the racket down.

He chose a sniper's roost across the avenue and one block east, in another high rise that would offer him an unobstructed field of fire. He left his car downstairs in an underground garage and rode up in the service elevator, wearing denim coveralls with a generic name tag on the breast and the logo of a nonexistent cleaning service stenciled on the back. In case he met a native, Blancanales had prepped him with a dog-eared business card explaining he was deaf and mute. His bulky toolbox weighed more than it should have under ordinary circumstances, and the slight bulge in his right-hand pocket was a cordless telephone.

He made it to the roof without mishap and chose his spot, a corner of the building facing west. He knelt and opened up the toolbox, lifted out a tray of screwdrivers and wrenches to reveal the folding-stock Galil sniper rifle beneath. In seconds flat he had the piece unloaded and ready to rock.

The Galil was a working sniper's weapon, designed by the Israelis with an eye toward reliability in the worst of battlefield conditions. Chambered in 7.62 mm, it retained the 20-round box magazine of the original Galil assault rifle, with provisions for a muzzle brake and silencer, ten-power telescopic sight and a folding bipod to provide stability when firing from the prone position. While it lacked the modern lines of certain other models, like the Walther WA-2000, the Galil would serve when others failed to make the cut in jungle, desert or the urban killing ground.

He sat and sighted through the rifle's scope, scanned several windows on the target office block before he found the one he wanted. Calderone was seated at his desk, a long cigar protruding from his swarthy face, while two young men stood facing him and hung on every word he spoke.

Bolan palmed the cordless phone and tapped out Calderone's private number, one more bit of information Juliana Alegrete had been able to provide before she disappeared. He watched as the man was interrupted by the telephone beside his elbow, frowning as he lifted the receiver to his ear.

"They tell me you speak English," Bolan said.

"Who is this?" Calderone asked, reaching up to take the fat cigar out of his mouth.

"We haven't met, but I'd like to help you anyway."

"Help me?"

"To stay alive."

"I don't like jokes," the big man snarled.

"Who's joking, Ciro? Would you rather die than take a simple message to Luis Obidos?"

"Am I supposed to be afraid because you call me on the telephone and threaten me? Come here and face me like a man—I'll show you something."

"I can do the next-best thing," Bolan said.

Even as he spoke, he set the cordless phone aside and wrapped his hand around the pistol grip of the Galil. His finger found the trigger as he swung the muzzle, heavy with its oblong silencer, a few clicks to the right.

The cross hairs of his telescopic sight were centered on the profile of a young man in his twenties. He was too well dressed to be a cop, which meant that he was one of Calderone's direct subordinates, a gofer with a gun. The bulge beneath his jacket, on his hip, left no doubt that the man was armed.

A simple squeeze, and Bolan felt the rifle lurch against his shoulder. With the silencer in place, the muzzle hardly jumped at all. He saw the plate-glass window shiver, watched the young man crumple as his face exploded, spewing crimson like a liquid halo as he fell.

They wouldn't hear the shot, of course, and target number two was still recoiling from his unexpected bloodbath when a second bullet closed the gap and drilled a tidy hole below his jawline, shattering the vertebrae and opening a four-inch exit wound behind his ear as it burst free. Another body hit the floor, and Bolan grabbed the cordless telephone before Calderone had a chance to grasp what he was witnessing.

"I hope we understand each other, Ciro." He had to repeat it once before the big man on the other end remembered where the voice was coming from and turned to face the shattered window, panic in his eyes.

"You've got a choice," Bolan said. "You can take a message to Obidos for me, or I'll let you join your friends and find myself another errand boy. What will it be?"

He reckoned he could hit the dazed gorilla at least twice before he ducked from sight behind the desk, but Ciro wasn't going anywhere. His fear had taken over, paralyzing him. It was a minor miracle that he could get his vocal cords to function.

"I will take the message to Luis."

"A wise decision. Here it is—your people have a friend of mine. Her name is Juliana Alegrete. If she's harmed, I plan on killing every member of the death squad I can find. I'll make it my career, you understand? The smart thing for Luis to do is let her go right now. You follow me?"

"It's clear."

"I hope so, Ciro. If I have to call you back, there won't be any second chances."

Bolan severed the connection with a click that left his target flinching, fumbling with the telephone. He watched as Ciro punched a button on his intercom and started shouting for assistance. Other gunmen barged in a moment later, startled at the scene of carnage waiting for them in the big man's inner sanctum.

He had seen enough to be convinced that Calderone would take the message back to his superiors. It was another job well done, but he was far from finished. There were other bases left to touch before he called Luis Obidos personally to discuss a deal.

It could go either way from there, he realized, and he would have to be prepared for any choice the death squad's leader made. If Juliana was released in decent shape, so be it. On the other hand, if her abductors tried to tough it out, he was prepared for total war.

Scorched earth.

And he would lend a whole new meaning to the notion of a death squad by the time he finished up in Rio, either way. The worm was turning with a vengeance, growing fangs, and it was out to bite Luis Obidos on his vigilante ass.

TEN MINUTES LATER, in his villa on the outskirts of the city, Luis Obidos sat down with his second-in-command to ponder a solution for the problem that was clearly getting out of hand.

"What do we know about these crazy bastards?"

Jose Campos occupied the hot seat, knowing that his leader wanted answers, needed answers, swiftly, if he meant to head this problem off before they lost control.

"They seem to be Americans," Campos said, starting with the basics. "We have only one report of an assailant speaking Portuguese."

"I know that! Is there nothing else?"

"I've spoken to our contacts in Brasília," Campos answered. "They weren't advised of any operations pending in the country. That means nothing from the CIA or drug-enforcement people, no reports from Interpol."

Obidos sneered. "As if they would inform those idiots of their intentions. Use your brains, Jose. It certainly will not be Interpol. As for the others . . ."

"The Americans?"

"Who else? Their administration is deceptive, smiling in your face while one hand comes around to stab you in the back. See what they did to Haiti and the Chinese dissidents, to their own homosexuals. They promise one thing and immediately do another. You can tell their President is lying if his lips are moving."

"If you're right, sir, why the sudden change in policy? Why should they care about some homeless brats in Rio when they have so many of their own."

"You still don't understand Americans, Jose. It is their nature to involve themselves in other people's private business. See the way they shook a righteous finger at South Africa for treatment of the native blacks, while blacks in the United States are filling up the jails. Last year they added sixty new offenses to their list of capital crimes, yet they criticize other countries for executing traitors and subversives. The

Americans are hypocrites with too much time and money on their hands. Understand that, Jose, and nothing they do will surprise you."

"Even so," Campos said, "this isn't their usual approach. I would expect some kind of diplomatic overtures, perhaps a threat of economic sanctions. Military action is a last resort, and they prefer to have an international consensus. They would never try—"

Obidos interrupted him. "You haven't read your history, Jose. It isn't that Americans don't care for covert action every now and then. It stimulates them, but they simply don't like being caught. Patrice Lumumba was before your time, and the attempts on Castro, but you should know something of their operations in Colombia, Bolivia, Peru. They love to plot and scheme, these Yankees."

"Then it's hopeless," Campos said, his tone and aspect glum.

"Not quite." Obidos smiled. "The disadvantage of a covert program is that it must stay covert or risk embarrassing the men responsible for its inception. Washington will not acknowledge its participation in the recent incidents, which means that it cannot complain—or offer any help—if their clandestine agents come to harm. The trick in stopping them," he said, "is knowing what they want."

"They want the woman," Campos said.

Obidos nodded. "Juliana Alegrete. Do we have her?"

Campos blinked. "She was abducted from the shelter, as you ordered."

"I know that, Jose. But is she still alive?"

A jerky nod from Campos. "Yes. I checked on that first thing and told our people not to damage her without direct instructions."

"Very good. You see, we have a weapon now we can use against our enemies."

"But how—"

"I'll tell you," Obidos said. "You must listen carefully, Jose, because I'm placing you in charge, with personal responsibility. You understand?"

He wasn't thrilled about it, but the young man nodded.

"Yes."

Obidos smiled. "Then here is what you do...."

THE SANTO ANDRÉ SUBURB of São Paulo is a city in its own right, seat of government for the subdivision of São Paulo Province—equivalent to a large American county—that bears its name. The death squads have their way in Santo André, as in larger cities, using the same combination of ideology and fear to quell any meaningful opposition. No body count was readily available, but estimates of death-squad murders in the area ranged upward from one hundred fifty victims in the past two years.

This afternoon Carl Lyons hoped to score a few points for the other side, help balance out the stats a little. Anyway, he meant to try.

It amused him, in a sickly sort of way, that members of the death squad—so incensed by any kind of crime that they had executed litterbugs and petty van-

dals—also sold protection to selected Santo André
pimps. The fact didn't surprise him, based on his experience with law enforcement in the States and elsewhere, but the irony still made him smile. It also gave
him something he could work with, maybe add the
sharp sting of embarrassment to his next move.

He started with a phone call, letting Pol take care of
the translation, tipping off a local tabloid journalist
about the scoop that could be his if he showed up at a
particular address, with a camera crew, at half-past
four. The timing had to be precise, no fudging, or the
story would go up in smoke.

Step two was moving on the brothel well before his
journalistic ally made the scene, to get things rolling.
Lyons knew from Juliana Alegrete's briefing that the
death squad not only protected Alano Diego's whore-
house, but its soldiers also patronized the place in
force. It was a rare occasion when you couldn't find
at least a dozen vigilantes hanging out and laying pipe,
all on the house. A number of them would be active-
duty officers, and some showed up in uniform, so
confident were they that no one would complain.

And they were right.

Lyons wasn't lodging a complaint; he simply meant
to kick their asses while the district's sleaziest newspaper trumpeted the details far and wide.

He went in through the back at 4:20. No point in
showing up too early, after he had sworn the newsies
to arrive at four-thirty. With any luck at all, ten minutes in the house should get it done, and he could find

an exit while the warriors of the Fourth Estate were snapping photographs and taking names.

The Ingram M-10 submachine gun came with a MAC suppressor, but he left it in the car. Some racket wouldn't hurt this time; in fact Lyons was counting on it, trusting panic to evacuate the "innocent" while he dealt with the rest.

The place was old, two stories, with a staircase on his right as he went in. He took the steps two at a time and made no effort to conceal the Ingram as he reached the upstairs landing, moving toward the far end of the hall. It made more sense to work his way back toward the stairs and flush his prey in front of him than to corral them on the second floor while he cut off their access to the only exit.

Strategy.

Six doors were on either side, which meant there would be other rooms downstairs. He started on the left, barged in and found an agile couple working up a sweat. The man was thirty-something, and his khaki uniform, complete with gun belt, had been neatly draped across a straight-backed chair.

"Hey, Marshal," Lyons hailed him, "rise and shine!"

The guy bailed out of bed as if his life depended on it—which in fact it did. He tried to reach his pistol, but he never had a chance. The Ingram stuttered, five or six rounds reaching out to slam the naked man against a chintzy chest of drawers. His playmate started screaming as he toppled forward, sprawling face-down on the floor, and Lyons left her to it, confident that she was neither brave nor interested enough to grab the dead man's side arm and come looking for revenge.

Across the hall he kicked the second door and crossed the threshold in a rush. The red-faced trick who spun to face him was an obvious civilian, recoiling in panic at the sight of a weapon. Lyons didn't know if he spoke English, and it hardly mattered.

"Up and out!" he told the guy. "The party's over."

Leaving Senhor X to scramble for his clothes, Lyons moved on to the next room in line. It was empty, and he doubled back across the hall. He didn't have a chance to try the door before it opened and a glaring face confronted him, a pistol rising into view.

They fired together, Lyons squeezing off a short burst from his Ingram, opening the gunner's chest. His adversary triggered two quick rounds as he was going over backward, but his bullets slapped into the ceiling, raining plaster dust.

A glance inside the room showed no one but the woman assigned to work that station, and he left her there, wrapped in a sheet and staring at the dead man on the floor.

Six minutes had elapsed since he had entered, and the news team would be rolling up outside before much longer. Lyons had the upstairs hallway covered when the next two doors flew open simultaneously, one on either side, disgorging gunmen clad in underwear. They looked ridiculous, but there was nothing laughable about their weapons, one a semiautomatic pistol and the other a revolver. Both weapons looked locked into target acquisition in a flash.

He hit the deck and opened fire. The Ingram stuttered, bucking in his fist, brass streaming out of the ejection port and bouncing on the floor around him.

On the left, his target with the autoloader took four hits across the chest and vaulted backward, shoulders touching down before his rump and heels. The other gunman flinched from Lyons's flashing SMG, his free hand rising like a puny shield to intercept the bullets, but it didn't do any good. A stream of parabellum manglers spun him like a top and dropped him with his face pressed flush against the stucco wall.

The Able Team leader scrambled to his feet and ditched his empty magazine, reloading on the move. Excited voices at his back made Lyons turn to check it out, but there were only hookers, peering from their doorways at the carnage, speaking excitedly in frightened tones to one another, ducking back and out of sight when Lyons spun to face them.

Nobody tried to stop him from leaving, and no one waited for him in the alley as he cleared the exit in a rush, turned left and sprinted for his waiting vehicle. His wristwatch made it 4:29, and if the news hawks were on time, they should be able to obtain some decent photographs before police arrived to cordon off the scene and put their standing plans for damage control in action.

Lyons wished them luck and left them to it, his mind already focused on his next hit down the line. Behind him there was meat enough for any vultures in the neighborhood, and he wasn't done yet by any means.

THE PRIVATE NUMBER for Luis Obidos was among the items Juliana Alegrete had supplied to Bolan and his team. It took three rings before somebody picked up on the other end and offered salutations in Portuguese. He answered back in English, cutting to the chase.

"Put Luis on the line," he demanded.

"I may say who's calling?"

"Be my guest," Bolan said. "I'm one of the men who's been giving him headaches since yesterday. Now we can talk, or I turn up the heat. It's his choice. Tell him that."

He listened to the distant telephone receiver thump against some solid surface as the gofer put it down. There was a snatch of muttered conversation, unintelligible, and a moment's silence before another voice came on the line.

"Hello?"

He didn't have to ask if he was talking to the man in charge.

"I want the woman back, Obidos, safe and sound."

"Your several messages have been received. What is this peasant child to you?"

"Let's say I like her style. I wouldn't want to see her wind up like her brother."

"Ah, Lorenzo. Accidents will happen, yes? I find this to be true. Whenever someone picks a risky occupation, he has no one but himself to blame for the results."

"You're learning that firsthand, I guess."

Obidos chuckled. Bolan thought it sounded forced. "I won't deny that you have caused me certain inconvenience," said the death squad's leader, "but I will survive. The movement will survive."

"I hope you're taking bets on that. I'd like to get some money down."

Another chuckle, definitely forced this time. "We have a problem, you and I," Obidos said. "If I knew where this woman was, the one you seek, and felt inclined to help you find her, there is still the matter of arranging for delivery. I don't know who I'm talking to or where you can be found."

"Another inconvenience, I imagine," Bolan said.

"If we agreed upon a meeting place, perhaps there would be something I could do to help you. I am not without resources, after all."

"They're getting whittled down, though. Running shorter all the time."

"A simple matter of accommodation. I admit no part in any action that precipitated your—how shall I say?—*unusual* behavior. If I found a woman being held against her will, I would of course make every effort to release her and return her to her loved ones."

"Chivalry's not dead, I see."

"In fact," Obidos said, continuing despite the interruption, "let's assume I can find such a damsel in distress. When would her friends desire to have her back?"

"As soon as possible," the Executioner replied.

"Two hours, perhaps?"

"That's pretty quick for theoretical solutions."

"As I said, I'm not—"

"Without resources," Bolan finished for him. "Right, I heard. That leaves the meeting place."

"Your choice," Obidos said. "I'm feeling generous today."

"Let me think about it for a second."

He was stalling, but he had to work out at least a couple of the details before he was committed to a rendezvous. Two hours should be ample time, he thought. The Able Team warriors were already on their way back from São Paulo, but the meeting would require some preparation on their part.

He tried to picture Rio de Janeiro in his head, a bird's-eye view or satellite projection, laying out the major streets and public buildings, parks and tourist attractions. When the notion came, it seemed so natural that Bolan wondered why he hadn't thought of it at once.

The contest—this phase, anyway—would be resolved where it began.

"The Jardim Zoologico," he told Obidos. "Meet me at the monkey house two hours from now."

Before his enemy could answer, Bolan cradled the receiver, walking back in the direction of his car. He had to get in touch with Able Team as soon as they were close enough to copy his transmission.

They were going to the zoo again, and this time Bolan knew that it would be a trap. The only question left to be resolved was who was trapping whom.

CHAPTER EIGHT

Juliana Alegrete didn't know where she was going, any more than she knew where her captors had confined her. They had taken all her personal belongings, watch included, and she didn't have a clue what time it was when they came in to fetch her, pistols drawn, their seeming leader carrying a two-foot piece of black cloth in his hand.

"You have good luck," he told her, smiling. "We've been ordered to release you. Will you put this on, or must I do it for you?"

He was holding out the blindfold as he spoke, and Alegrete saw a feeble glint of hope. If they were still concerned about the possibility that she could afterward identify her prison, then they had to truly mean to set her free. Otherwise, why waste time with a blindfold when they could simply shoot her where she stood?

"I'll do it," Alegrete told him, reaching out to take the blindfold, careful not to let her fingers touch his hand. She wanted no more contact with these animals than absolutely necessary.

She wrapped the cloth around her head so that her eyes were covered and tied an awkward knot in back. The blindfold fit her snugly, cutting off all light, and Alegrete had barely finished tying it when she fell prey to second thoughts. Suppose they meant to shoot her now, the blindfold a diversion, something to distract her from resisting, fighting back? She couldn't even see now if one of them had raised his weapon, aiming at her face.

She flinched involuntarily when one of them stepped closer, reaching for her arm. The touch made her skin crawl, but she didn't pull away. Instead, she tried to fix the man's position in her mind, in case she had to strike out blindly, groping for his face or groin in self-defense.

They didn't need to touch her, guide her from the little cell as they were doing now, if they were bent on killing her. Unless, of course, they meant to murder her outside, thus keep from smearing blood around the floor and walls.

Alegrete let herself be guided through the doorway, turning left, continuing along a corridor that smelled familiar from the short trek when she'd arrived.

She bumped against some heavy piece of furniture, a couch or easy chair perhaps, before they reached the exit. Cool, fresh air washed over her as the door was opened and her faceless guide took her outside. She heard the others close behind and made no attempt to bolt or lift her blindfold as they led her to a waiting car.

It was a different vehicle from that used in her kidnapping. More legroom, for a start, and it smelled new, like polished leather. She felt sealed within a vacuum when the doors closed, one on either side of her and one in front. The driver, she surmised. The engine had more power to it than the vehicle in which she was abducted from the São Martinho shelter. Possibly a limousine—it seemed to have the weight and solid feel. It also meant there would be tinted windows, hence the fact that she hadn't been forced to lie down on the floor this time.

"Where are you taking me?"

"To see a friend," one of her keepers said. "He's very anxious for your safe return."

Belasko? Alegrete wondered. Who else could it be? But how had he persuaded them to set her free?

"But where...?"

"You like the animals, I think." It sounded like the leader talking. "At least, you try to save them from the march of progress."

"Yes, that's right."

"You should be happy, then," he said. "We're going to the zoo."

THE MONKEY HOUSE WAS jumping when he got there shortly after feeding time, and Bolan took advantage of the modest crowd to reconnoiter the place. There would be lookouts spotted somewhere close at hand... or would Obidos wait and try to seal off the killing ground after everyone arrived? It could go either way, a setup or a suck, and Bolan did his best to search out any gunners waiting for him at the scene.

The men of Able Team were scattered, each one covering a main approach to the exhibit, blending with the tourist crush as it began to thin out toward closing time. They had another thirty minutes before zookeepers started circulating through the grounds, inviting visitors to leave. With any kind of luck, the enemy would be on time, and they could wrap this up without innocent civilians getting in the line of fire.

It crossed his mind that Juliana might not be among the gunners when they came. It would be simple for Obidos to dispatch an army while the woman stayed behind, safe under lock and key. Or what if she was dead by now, another grim statistic in the death squad's reign of terror?

Bolan didn't dwell upon that line of thought. If Juliana had been killed, or if she was prevented from appearing at the rendezvous, then he would have to fight his way out of the trap, resume his blitz against Obidos and the death squad, no holds barred. And next time, the Executioner vowed, there would be no reprieve, no warnings, no white flags.

A subtle movement at the corner of his eye cut through the reverie. He kept it casual as he began to turn, see what it was that triggered the alarm inside his head.

Four men were ambling toward the primate house, a woman in their midst, surrounded, like a witness on her way to court in some high-profile trial, with bodyguards to get her there alive. Except, thought Bolan, these gorillas would have rather different orders from their chief.

Juliana Alegrete wore a lightweight jacket, with a yellow blouse beneath and a skirt that stopped an inch or two above her knees. Dark glasses hid her eyes, but they couldn't disguise the other bruises on her face.

The sight made Bolan grit his teeth in anger, but he kept his wits about him. He fell back a few steps as the enemy came on, his lips barely moving as he told the tiny microphone on his lapel, "They're here."

"They've got some company," Lyons said, speaking through the earpiece Bolan wore. "Three heavies coming your way, past the bear pits."

"Three more moving past the reptile house right now," Schwarz added.

"I feel left out," Blancanales said. "Nobody visible on this side."

"Some guys have all the luck," Schwarz said.

"Close up," said Bolan. "Everybody wait for me."

At last he turned to face the gunmen and their hostage, let them know that he was wise to them. Three held their ground, one taking Juliana by the arm to hold her back, while number four—the leader, Bolan recognized—came forward to negotiate.

The man wasn't Luis Obidos, but it came as no surprise to find the death squad's master missing from the scene. He wouldn't be the kind who got his own hands dirty, risked his life while there were grunts on hand to get it done.

The raincoat Bolan wore was black, lightweight and loose enough to hide the Uzi on its swivel rig beneath his arm. The right-hand pocket had been cut away, allowing unobtrusive access to the SMG. His hand was wrapped around its pistol grip as he stood waiting for the leader of the team to speak.

"You're an American?" the gunner said.

"That's right."

"You wait for us, I think."

"Could be."

"Where are your friends?"

"What friends?" Bolan asked, glancing past the man toward Juliana. "Maybe I'm alone. You let me have the woman, and we can wrap this up right now."

His adversary smiled at that. "It's not that simple, I'm afraid. You really should have brought your friends along to help."

The guy was reaching underneath his jacket for a weapon, while the goons behind did likewise. Bolan felt the first jolt of adrenaline as he revealed the Uzi and aimed it at the leader's chest.

"Well, maybe so. If you insist." He fired a 3-round burst that struck the man dead center, slammed him over backward on the cobbled path. Behind the writhing body, one gorilla had a grip on Juliana's hair, a pistol in his right hand, dragging her toward cover while the other two stood fast with weapons drawn.

And this, Bolan thought, is the way it goes to hell.

CARL LYONS WAS behind his targets as they passed the bear pits, moving toward the monkey house. He had a box of popcorn in his left hand, more or less forgotten as he homed in on the gunners, his right hand rising toward the big Colt Python in its shoulder rig.

The sudden rattle of machine-gun fire changed everything. Before the loud staccato sound, his targets were proceeding slowly, almost casually toward their destination, acting as if they didn't have a worry in the world. No sooner had the din of shots erupted, though, when they drew weapons, breaking toward their mark like sprinters in the last yards of a desperate race.

He had to stop them before they closed on Striker's blind side and caught him in a cross fire. Lyons dropped his popcorn and palmed the big .357 Magnum in a firm two-handed grip. He lined up on the right-hand gunner, squared his sights between the target's shoulder blades and squeezed the trigger once.

The Python bucked and roared, its recoil tingling in his wrist and forearm. Lyons saw the bullet hit, watched fabric ripple from the impact, staining instant crimson as the guy pitched forward on his face.

Which still left two, both turning to confront the enemy behind them, semiauto pistols in their hands. The middle gunner got off two quick shots, not aiming, but he still came close enough to make Lyons flinch from angry hornets buzzing past his head.

The Python answered, slamming two rounds through the gunner's rib cage, lifting him completely off his feet. He vaulted backward like a rag doll in a windstorm. Scarlet geysers spouted from his wounds, blood spattering the cobblestone like viscous rain.

The third man was intent on running for his life, more anxious to escape than duel with Lyons, though he squeezed off several aimless shots by instinct as he ran. There wasn't much in terms of cover to be had, but he was desperate, leaping for the nearest waist-high railing, down into the pit.

There was a loud splash as he found the moat, then thrashing sounds and an angry stream of Portuguese that Lyons took for cursing. Seconds later, while he was advancing toward the pit, a rumbling snarl eclipsed the gunner's voice. The curses turned to screams, the screaming interspersed with muffled gunshots.

Lyons made the rail, peered over, leading with the Python just in case. He found the shooter grappling with a giant polar bear, his point-blank pistol shots no worse than bee stings to the snarling bear as it gnawed his left arm to the bone and used three-inch claws to rake his flanks.

All things considered, Lyons was surprised how long the gunner lasted in that grim, uneven contest. Shock apparently kept him from feeling it when the bear ripped his arm out of the socket, pumping blood into the moat. The slide locked open on his pistol when the last round went, but he reversed it, swung the butt against his massive adversary's skull. It was a bold but risky move, which let the bear chomp down on his remaining arm and hold fast while it began to bludgeon him with sweeping roundhouse blows from left and right.

Lyons never knew how many swings it took to crush the gunner's skull. No more than three or four, in any case, and he was a limp corpse in the bear's unyielding grasp.

Snack time.

Lyons felt his stomach knotting and turned away before the Arctic predator began to feed in earnest. Fumbling with the Python's cylinder release, he dumped the empty cartridges, reloading on the move as he proceeded toward the monkey house.

Three down, but they weren't yet in the clear. Seven gunners remained that he knew of, and they couldn't rule out backup teams sequestered somewhere on the grounds.

Too bad he couldn't take the bear along, Lyons thought, for a small diversion on the way, but the brute was occupied.

The Ironman would be forced to deal with any other gunmen on his own.

THE BULLETPROOF VEST had saved his life, but Jose Campos felt like road kill, stretched out on the cobblestone, ribs aching from the impact of the bullets that had knocked him sprawling. It required an effort just to breathe, and pain lanced through his torso with each breath.

Still, he could move, if only with a grueling effort, and his enemy was still alive, still firing on his men. Campos could stop him yet if he was swift and sly enough.

The sly part was no problem. *Swift*, however, took some doing in his present state.

Campos heard the others running, firing, cursing, and he wondered if they had been smart enough to keep a firm grip on the woman. Never mind. She would be dead before they left the zoo, in any case. His first priority was taking out the stranger who had nearly killed him with the hidden submachine gun.

Campos strained his neck to scan the battlefield. His adversary was some thirty feet away, crouched behind a pair of trash cans framed in tidy brick. It made for solid cover, but he lacked mobility and had to put himself at risk each time he rose to fire the Uzi. Campos was behind him, at an angle. He could take the man down, if...

For a moment he was panicked, fearing he had lost his pistol when he fell. Relief washed over Campos when he felt it, wedged between his buttocks and the cobblestone. He shifted slightly, took the weapon in his hand and brought it into line with his intended target.

No, it wouldn't work. His hand was trembling, and the painful spasms in his rib cage made it difficult, if not impossible, for him to aim. Campos would have to use both hands, and that meant sitting up, at least. His chances would be better if he knelt or stood, and that meant risking everything.

He bit his lip, deciding he would have to take the chance.

It cost him everything he had in terms of energy, but Campos sat up slowly, trying to avoid the sudden movements that would draw his adversary's eye. He was about to try the shot while sitting upright, elbows braced against his knees, but it felt shaky, and he knew there might not be a second chance.

Campos got his legs under him, leaned forward on his hands and pushed off. The pistol scraped on stone as he was lurching to his feet. The sound seemed to echo through the park, but his intended target didn't notice, squeezing off a short burst from his Uzi just before. Small favors, Campos thought, and struggled to remain upright on legs that felt like rubber. If he could only keep his balance for another moment . . .

At the end he rushed it, ruined everything with haste. He had a perfect fix on the target's profile, framed directly in his gun sights, but he lost control and jerked the trigger back instead of squeezing it with care. The bullet missed his mark by inches, sprayed the target's cheek with brick dust as it ricocheted.

And that was all.

He was about to try again, pour out the next few rounds in rapid fire, but Campos never got the chance. His adversary swung around to face him, rocking backward on his haunches to present a smaller target even as the submachine gun started spitting death in his direction. Two or three rounds nailed his legs, and he was falling, arms thrown out to catch himself, the pistol spinning out of reach, when yet another bullet drilled into the space between his collarbone and shoulder blade.

He felt the white-hot lance inside him, knew that he was dying, even with his foggy knowledge of anatomy. The leaden fullness in his throat and chest was blood, exploding from a severed artery to flood his lungs. It was an eerie feeling, this one, drowning on dry land.

At least, Campos thought, he wouldn't be forced to tell Luis that they had failed.

He was actually smiling when he died.

BLANCANALES HAD TO JOG from his position near the alligator pits to catch up with the action. It was ten to three without him, otherwise, and that was ten they knew about, with the potential for a backup team still preying on his mind. Now, ten on three weren't the worst odds in the world, considering the three consisted of Mack Bolan, Gadgets Schwarz and Carl Lyons. It was more like even money when he thought about it, but the Politician didn't feel like being left out of the game.

No way.

So he was jogging past the alligators, then around a wide enclosure housing antelopes and zebra. Somewhere in the background, he could hear hyenas cackling at the swift approach of night.

The sounds of gunfire turned his jog into an all-out sprint. A submachine gun first, with pistols answering, and then, from Lyons's direction, loud reports from what could only be his Colt Python. Which way should he go? And what was Gadgets doing all this time?

As if in answer to his silent questions, more guns started going off immediately to his left, from where Schwarz had been stationed, near the reptile house. Pol made his choice and swerved in that direction, pouring on the speed. He had his pistol drawn and ready, scanning for a target, so intent on helping Gadgets that he missed the danger close at hand.

The two young men came out of nowhere, stepping from the shadowed doorway of a public rest room. One of them, the guy in front, was carrying a shotgun, but he got a little hasty with it, counting on the spread to compensate for mediocre marksmanship. Instead of lining up a decent shot, he braced the cut-down stock against his hip and started blasting like a gangster in the movies. Out in Hollywood, however, they had editors and FX men to score the hits, no matter where you aimed. In combat, when your life was riding on the line, it didn't quite work out that way.

He almost nailed the Politician, even so. Pol felt a pellet slap the left cheek of his buttocks, tearing up his wallet, others plucking at his jacket. It was all the warning he required to launch himself into a head-long dive, no cover handy, but at least the change in elevation ought to spoil his adversary's aim.

The shotgun's muzzle-flash gave Pol his target, firing as he fell, three rounds away before he hit the cobblestone. He saw the gunner reeling, slumping backward, maybe not disabled, but the shock of impact punched him off his feet. Behind him, in the shadows, number two was ducking, dodging, trying for a clear shot with a shiny automatic.

Blancanales didn't give him time to set it up. He triggered three more shots, still lying prone, and watched his target jerk, then drop to his knees. He executed a slow roll forward, so that he was lying on his face, the gun wedged underneath him somewhere.

It was all the edge Pol needed. He leaped to his feet and rushed toward the rest room. He was right about the hardman with the shotgun. He was still alive and gasping like a grounded trout, blood soaking through his white shirt from a chest wound that might kill him if the Politician gave it time.

Unfortunately for the gunner, he had no time left to spare.

He put a mercy round between the young man's eyes and turned away without a backward glance. Those two were dead, but there were others still alive and kicking, trying desperately to kill his friends.

Pol ran to join the nearest battle he could find.

THE HELL OF IT, Gadgets thought, was that he let himself be cornered with a bunch of snakes and lizards. There he was, on top of it, a clear shot at his targets, and he hadn't noticed number four, some forty yards behind the other three. A straggler, right, but that was no excuse for negligence. No sooner had he dropped the gunner on his left, a clean shot through the head, than Mr. Backup started blasting from his flank and drove him under cover, back into the reptile house.

Which brought him to his present situation, crouching near the open doorway, wishing he had something more than the Beretta 93-R to defend himself when the odds were three on one. Beside him, in a large terrarium with glass up front, a cobra reared and spread its hood to challenge this invader on its turf. Around him, high and low, more cages seethed and rippled with the vipers, mambas, adders, kraits and coral snakes that exerted such a pull on tourists at the zoo. The occupants of half a dozen cages here could lay a company of soldiers to waste in nothing flat.

He leaned around the corner, winged a shot in the direction of his enemies, but had no hope of scoring when he couldn't even aim. They had him bottled up, but worse than being cornered was the knowledge that his good friends were in jeopardy because of his mistake. One man could pin him down here, while the others went to deal with Lyons or the Executioner. Outflank them, maybe, come up on their blind side for a sneak attack.

Gadgets knew there had to be something he could do. Another exit from the snake house, right! The traffic was supposed to run one-way, and he was crouching by the normal exit, where they saved the heavy killer snakes for last. If he retreated, made his way out through the entrance, there was still a chance he could surprise his adversaries, shift the balance, maybe take them down.

He figured it was worth a try.

Gadgets fired another aimless shot around the doorjamb, just to keep their heads down, then he rose and moved along the corridor between glass-fronted walls.

He eventually came out into fading daylight, with the square bulk of the reptile house between him and his enemies. Schwarz circled to his left and kept going, leading with the Beretta as he came around one final corner and beheld one of his adversaries kneeling on the cobblestone, no shelter, covering the building's exit with an SMG.

It was an easy shot from thirty feet, and Schwarz couldn't resist. He sighted down the 93-R's slide, took a good two-handed grip and slammed a parabellum round into his target's skull. The guy was still in motion, going over on his side, when Gadgets poked his head around the corner, looking for the others, half expecting to discover they were gone.

Not quite.

The other two cut loose with automatic weapons even as he showed himself, the bullets chipping brick and whining off the cobblestone. He ducked back under cover, wondering if he was better off or in a worse position now, when it was down to two on one but he wasn't surrounded by the safety of brick walls.

He had to work with what he had, and that meant exposure, maybe rushing them. Or should he try to drag it out and keep them occupied while Bolan and the others wrapped up their end of the confrontation, bagged the woman and got out clean? At least this way Schwarz knew his two remaining enemies wouldn't be stalking someone else.

Unless they killed him first.

The rush was unexpected, both men firing from the hip to keep his head down, charging toward the reptile house, intent on finishing the duel once and for all. The double stream of fire kept Schwarz from sniping back. They would be on him in another moment, two against his one.

He was about to bolt for cover when the flat reports of pistol fire cut through the rattle of their SMGs. Not another one! But there was something different now. Excited conversation from Schwarz's enemies, and while they kept on firing, no more rounds were swarming his position. They were firing somewhere else, at someone else.

He risked a peek around the corner, saw Pol Blancanales dodging, weaving, firing as he ran. One of the gunners staggered, then dropped to his knees, still pumping bullets from the submachine gun even as he fell. The other was retreating toward the snake house, running like an all-pro quarterback.

Schwarz rose to meet him, squeezing off three quick rounds from the Beretta and scoring with all three. His man broke stride and appeared to stumble, sprawling lifeless on the cobblestone. That still left one, but Pol was dealing with him, ducking the sporadic bursts of automatic fire and putting two more rounds on target for the kill.

"Are you okay?" he called across the bloodstained killing ground.

Schwarz grinned. "I'm getting there."

THE LEADER of the hit team almost nailed him, coming back to life that way, but he was shaky on his aim, and Bolan made sure he was finished on the second try. You couldn't miss the blood that pooled around his face and ran between the cobblestone, bright crimson pulsing from the blowhole in his neck.

Two down, but one of those remaining still had Juliana in his grip. He used her like a shield, retreating in a search for better cover, while his sidekick tried to keep the Executioner pinned down. The barricade of brick and trash cans kept him safe enough, but it restricted his mobility, and Bolan feared that it was giving Juliana's captor time to slip away.

He had to put a kink in that equation before the two surviving members of the team got wise and bugged out with the woman. It meant a mortal risk, but that was nothing new for Bolan. Every day he woke and put his pants on meant another dance with death.

This time, at least, he knew the risk involved a worthy cause.

He switched mags on the Uzi, held it steady in his right hand as he broke from cover. As he dived out into the open, lumpy cobblestone immediately bruised knees and elbows. To his right the rearguard shooter tried to pivot, tracking him, but Bolan got there faster with the SMG and stitched him with a rising burst from crotch to throat. The guy went through a jerky little dance and sat down hard, his weapon clattering beside him on the walk. As he slumped over backward, there was no life in his eyes.

And that left one—the most important one, if only for the hostage in his grasp. It took a heartbeat for the Executioner to switch his weapon's fire-selector switch to semiauto, following the nervous shooter with his sights.

The shooter played it cautious, keeping Alegrete right in front of him, but he couldn't decide which way to point his pistol. First he held the muzzle pressed against her cheek, then waved the gun in Bolan's general direction for a beat or two before he brought it back to the woman's head.

Coordinating hand and eye could be the tricky part with a precision shot, no matter what the range. In this case Bolan's target was no more than forty feet away, but tagging him meant watching both his feet and hands at the same time. The only decent target Bolan had would be the gunner's legs, where they were visible between Juliana's, and even that shot would be dicey, with a risk of wounding her. A leg wound, even so, was better than a bullet in the head.

He had to take the chance.

Another step, one more, and Bolan caught the flicker as his adversary took the gun away from Juliana's head once more, as if to try a shot. There was no time for hesitation, as a denim thigh came into view, and Bolan squeezed the Uzi's trigger once. A parabellum shocker burned in on target, drilling flesh and shattering the femur in a burst of crimson.

Bolan saw his target stagger, listing, Juliana spinning from his grasp and sacrificing one sleeve of her blouse to break away. He concentrated on the gunner, firing three more shots on single shot as the man went down, saw two of them strike home, almost dead center on his chest. The shooter lost his pistol as he hit the deck, but was long past retrieving it.

Alegrete ran into Bolan's arms as he rose, momentum almost downing both of them. He held her close, felt tears against the hollow of his neck. Behind her, coming into view around the north side of the monkey house, was Carl Lyons. He scanned the bodies, checking each in turn before he tucked his Python out of sight.

"All done?" he asked.

"Looks like," the Executioner replied.

"We'd better roll."

"The others?"

"Here they are." Lyons nodded toward Pol and Gadgets, late arrivals on the scene.

"All hostile troops accounted for?" Bolan asked.

"It's a clean sweep," Gadgets said, "as far as I can tell."

"Okay, let's move. We've got a plane to meet."

CHAPTER NINE

Juliana Alegrete was reluctant to leave Rio, but she had no viable alternative. The death squad had her marked for execution, and she didn't wish to join her brother in the Great Beyond just yet. The charter flight to Nassau was arranged by Bolan, with some help from Stony Man, and the woman had a tight-lipped escort waiting at the airport, courtesy of Hal Brognola's contacts in the CIA.

Her mood was solemn as they sat together in a corner of the large departure lounge at Santos Dumont Airport. Lyons, Schwarz and Blancanales had the layout covered, while the man from Langley watched the plane as it was being fueled. There would be no surprises this time in the cargo hold.

"I can't believe they've really won," she said at last.

"How do you figure that?" Bolan asked.

"My brother's dead, and now they're forcing me to leave my home. They've beaten me."

"Consider this an overdue vacation," Bolan said. "You'll be home soon. I think you'll find some changes by then."

Alegrete frowned. "You've done so much already. The best thing is for you to leave right now. There are too many of them, everywhere you turn."

"Seems like their numbers kept on getting smaller all the time," Bolan said.

"And how many can you kill? A thousand? Two?"

"As many as it takes," he said.

The woman shook her head. "I used to think there was another country, one the death squads didn't own. But I was wrong. They *are* Brazil. Look at our history if you have any doubts. There's nothing else."

"Your brother didn't think so."

"And it cost his life. Where is he now?" A single tear rolled down her cheek.

"I don't have any theories on the afterlife," Bolan said. "As it is, I've got my hands full, living day to day. But one thing I can tell you from experience, and that is that the hard men never really *own* a country or a people. Look at Hitler, or the Russian Communists. They may hang on for years, until it feels like nothing else exists, but in the end they always fall. You want to phone up Obidos and ask him how he's feeling at the moment?"

"No." She tried a cautious smile but couldn't make it stick. "I'm frightened."

"Don't worry, you'll be fine in Nassau."

"No, I don't mean for myself." She reached out, took his hand and squeezed it. "You don't realize the danger."

"Sure I do," Bolan said, "but the best way anybody ever found to take a bully down is just keep punching till he drops. We're halfway there. I'm not about to let up now."

"You'll all be killed."

"We may surprise you," Bolan said. "Obidos and his army haven't done that well so far."

"I wish you'd just come with me." Alegrete hesitated for a beat before she added, "All of you."

"I wouldn't mind a few days in the sun, but I've got a job to do."

"You risk your life for strangers."

"Not quite," Bolan replied, holding her gaze with his own.

"And if you win," she said, "what happens afterward, when you are gone?"

"Brazil will still have you and thousands more who value human life, a civilized society without the death squads or the slash-and-burn economy. I wouldn't be surprised if you helped organize them somewhere down the line."

"I'm not a politician," the woman told him.

"Better yet. An honest woman couldn't hurt."

She did smile then. "How is it that you have such faith," she asked, "when you have seen the worst that men can do?"

"It's all a matter of perspective," Bolan said. "If there's a worst, it means there also has to be a best. You'd be surprised how often that shines through. It's hard to beat."

She beamed at that and said, "You're an idealist, after all."

"Don't let it get around," the Executioner replied. "I've got an image to protect."

"Your secret's safe with me."

"I thought it might be."

From the corner of his eye, he saw the Politician moving closer and Lyons shifting in the background to protect their flank.

"The plane's all set," Pol said.

"Okay, let's do it."

Bolan rose, took Alegrete's bag and led her from the terminal across the runway apron to the Learjet that waited for its solitary passenger. There was another moment's hesitation at the loading stairs while she stood on tiptoes, brushing Bolan's cheek with soft, warm lips.

"Be careful, please."

"I always am."

Alegrete didn't argue with the barefaced lie, but simply squeezed his hand and turned away, not looking back again before the door closed on her escort from the CIA.

"The lady has some nerve," Gadgets said as they walked back to the terminal. Behind them Bolan heard the GE turbojets begin to rev, a high-pitched whine that would become a scream in seconds flat.

"She'll do all right," Lyons stated, glancing back in the direction of the jet as it taxied toward the runway, getting ready to take off.

"I wouldn't be surprised," Bolan said, keeping both eyes on the terminal.

It helped that Juliana would be out of sight and mind before they started on the next phase of their mission in Brazil, one less distraction when he needed to be focused on one goal: the swift eradication of his enemies.

The war in Rio might be winding down, but it had only been phase one of Bolan's campaign from the start. The action in Brazil wasn't confined to city streets and high-rise office blocks. There was a wide, wild world out there, and it was waiting for a visit from the Executioner and friends.

LUIS OBIDOS NEEDED someone he could punish, chastise for the failure of his latest plan. He never thought to blame himself; his strategy was perfect, plotted out in every detail. If it fell apart, he reasoned, someone had to have bungled on the execution. Otherwise, Obidos wondered, fuming, how could everything have gone so wrong?

Blame had to lie with someone on the strike team— that was obvious. Jose Campos had either bungled the assignment or had chosen badly when he picked his soldiers. Either way, the field commander on a mission took responsibility for its success or failure.

Yes, Obidos told himself with satisfaction, someone on the team was certainly to blame.

The problem was that Jose Campos and his men were dead. All twelve of them, stretched out on tables at the crowded city morgue. Obidos didn't plan to claim the bodies. That would mark the raid as his responsibility, and he had no use for another headache at the moment, thank you very much. If any of the bunglers had surviving relatives, it would be their job to make funeral arrangements, answer any questions the authorities might have.

In time, of course, Obidos knew that he would have to answer certain questions of his own. It was no secret in the city that Campos had been his second-in-command. It wouldn't take a Sherlock Holmes to solve *that* puzzle, and he guessed that homicide investigators would be knocking on his door by breakfast time. Obidos didn't fear them, knew that most of the police in Rio—in Brazil—were sympathetic to his cleanup efforts, but he also knew this incident was very different from the average shooting in the streets.

For one thing, it was members of the death squad who had died, most of them ex-policemen or ex-soldiers, men with families, some of them known and well respected in their home communities. The fact that they were gunned down in a public place, while armed and doing God-knew-what would prompt reporters to start digging. How long would it take before they linked the action at the zoo to Juliana Alegrete's disappearance?

This was trouble, Obidos thought. First the brother died, and it would take an idiot to buy the "accident" scenario. The left-wing press was sniffing closer to Lorenzo Alegrete's death each day, and now his sister disappeared, leaving members of the death squad scattered in her wake like broken toys.

Where was she?

Was she even still alive?

If so, how long before she surfaced, giving statements to the press in Rio? In America?

Obidos wished that he had never forged his pact with Daniel Nazare to support Nazare's empire in the jungle. Life was good when he confined himself to hunting petty criminals, street children and subversives. No one really gave a damn what happened to them, anyway. A few old nuns, perhaps, or the American "politically correct" brigade of snoops who minded everybody's business but their own. Things had been simple, then, from running down targets to fixing cases in the courts on the rare occasions that a member of his private army was arrested.

Now, though, with Nazare in the picture, everything had changed. There was big money on the table, and the risks increased proportionately. Targets like the Alegretes were selected from the upper strata of society in Rio de Janeiro, and their deaths or disappearance couldn't be shrugged off as if they were a pair of homeless beggars. Once, perhaps, a flimsy explanation might get by with help from the police, but twice was definitely stretching it. And now, if Juliana Alegrete was alive, what stories she could tell of her captivity, perhaps identifying Campos and the others as her kidnappers?

Obidos slammed his fist into the padded headrest of his favorite easy chair. It brought back pleasant memories of punching suspects in the kidneys, when he wore a uniform and drew his salary from the police force. In the good old days, before "democracy" crept in and ruined everything.

It felt so good, in fact, that Obidos kept on punching until his knuckles ached and there were sweat stains at the armpits of his long-sleeved shirt. He stepped back, winded, checked for signs of damage on the chair and saw nothing.

It was just like Rio lately. Anything he did, the effort still fell short. The tide of decadence and lawlessness was overwhelming civilized society. Obidos felt hard-pressed to hold the line, much less reverse the deadly tide.

Obidos crossed the room and poured himself a double shot of whiskey, tossed it back and poured another. When the alcohol had kindled fire inside him, he felt better. Not relaxed, by any means, but better in the sense that he could organize his thoughts without an angry buzzing in his ears or the crimson film of rage obscuring his vision.

Who to call?

It would be simple for Obidos to upbraid his various subordinates, but they had no part in the failure of his recent plan. Who, then? Who better than the man who'd gotten him into this predicament to start with?

It was after nine o'clock, which meant that Daniel Nazare would be "entertaining" at his home. Young women, sometimes two or three at once, were chief among the houseguests he preferred. In Rio, when you had a bank account the size of Daniel Nazare's, buying love—or renting its facsimile, at least—wasn't a problem. Any difficulty he encountered would revolve around the process of selecting special women from the crowd of applicants.

Obidos knew before he made the call that Nazare wouldn't appreciate the interruption. That was sim-

ply one more reason for the call. If Obidos couldn't
rest, relax, enjoy himself, why should Nazare have that
luxury? This trouble had begun with him and his in-
sistence that Lorenzo Alegrete had to be permanently
silenced. Well, the job had been done as ordered, but
the cleanup chore was getting out of hand. He had lost
count of the number of his soldiers killed the past two
days in Rio and São Paulo, while his faceless enemies
ran free without a single casualty.

It was enough to try the patience of a saint, and Luis
Obidos made no claims to sainthood. Quite the opposite, in fact. He felt more like the devil most of the
time.

Obidos took another drink for courage, just a single shot, and walked back to his desk. He picked up
the telephone receiver, tapping out Nazare's home
number from memory. He listened to it ring three,
four times before one of the servants answered.

"Yes?"

"I need to speak with Daniel. Put him on the
phone."

"Mr. Nazare isn't taking calls tonight."

The snap inside his skull was almost physical in its
intensity. Obidos clutched the telephone so tightly that
his knuckles blanched, his teeth grinding as he snarled
into the mouthpiece. "He *will* take my call. Go tell
him that Luis Obidos needs to speak with him at once.
You understand? Immediately! Do it now! Your job
depends on it!"

He would have liked to say *Your life depends on it,*
but he had done the trick already. There were muffled

noises as Nazare's servant put the handset down and went to fetch his master. Moments later, when he answered, Daniel Nazare sounded cool, at ease.

"What is it, Luis?"

"We have trouble."

"*We* have trouble?"

"With the woman. She's escaped."

"How careless of you."

"Careless, nothing! I've another dozen soldiers dead, Jose among them. At the zoo, for God's sake! Killed in public! Do you understand what this could mean?"

"It means you're running short of soldiers, I suppose."

He felt like reaching through the line and striking at Nazare, driving over to his house and breaking down the door to kill him in his own posh bedroom while his woman of the evening watched.

"I'm not alone in this, you understand? I have this trouble now because of *you.*"

Nazare's voice took on a sharp edge for the first time as he answered. "I am not responsible for your misfortunes, Luis. If your men are so incompetent they can't go out of doors without somebody killing them, what fault is that of mine?"

"I won't be spoken to this way, you insolent—"

"Do not forget yourself, Luis."

There was menace in Nazare's tone, a threat that needed no expression to be recognized. Obidos was surprised and instantly ashamed to find that he was trembling where he stood.

"I'm not sure I can deal with this alone," he said at last, some of the anger fading from his voice. "You understand?"

"Of course," Nazare said. "If you need help, I'll do my best. It's in my own best interest, after all. About *that* other problem, while I have you on the line . . . is everything prepared?"

Obidos had to stop and think for just a moment, figure out what other problem Nazare was referring to. He had it now, amazed that he could be expected to proceed on yet another front when he was facing such a crisis there in Rio.

"I assumed there would be a delay," he said.

"Nonsense. One thing doesn't affect the other in the least. There's no time like the present to dispose of an unwelcome pest. Get on with it, by all means. I look forward to reports of a successful mission by tomorrow night."

Obidos wanted to object, refuse, defy this cocky bastard who was giving orders to him like a sergeant talking to a lowly private in the midst of basic training. Still, defiance would be costly at the moment, when he needed all Nazare's help and influence to salvage something from the chaos that surrounded him in Rio. It was better if he simply played along and did the job he had agreed to.

Anyway, Obidos thought, an easy victory would boost morale among his troops, with all that they had suffered recently. What better medicine for fighting men than to unleash them on a helpless enemy and let them run amok?

He would consider it a course of therapy, for which Nazare would be picking up the tab.

"It shall be done," he said, and cradled the receiver instantly, before Nazare could say more, demand some new act of subservience.

One mission at a time was all he needed at the moment.

And before that mission, he would need another drink.

"So, WHAT'S THE PLAN?" Carl Lyons asked when they were all together in one car and cruising aimlessly, with Gadgets at the wheel.

"I think we need to go upriver," Bolan answered. "Pay a little visit to the wild frontier."

"The forward team?" Blancanales asked.

Bolan nodded. "We can check it out, see for ourselves what's happening to the interior."

"Why don't we just take out Nazare?" Lyons asked. "I could smoke him at his office, save us all a jungle hike."

"That's not much of an object lesson," Bolan said.

"You figure we can educate this asshole?"

"Nazare?" Bolan frowned and shook his head. "No, I was thinking of his understudies waiting in the wings. Eliminate the man on top, they're lined up twenty, thirty deep to take his place."

"So blitz the wings," Lyons said, cutting to the chase as always.

"It's not the people," Bolan replied. "Not most of them, at least. You have to try and blitz the attitude."

"A greed-reduction program?" Blancanales sounded highly skeptical.

"To kill the attitude, you'd have to smoke the whole damn race," Lyons said. "We could still start with Nazare, for the hell of it."

"You've got a one-track mind," Pol said.

"Damn right. And Nazare's sitting in the middle of the track."

"We'll get around to him," Bolan said, "but it's early yet. If he goes down too soon, without the proper groundwork, he could wind up looking like a martyr. His buddies in the capital could blame eco-terrorists, you name it. I prefer to take a look from the supply side, at the heart of the machine. Nazare may not shine so brightly once we broadcast what he's doing to the country—and especially the native tribes."

"I get a feeling," Gadgets interjected, "that they're not exactly top priority with anyone from *Who's Who in Brazil.* In fact the government would probably appreciate a chance to wipe them out once and for all."

"Forget about the government," Bolan said. "Think about the people for a minute. Some of them already know what's going on upriver. Some of those don't care. A few, like Juliana and her brother, pick a side and take a stand."

"Which leaves the great majority fence-straddling as usual," the Politician said.

"That's right. We need to shake them up a bit and see which way they fall."

"The thing is," Lyons told him, "we've all seen TV specials on the vanishing rain forest, the endangered species, aborigines in danger—hell, you name it. Why should one more headline wake them up or change their minds?"

"I want to rub their noses in it," Bolan said. "I don't know how we'll do at winning hearts and minds, but we can show Nazare up for what he is, spotlight his corporate connection to the death squads. I'll be interested to see how Wall Street feels about financing genocide."

"The bottom line is still the bottom line," Schwarz said.

"Maybe. They trade as much on reputation as on the profit margin, though. This kind of black eye never helped a company that I know of."

"Suppose it doesn't work?" Lyons asked, playing devil's advocate.

"We still know where to find Nazare and Obidos any time we want them," Bolan said. "I can't see giving either one of them a pass."

"You had me worried for a second there," Lyons told him. "I've got those pricks measured for a hole."

"Same here," the Executioner replied. "It's just a point of strategy, deciding when and where to dig."

"I guess a little nature walk won't do me any harm," Lyons said at last.

"Suits me," the Politician echoed.

"Guess I'll need someplace to stash the car," Schwarz said.

"Okay," Bolan said, satisfied now that they were all on board, "here's what I had in mind."

It took the best part of an hour to lay out his plan, refine details, listen to input from his trusted friends. When they were finished, all the fine points memorized, he knew that there were still a thousand different things that could go wrong. A battle plan wasn't a blueprint in the sense that everything remained the same from the initial brainstorm to the final act. Unlike construction work, warfare was fluid. Soldiers had to constantly adapt themselves to changes in terrain and climate, to the shifting tactics of their enemy. A house would sit and wait if you ran into trouble with the weather, ran short of supplies or simply felt like sleeping in one day. A living, breathing enemy would seize upon your weakness, indecision, negligence, and ram it down your throat.

For now they still had the initiative, but that could change at any moment. Bolan's only hope for keeping up the pressure lay in forward motion, nonstop action to confuse, harass and decimate his adversaries.

Some time back, there was a slogan popular on T-shirts and bumper stickers that said He Who Dies With The Most Toys, Wins. It wasn't like that in the hellgrounds, though.

Dead men were always losers on the battlefield, regardless of their uniform.

The Executioner intended to survive and fight another day.

Which meant his chosen enemies would have to die.

CHAPTER TEN

Daybreak on the Xingu River takes a while to filter through the treetops and warm up the ground a hundred or two hundred feet below. The forest floor is never really bright, except in clearings where a giant tree has fallen, and the sunlight lances down to earth like something from an illustration in the more expensive Bibles, with their painted scenes of Glory beaming from on high.

On a tributary of the Xingu, near the point where Pará Province butts against the Mato Grosso, Jacob Reese awoke at dawn. His internal clock rarely failed him, except on mornings after he had stayed up late with the Parañas, drinking native beer. On those days everyone rose an hour or two later and started any chores where they had broken off the day before. It was an easygoing life, all things considered, with no time clocks to punch, no deadlines to meet beyond those imposed by hunger and the changing elements. There were no seasons here, as North Americans would understand the term: no autumn leaf-fall, winter snow or obvious rebirth in spring. The rainy season was a matter of degree, more rain than in the "dry" season, when it still rained almost every day.

There had been no beer-drinking the previous night in the village where Reese had resided for the past two years. The people whom he thought of as his family, *his* tribe, were on the verge of being forced to move again—the third time in as many years. Each day the distant smoke grew closer as a service road was hacked out of the forest, great trees cut and burned to make way for the dubious blessings of "civilization."

The Paraña tribe wasn't included in those blessings. Rather, they were seen as obstacles to progress, something to be moved or else plowed under, preferably out of sight and out of mind forever. "Relocation" was the standard tactic; it sounded like a peaceful move from one home to another, possibly with government assistance, but the stark reality was something else. The Indians could either move or see their village bulldozed flat, with their belongings still inside. They had the whole great forest of the Amazon in which to settle, if they chose, except that there were other tribes to deal with, any way they turned, and the great Amazon forest wasn't as vast as it used to be. Each year the largest natural rain forest in the world was shrinking, huge tracts transformed into a charcoal wasteland where fences, homes and oil rigs sprouted in the place of trees.

There was no room for "savages" in the new Amazon basin. In official parlance, they had outlived their time. The end of the road was at hand. The Indians who fled their homes were forced to battle other tribes for living room, dislodged from hunting grounds and left to starve, while constant travel and privation slashed the birth rate. Those who stood their ground and fought were labeled enemies of progress, marked for swift extermination by the army or the extralegal death squads.

Reese had come to Brazil in pursuit of his doctoral thesis in anthropology, taking time to earn the trust of the Parañas in an atmosphere where faith in men of any race—much less the hated whites—was hard to find. He learned their language, lived as the Parañas lived, made no attempt to judge them or impose his Anglo values on a culture older than his own. If they were primitive in terms of scholarship, technology and hygiene, Reese discovered they were also better off in many ways. There was no crime to speak of in the jungle, and the wars "his" people fought were strictly territorial, a matter of survival in a world of shrunken hunting grounds. The tribe was ignorant of politics, Judeo-Christian morals and the endless guilt trips that inevitably followed on the heels of spiritual "salvation." Reese was happy with the tribe, supremely happy for the first time in his life—until he learned that they were on the verge of being driven to extinction.

Somewhere along the way, his life and goals had changed. His Ph.D. fell by the wayside, interviews and notes forgotten as he pitched in with a will to help the tribe survive. He sensed that some of the Paraña didn't trust him still, might never take him to their hearts completely. Who could blame them? It was *his* race, more or less, that stalked them like wild animals, with guns and sensors tuned to pick out human body heat from several hundred feet above the forest floor, with poisoned food, disease-infested clothing.

There was more trust, granted, now that he had killed on their behalf.

Reese thought about the killing as an accident, but it was clearly more than that. It had been his idea, however ill advised, to meet the foreman of the road crew and discuss his rape of the environment as a thinking human being. Violence was the last thing on his mind the day he'd hiked out of the forest to the road head, met the foreman in his hard hat, faded denim jeans and steel-toed boots.

At first the stout Brazilian looked at Reese as if he were insane, amusement fading into anger when he understood that Reese was serious, suggesting that the crew stop work immediately, turn around and head back to Brasília. Anger led to shouting, and from there to violence, the foreman calling members of his crew to teach this foreigner some respect. They rushed him, swinging bony fists, and Reese, stunned, fought back the best he could. With four on one, he never gave a second thought to drawing his machete, lashing out with desperate strokes to left and right.

One member of the road crew lost three fingers, while another had his cheek laid open to the bone, and still they pressed home the attack. The foreman called for guns, and it was then that Reese struck him, barely conscious of the action, putting all his weight behind the blow that nearly took off his adversary's head. Four Parañas watching from the safety of the trees as Reese left the man dying, turned and ran for cover in the forest.

He was something of a hero to the tribesmen after
that. A few had blamed him when the tribe was forced
to move that time—Reese blamed himself—but most
had come to treat the march of white man's "progress" as a fact of life. They had no concept of the forest's finite size, apparently believing there would
always be more land, more trees, no matter how far
they were driven from their starting place.

Reese did his best to disabuse them of that notion,
bring them into touch with harsh reality, but it was
difficult. He had already given up on forging any kind
of union with the other tribes to organize resistance on
a broader scale, but the Paraña had begun to come
around a bit in terms of picking up on his philosophy.

The killing at the road head had changed Jacob
Reese, as well. From shock and horror, he had come
to view resistance—*armed* resistance—as the only
logical and honorable course of action. Granted, it
seemed hopeless, but the quality of life for people ever
on the run was scarcely an improvement over death.
Selective action, well considered, planned out in advance, might yet delay "society's" destruction of the
forest that was so much more important to the planet
than a mere retreat for scattered bands of aborigines.

Somehow, almost without a conscious effort, Jacob Reese had moved from working anthropologist to
ecoterrorist. The strange thing was that he didn't regret the change.

Not in the least.

This morning there was snake for breakfast, with a
side order of fruit. The fires were lit, a number of the

women up before he woke, and Reese hiked from the village to the nearby river, where he washed his face and found a private spot to do his business.

He was returning to the village proper, looking forward to the tasty snake meat, when he heard the sound of helicopter rotors closing from the west.

He mouthed a curse and started sprinting back to warn his large adopted family before it was too late.

FERMIN CONSTANZO WATCHED the treetops skimming past below the helicopter, leaning on his FN automatic rifle while the wide strap of his safety harness cut into his shoulder. You could hide an army down there, in the forest, and surveillance from the air would never find them—if the searchers used their eyes alone. It pleased Constanzo that technology made hunting easier, less trouble for the men who had to do the job.

"Another hundred yards," said Berto, hunched above the sensor for the infrared device that had been specially designed to pick out thermal "prints" from body temperatures within the normal human range. It didn't work on reptiles, and was sensitive enough to tell an educated user whether he had sighted on a man or, say, a jaguar prowling the forest floor two hundred feet below.

"How many?" he inquired of Berto, leaning closer, shouting to make himself heard above the noise of the engine and rotors.

"Forty, forty-five at least," Berto said, grinning like a hungry caiman. "Maybe more. It gets a little hard to read when they're all bunched together."

Breakfast time, Constanzo thought. His lips turned upward in a narrow smile, devoid of mirth. What better way to start the morning than by killing off forty or fifty forest dwellers?

"Where can we land?" he asked the pilot, speaking through the tiny microphone he had been given for that purpose.

"I can put you down beside the river," the pilot replied, searching for a closer opening among the trees. "This canopy's too close for setting down on top of them. They know that, I suppose."

"The river, then," Constanzo said, "and hurry."

This was more than just another mission, one more stinking village to be blasted off the map. He knew about the mess in Rio, Jose Campos and the others dead. It bothered him, but at the moment Constanzo's first thought was of power vacuums at the top. With Jose Campos gone, there was an opening to fill. He might be too ambitious, hoping for a spot as second-in-command, but he had done his time, come through when others offered only lame excuses, worked his way up through the ranks to wear a sergeant's stripes. It wasn't much, per se, but if he proved himself once more, on an important mission, then Obidos might consider him for something better. It was worth a try, at least.

Besides, Constanzo enjoyed hunting Indians. They were like big-game animals, with greater cunning and intelligence. Their weapons were peculiar, primitive, but still effective if they crept in close enough. It made the hunt more interesting, exciting.

But Constanzo wasn't looking for a thrill this morning. What he needed was a quick, decisive victory, for which he would take credit with Obidos.

Simple.

"Here we go."

The Army-surplus Huey from America heeled over, circled into its descent. Below, Constanzo saw the winding watercourse, a tributary of the Xingu, which in turn went on to feed the mighty Amazon. The village would be several yards east and hidden from the river, already alerted by the helicopter's noise.

Sneaking up on Indians was practically impossible when you were forced to fly for time's sake. With luck, though, they could still make up in speed what they lacked in surprise.

Constanzo felt his stomach rolling as the helicopter dropped a hundred feet, finally hovering some three feet off the riverbank. Its rotor wash beat down surrounding ferns and bushes, flattening potential cover for their enemies. Still, they would have to be alert for arrows launched back in the shadows of the forest, maybe even darts from blowguns. Nothing could be taken for granted in dealing with the forest dwellers, even if they were no more than clever animals.

Constanzo jumped and landed in a crouch. He faced the trees and moved a few steps closer, waiting for his men to group behind him. There were fifteen men besides himself. They would be outnumbered by the Indians, but it wasn't a problem. Two-thirds of the average tribe were noncombatants—women, children and the elderly. No matter, though, since modern weapons—automatic rifles, semiauto pistols, hand grenades—made all the difference in the world.

Still, he could feel a certain apprehension as his men gathered behind him, waiting for the signal to advance. Constanzo chose a point man and waved him forward, the others following while their leader made a point of marching near the middle of the group. If they met armed resistance, he would have a measure of protection now, a fair chance to defend himself. No one expected a commanding officer to lead the way on hostile ground.

Constanzo smelled the village well before he saw it. They had something on the fire for breakfast, but it wasn't simply cooking meat he smelled. There was the *other* smell, which he had noted in a score of confrontations with the forest dwellers. Unwashed bodies, offal decomposing in the humid climate, all the smells that went along with people who were innocent of the hygienic niceties.

How would the "green" fanatics feel about these Indians if they were forced to deal with them up close? Constanzo understood hypocrisy, the trademark of a so-called liberal who loved minorities but always from a distance. It was much the same in Rio, in São Paulo and Recife, where advocates for the civil rights of homeless children did their talking at black-tie banquets, steering well clear of the neighborhoods where their pet urchins robbed, raped and killed.

The beef served at those banquets had to come from somewhere, as did the gasoline that fueled their luxury sedans so they could spend their evenings in the company of Communists who claimed a grudge against technology. Where else but from the land now being cleared for cattle ranches, oil fields, up-scale housing tracts?

Each hour of every day, Constanzo knew, deforestation teams would clear an area the size of an American football field, leaving others to clean up in their wake. It meant less jungle: fewer snakes, mosquitoes, spiders, flies. So what was the problem?

He reckoned they were halfway to the village now, no stealth to speak of in their swift approach, but he didn't expect to catch their targets napping. Let them scatter if they had the energy and common sense. It wouldn't stop his soldiers burning down their filthy huts, destroying any animals or tools they left behind. And if the savages were fool enough to make a stand, so much the better. It would certainly impress Obidos more if he could claim a decent body count.

Constanzo thumbed off his rifle's safety and curled his finger through the trigger guard. A few more seconds remained until they reached their destination. He picked up another odor now, besides the reek of human filth.

It smelled like victory.

REESE GUESSED that half of the Parañas had already taken to the trees before he reached the village, running like a madman with imaginary demons on his heels. Some of the others were intent on saving their possessions, meager as they were: a bit of brightly colored cloth, some trinkets, handmade tools or weapons. Half a dozen of the warriors had their spears in hand, prepared to fight, and Reese began with them, imploring them to run before the white men came.

The warriors were a stubborn lot, proud of their achievements on the battlefield. They understood that this was different—bows and spears against the modern weapons of their hated enemies—but for some of them, at least, it was worse to run away than to remain and sacrifice their lives.

Reese knew that time was running out. He ran back to the hut he occupied alone, built with his own two hands, and rummaged in his sleeping bag until he found the pistol he had stolen on a foray to the camp of the construction crew a few weeks after he had killed the foreman. It was war, and he had sought to arm himself, his people, but the heavy weapons had been under lock and key. At last he'd settled for a .38 revolver, half a box of ammunition and a holster that he never wore around the camp. This morning, when he strapped it on, he felt as if his enemy had reached inside him, soiled a portion of his soul.

Outside, the sleeping bag rolled up beneath his arm, he faced the warriors once again. They scowled and muttered when he urged them to hide with him among the trees, but two agreed as they watched other members of the tribe evacuating, heard the helicopter rotors change their pitch, indicating their descent somewhere near the river. Four others stood their ground, refusing to be frightened off, and there was nothing Reese could do or say to change their minds.

He stopped with his companions ten or fifteen yards beyond the outskirts of the village, sheltered by a fallen tree that had to have been twelve feet across its base. The ancient bark was overgrown with moss and riddled with the tracks of insects, but its bulk provided temporary shelter from their enemies. Reese drew his weapon, broke the cylinder to check its load, then snapped it shut again. He prayed the gun would fire upon demand, that damp and dirt wouldn't impede its function as a killing tool.

The gunmen were approaching. He could hear them coming through the forest with a rattle of equipment, voices raised from time to time. They made no effort to surprise the village, knowing that their helicopter would have spoiled the effort. Reese found he was trembling as he lifted the revolver, sighting down the barrel with his forearms braced against the fallen tree. On either side of him, his young Paraña allies fitted arrows to their bowstrings, waiting for a target to reveal itself.

The soldiers came in firing from a range of twenty yards, their muzzle-flashes visible before the men themselves. They had the four Paraña warriors spotted from a distance, and it was too late for the Indians to cut and run once bullets started whispering around them, smacking into sun-bronzed flesh.

Reese watched them die and cursed himself for knowing there was nothing he could do to help them.

Four fewer members of a tribe already whittled by attrition, never large to start with, growing smaller every year. His two companions watched the murder of their friends in silence, drawing back their bowstrings and waiting for a solid target to reveal itself.

At last the point men for the raiding party reached the clearing, fanned out to inspect the vacant huts. One checked the fallen warriors, firing twice at each of them in turn. When his companions left a hut, smoke billowed out behind them, bright flames appearing moments later, eating up the thatch.

Men in camouflage fatigues cavorted in the village like a group of rowdy children on a day out in the country. They were clearly disappointed to have missed more human targets, but they took malicious pleasure in destruction of the village, laying waste to lives and property.

It was enough. No marksman, Reese still reckoned he could do the job at this short range. He chose a target, aimed for the center of the soldier's torso and thumbed back the weapon's hammer, remembering to squeeze instead of jerking on the trigger.

The pistol jumped, and there was only time for Reese to see his target falling. His two Paraña allies had unleashed their arrows, reaching back for more as their adversaries scattered in search of cover. Reese fired two more shots and was rewarded with the image of a second gunman clutching at his face. He knew then that it was time to run.

A terse command to the Paraña bowmen, and he felt them close behind him as he fled. The enemy was firing now, without a clear-cut target, bullets swarming through the trees like hungry insects out for blood. Reese heard one of the rounds strike flesh and glanced back and saw the older of his two companions sprawl facedown, unmoving on the turf. He doubled back, knelt and tried to find a pulse, but there was none.

He stood and ran, the other bowman well ahead of him. He kept running even when he knew their enemies had given up the chase, afraid of venturing too deep within the forest where they could be ambushed and cut off.

Five were dead, and the village up in smoke. Reese knew he would have to take some action, turn the tables on his enemies before they had a chance to massacre the last of the Paraña tribe.

But what could he achieve against so many, so well armed, well funded, with the government and army on their side? Would he be wiser just to cut his losses, make his way back to Brasília while he could, before the hunters had some concrete proof of his identity, and catch a flight back to the States?

Of course. It was the smart decision, but he couldn't bring himself to do it. Not when he had seen and learned so much. Not when the very lives of those whom he had come to love were riding on the line.

There had to be another way.

If he was branded as a terrorist, then he would live the part, beginning now.

The war was waiting for him, somewhere in the forest up ahead.

CHAPTER ELEVEN

The jumping-off point for their trek into the rain forest was Pôrto Nacional, a frontier town on the Tocantins River, in Goiás Province. There were half a dozen bush pilots to choose from in the town, and Bolan left Blancanales to select one who could do the job *and* keep his mouth shut afterward. It cost a little extra, but between the payoff and an "accidental" glimpse of military hardware as they stowed their gear aboard the plane, they got their point across.

The pilot would assume they were affiliated with the death squads, or perhaps drug runners flying out to guard a shipment, maybe settle some old quarrel with rivals in the wilderness, where Mother Nature would dispose of any evidence. In any case, the fly-boy knew there was no profit for him in spreading the tale around town, potential disaster lying in wait if he spoke out of turn.

From Pôrto Nacional, they flew northwest across the Serra do Estrondo, crossed the Braço Maior Araguaia where it marked the boundary line between the provinces of Goiás and Pará. Another hundred miles, and they were dropping toward a jungle airstrip that was barely large enough for the little Cessna to taxi in and turn around. The pilot seemed relieved when their gear had been unloaded, leaving him at liberty to fly back home.

They would be traveling on foot from there, some thirty miles with nothing in the way of roads to guide them toward their target. One of Daniel Nazare's crack deforestation crews was working up ahead, a hundred men or so with bulldozers and other heavy gear to help them push the jungle back. A giant scar already stretched behind them, back to São João do Araguaia, to the east.

The hundred-man road crew was merely an advance party, blazing the trail for those who would follow like a swarm of driver ants, devouring the virgin forest with their axs, chain saws, flamethrowers, explosives and chemical defoliants. Nothing but the smaller insects would survive when they had done their work. Some forest species would be driven back, in search of safer hunting grounds, while others disappeared entirely.

Bolan knew the arguments on both sides of the controversy, and he didn't rank himself among the Earth First types who felt that any logging, any use of natural resources was a crime against the planet, suitable for intervention by extremists spiking trees or bombing boats that put to sea in search of fish. He knew that some experiments on laboratory animals were brutal and redundant, others holding out potential cures for cancer, AIDS and countless other plagues that claimed a steadily mounting toll in human lives. If asked, he couldn't have provided details on the cur-

PLAY

GOLD EAGLE'S

LUCKY HEARTS GAME

AND GET

★ **FREE BOOKS**
★ **A FREE SURPRISE GIFT**
★ **AND MUCH MORE...**

TURN THE PAGE AND DEAL YOURSELF IN

PLAY "LUCKY HEARTS" AND GET . . .

★ **4 Hard-hitting, action-packed Gold Eagle® novels —FREE**

★ **PLUS a surprise mystery gift —FREE**

THEN CONTINUE YOUR LUCKY STREAK WITH A SWEETHEART OF A DEAL

1. Play Lucky Hearts as instructed on the opposite page.

2. Send back this card and you'll get hot-off-the-press Gold Eagle books, never before published. These books have a total cover price of $17.48, but they are yours to keep absolutely free.

3. There's no catch. You're under no obligation to buy anything. We charge nothing — ZERO — for your first shipment. And you don't have to make any minimum number of purchases — not even one!

4. The fact is thousands of readers enjoy receiving books by mail from the Gold Eagle Reader Service™. They like the convenience of home delivery…they like getting the best new novels before they're available in stores…and they love our discount prices!

5. We hope that after receiving your free books you'll want to remain a subscriber. But the choice is yours — to continue or cancel, anytime at all! So why not take us up on our invitation, with no risk of any kind. You'll be glad you did!

THE GOLD EAGLE READER SERVICE: HERE'S HOW IT WORKS

Accepting free books places you under no obligation to buy anything. You may keep the books and gift and return the shipping statement marked "cancel." If you do not cancel, about a month later we will send you four additional novels, and bill you just $14.80 that's a saving of 16% off the cover price of all four books! And there's no extra charge for shipping! You may cancel at any time, but if you choose to continue, then every other month we'll send you four more books, which you may either purchase at the discount price... or return at our expense and cancel your subscription.

*Terms and prices subject to change without notice. Sales tax applicable in N.Y.

If offer card is missing, write to: Gold Eagle Reader Service, 3010 Walden Ave, P.O. Box 1867, Buffalo, NY 14269-1867

BUSINESS REPLY MAIL
FIRST CLASS MAIL   PERMIT NO. 717   BUFFALO, NY

POSTAGE WILL BE PAID BY ADDRESSEE

GOLD EAGLE READER SERVICE
3010 WALDEN AVE
PO BOX 1867
BUFFALO NY 14240-9952

NO POSTAGE
NECESSARY
IF MAILED
IN THE
UNITED STATES

rent status of pollution, global warming or the dwindling ozone layer.

But somewhere, someone had to stop and draw the line.

When high-tech loggers, ranchers and petroleum prospectors fielded mercenary troops with orders to annihilate a race of people in the name of corporate greed, then it was time for men of conscience to respond. Discussions and diplomacy had failed to do the trick so far, and Bolan reckoned it was time to try a new approach.

A visit from the Executioner and friends wouldn't solve anything in global terms, but it could make a difference on the local front, where Daniel Nazare and his allies in the death squads set themselves above the law. They had a lesson coming, one that some of them wouldn't survive to profit from. It would be someone else's job to figure out if Bolan's efforts made a difference in the long run. Soldiers focused on the here and now, survival day to day, and left the fortune-telling to the statesmen with their crystal balls.

The forest felt like home, reminding him to some extent of Southeast Asia, where his youth had vanished in the pall of battle smoke. There was no great resemblance in terrain or wildlife; it was more a feeling for the wilderness, which, he suspected, would be much the same for any wild, unsullied place on earth. You simply had to listen, sniff the breeze or watch the brightly colored birds in flight to know that Nature ruled the roost here, as she had when dinosaurs were still alive and stalking one another through the forest glades.

This place was still unscarred, but it was fading fast.

No more than thirty miles from where he stood, a gang of city boys were working around the clock to pave the way for mankind's march of "progress"— meaning larger profits for the men in charge. If they were left unchecked, another ten or fifteen years could see the mighty forest of the Amazon reduced to theme-park status, stodgy "jungle rides" complete with wind-up crocodiles and tapirs à la Disneyland.

The Executioner had never viewed himself as a crusader, but he wouldn't stand aside and watch the predators grow fat and sassy, feeding on the misery of others while they jeopardized the very roots of life on earth. Daniel Nazare and Luis Obidos had been judged according to their works, and if the game had more at stake than Rio's children of the street by now, so be it.

Bolan always played for life or death.

It made the game more interesting.

DANIEL NAZARE'S lavish villa on the outskirts of Rio de Janeiro had cost him a cool million dollars to build. That didn't sound like much in California, but it meant a great deal more when visitors considered his connections to the government—which drove land prices down—or the fact that he supplied most of the various construction materials himself, using cheap native labor on the job. One million dollars in Brazil, at those rates, equaled ten or fifteen million in the

States, and every penny of it showed; polished marble floors, hanging tapestries, classic works of art, gold-plated bathroom fixtures, indoor-outdoor swimming pool, whirlpools in the seven largest bedrooms, with a tennis court and private airstrip out back. The stable for his breeding horses was another story, one more passion of a man who viewed life as a banquet arranged for his personal pleasure.

For all his possessions and wealth, Nazare was unhappy this morning. He wasn't worried; worry was beneath him, something that upset the common people. But he was concerned, not least of all about the recent failures of his colleague to identify and deal with their persistent, faceless enemies. It galled him that he had to invite Obidos to his home to discuss the latest blunders of the men who were supposed to be professionals. Nazare was considering a change of staff, but it would be a problem to replace the death squad's leader at the moment, when Nazare himself was under attack.

The way things had been going, he decided, there was some chance that the enemy would do it for him, clear the way for someone more efficient to step in and lead what Daniel Nazare had begun to think of as his private army.

For the moment, though, he was compelled to smile and act polite, pretend that he had faith in what Obidos told him. Maybe if the ex-policeman got his act together, he could salvage something from the present mess at that.

Nazare recognized his butler's knock and turned to face the study door. "Come in."

"Mr. Obidos has arrived, sir. Shall I bring him in?"

Nazare nodded, then turned back toward the window as the door closed softly at his back. He made a point of studying the flower garden just outside, deliberately showing his back to Obidos when the man was ushered into his study moments later.

"So, Luis. You lost the woman, another dozen soldiers *and* you still have no idea of who it is we're fighting, eh?" Nazare turned to face his guest and let the man experience his most imposing frown.

"I'm fairly sure they are Americans," Obidos answered.

"Fairly sure? That's something, I suppose. Are you implying a connection to the government, perhaps? Some covert action by the White House?"

"Who can say?"

"Indeed. That seems to be your answer to most questions, Luis. Who can say why all your men are being killing in Rio and São Paulo? Who can say why *I* have been selected as a target by these madmen? Who can say what's going on beneath your own great nose?"

Obidos stiffened, almost coming to attention. "You will not address me in that manner."

"No? Are you about to threaten me, Luis? Have you forgotten who it is that pays you so much money every month? Perhaps you need to stop and think about my contacts in Brasília, who would certainly be angry if I came to any harm."

Obidos stood and glared, the dark rage slowly fading from his eyes. "I did not threaten you," he said at last.

"Of course not. My mistake," Nazare told him, putting on a smile. "This business has my nerves on edge, the same as yours. Unfortunately, while your men have suffered injury, I also have been taking losses. Do you know the Yankee saying 'Time is money'? No? It's something you should think about, Luis. An interruption of my work in the interior costs twenty thousand U.S. dollars for an average day, before I calculate potential losses from my pending contracts in Brazil and the United States. You understand what I am telling you, Luis?"

"I do."

"Of course you do. The more I lose, the more you lose, Luis. It's very simple. You can easily replace the soldiers you have lost with new recruits. If I lose out on an important contract, though, the money simply disappears. It won't come back. That's why I must insist that you identify our enemies and deal with them at once. There's simply no more time for playing games. I hope we are communicating."

"There's a problem," Obidos said.

"Yes?"

"If these men *are* Americans, they may in fact have some official sanction from their government. Who knows. The CIA, for instance, often tries to hide its actions from the President and Congress."

"What's your point, Luis?"

"We're not equipped to fight a war with the United States. At first I thought these men were only fighting for the children, but they aren't such sentimental fools as that. They know my business—yours, as well—and strike where we are vulnerable. I believe they mean to kill us both."

"Have you made enemies in the United States, Luis?" Nazare smiled at the idea. "Does anyone outside Brazil know you exist? As for myself, I cultivate the very best of friends. Would it amaze you if I named the congressmen and senators who have gone hunting with me on my ranch in Texas or enjoyed my hospitality in San Diego?"

"No, Daniel. I'm saying that your friends may not have been informed about this plan to damage you."

Nazare thought about it for a moment, frowning. Anything was possible, of course. "You may be right," he said at last. "I'll make some calls, ask questions. Nothing too specific. In the meantime you have work to do. What's happening in Pará, with those savages—Paraña, is it?"

"My men found the village," Obidos said. "They killed several Indians, but most escaped. The village is destroyed. They won't be coming back. Three of my men were wounded."

"By the Indians?" Nazare was surprised at that.

Obidos frowned. "It's hard to say."

"What do you mean?"

"One took an arrow in the leg, which we expect from time to time. The other two were hit with bullets."

"So?" What was the mystery, Nazare wondered. "Now the Indians have guns."

Obidos shook his head. "Not the Parañas, Daniel. They are far too primitive. No one who knows them would provide such weapons to the tribe."

"A white man, then. One of the ecoterrorists I hear about each time I turn on the television."

"Perhaps."

"Again the answer seems so simple." He waited, while Obidos raised his eyes to meet his gaze. "You must go out and kill them, Luis. Kill them all."

"WE'RE DOING PRETTY WELL," Gadgets said when they took a breather an hour short of noon. "I'd say eight miles."

"Is that all?" Lyons groused. "God*damn!*"

The complaining didn't worry Bolan. It was SOP for soldiers when the grunt work came around, and he knew well enough that Lyons had the grit to march their butts off if he had to. Still, he had a reputation to uphold, and there was no point letting down when circumstance had given him a perfect opportunity to vent his spleen.

"I thought you looked a little rusty back there, Carl," Blancanales chided.

"Hey, I got your rust right here."

Schwarz changed the subject, sipping lightly from the first of his canteens. "So, what's the drill when we get where we're going, Sarge?"

"We'll have to see what's shaking," Bolan said. "Ideally I'd like to shut Nazare's operation down and run his bills up through the roof."

"If they want a fire," Lyons said, "we can give them one."

"Damn right," the Politician agreed.

"We have to get there first," Bolan said. "Save some of that energy for walking, while you're at it."

"Energy?" Lyons grinned. "Hell, I've got energy to spare."

"I hope so," Bolan replied. "You'll need it at the other end."

"One thing," Pol interjected. "While we're on the subject of the other end. That fly-boy isn't coming back for us, correct?"

"That's right," Bolan said.

"Yeah, that's what I thought."

"No sweat," Gadgets said. "Sarge always has a plan. That's right, hey, Sarge?"

"Truth is," Bolan replied, scanning faces, "I just planned on improvising when we finished with the job."

"Improvisation's cool," Blancanales said, "just as long as we aren't stranded in the bush a thousand miles from nowhere."

"Nowhere's in the eye of the beholder," Bolan told him. "We'll get by."

In fact their transport back to Rio was the least of Bolan's problems at the moment. He was looking forward to the next engagement with their enemy and wondering how many of them would be needing transportation when the smoke cleared.

If they lost it here, he realized, they would be in a world of hurt.

And that was no good place to be.

CHAPTER TWELVE

Pol Blancanales crept forward on his belly, careful not to make a sound as he neared his target. Fifty yards away, across a stretch of open ground, the vanguard of machines stood idle for the moment, like a group of dinosaurs relaxing in the twilight.

The Stony Man team was thirty miles from its insertion point, and Pol felt every yard of it—the aching muscles in his legs and raw spots on his shoulders, where the wide straps of his pack had chafed him. He put all of that behind him and concentrated on the target as he crawled the last few yards to reach the last good cover he could find.

The others would be close to their positions now, if not already on their marks. They had surveyed the road head as a team, before they separated, fanning out to flank the enemy and fix what Blancanales hoped would be a swift, effective cross fire. He was counting on surprise to help reduce those killer odds.

It was at least a hundred men from the looks of the expansive camp, with tents large enough for two or three men each lined up in rows, like something from a Boy Scout jamboree. The mess tent covered more ground than the others, shielding butane stoves, a serving table, stacks of metal trays and silverware.

They had guards posted, half a dozen visible from where Blancanales lay. He reckoned they were watching out for Indians, maybe guerrillas, standing easy with their automatic rifles in the twilight, several of them smoking cigarettes and looking bored.

So much the better, then.

Pol's weapon was an M-16 A-2, with an M-203 grenade launcher mounted underneath its barrel. Chambered for 37 mm rounds, the launcher could deliver smoke, high-explosive, incendiary rounds or buckshot on command, while the assault rifle kept his enemies at a distance with its stream of 5.56 mm tumblers, lethal well beyond a hundred yards if he could see that far. Between the creeping dusk and jungle flanking him, a killing range of half that distance seemed more realistic.

It would be open season on the guards and road equipment when the shooting started. Noncombatant members of the crew could either stay that way or find a weapon, join the party if they had a mind to, take their bloody chances with the rest. It would be nice, Pol thought, if most of them decided to evacuate the camp, run for their lives, but he would have to count on the machismo factor to produce some would-be heroes from the herd. How many? Only time would answer that one, and he would be forced to meet all comers with the same response.

Bail out or die.

Pol never liked the butcher work, but it was necessary. When the chips were down, and they were facing odds of twenty-five to one at best, there was no way to get around the killing. Under those terms, it was best to do your job effectively, forget about your enemies as human beings and do everything you could to help yourself.

Like now.

He waited for the signal, Bolan's overture to the explosive symphony of death. Pol kept his finger on the automatic rifle's trigger, picking out his target in the dusk. The nearest grader would be perfect, with its elevated cab. The massive blade might be impervious to anything except C-4 or thermite, but an HE round could damn sure trash the engine and controls. It would be no small job to winch the wreckage out of there when he was finished, either, should Nazare try to start from scratch.

Slow down now. First things first.

He wouldn't think about Nazare at the moment, snug and safe in Rio with his mistress of the moment, sipping chilled champagne and eating veal, maybe some caviar. There would be time enough for dealing with the big boy when they finished punishing his troops.

Assuming they were still alive.

He had been ready, waiting for it, but the first explosion still made Blancanales flinch. A heartbeat later he was back on target, with his index finger curling easily around the M-203's trigger, taking up the slack. He watched his HE round explode on impact, shearing off the grader's cab, bright arcs of flaming diesel fuel like fireworks in the night.

Blancanales reached back for another HE round to feed his hand artillery. The battle had been joined, and he was ready to take it to the limit.

BOLAN had worked out his major problem while they were hiking through the forest, some miles back. It stood to reason that Nazare's road crew and the bodyguards attached to it wouldn't be active-duty officers, since working cops would never find the time to spend a few weeks in the jungle cutting trees. It made things easier for Bolan, picking out his targets, and he knew that he could always reassess the situation if the cavalry arrived in uniform.

So far so good.

When they had finished checking out the camp, selected their positions, Bolan worked his way around to face his adversaries from the south. They left the rough road eastward, toward São João do Araguaia, open for whatever members of the team might choose to flee the campground when all hell broke loose.

Beginning any moment now.

He checked his watch, saw it was almost time and raised the Steyr AUG assault rifle with its MECAR 40 mm grenade attached to the factory-standard launcher. He didn't go directly for the heavy gear, but rather sighted toward the mess tent with its butane stoves and fuel tanks, where a number of the crew's armed guards were first in line to eat. With any luck, he thought, a measured dose of chaos at the start would keep his adversaries from regrouping later on,

thus shifting the advantage more in favor of himself
and Able Team.

At least, he thought, the ploy was worth a try.

He found his mark, squeezed off and watched the
high-explosive round detonate on impact with the
nearest butane tank. A ball of flame enveloped half
the mess tent, several blackened scarecrows flapping
wings of fire and screaming as they died. He dropped
one with a mercy burst, moved on in search of other
targets as the second butane tank caught fire, resisted
briefly, then went up like the world's largest cherry
bomb. Hungry flames spread to the rest of the tent and
beyond.

Another blast, away to Bolan's left, took out a giant road grader, shattering the driver's cab and trash-
ing the engine beyond repair. Seconds passed, then the
men of Able Team weighed in with HE rounds or
bursts of automatic fire, turning the once-relaxed
campsite into a mob scene from Dante's *Inferno*. Men
were dashing every which way, some of the guards
firing blindly toward the darkened trees while firelight made their giant shadows dance and quiver.

It was damn near perfect.

He broke from cover, moving closer, stalking human prey. One of the riflemen saw him coming, raised
his FN FAL and squeezed off two quick rounds before a short burst from the Steyr disemboweled him,
dumped him backward on the dark, uneven ground.
Away to Bolan's right, another pair of gunners were
approaching on the double, firing as they came. He

responded with a burst that missed both targets, then hastened to find some cover of his own.

How many shooters in a team this size? He guessed somewhere from a dozen to twenty guns, hired primarily to keep the local Indians at bay and make the noncombatant workmen feel at ease while they were savaging the earth. Distractions would be bad for business, and the team wouldn't maintain efficiency if workers had to watch their own backs all day long.

He went to ground behind a crane decked out with tracks, no doubt employed to clear the toppled forest giants, move them to the side, where other drones would douse the bark with gasoline and strike a match or maybe use a flamethrower to start the fire. The bulk of the machine gave Bolan ample cover, and he used it to good advantage, circling in what he hoped was the opposite direction from what his enemies expected.

In fact the two men had divided forces, breaking off to flank the crane on either side. He met one of them charging from the north, full tilt, knees pumping, lips drawn back in a snarl that resembled the rictus of death. The shooter opened up at sight of Bolan, but the AUG had found him by that time. The optic sights locked on his chest as Bolan stroked the trigger to release a 3-round burst. The 5.56 mm tumblers stopped him in midstride and punched him over backward, head and shoulders touching down before his rump and heels.

That still left one, and Bolan doubled back to greet him at the rear end of the crane. The gunner was unloading short bursts as he closed the gap between

them, trying hard to pin down his target, but Bolan
had too many options with the crane for cover. Leaping to the cab, he stepped across the driver's seat and
found himself with a fair elevated view of his enemy,
firing down at an angle close to forty-five degrees. At
thirty feet he nearly took the soldier's head off, dropping his lifeless body writhing in the mud. The odds
were getting better all the time . . . or were they?

Bolan was about to jump down from the crane's cab
when he heard another grim, familiar sound above the
hissing flames and crack of small-arms fire. He turned
and faced northward, toward the source.

And listened to helicopters, closing fast.

FERMIN CONSTANZO'S raiding party had been reinforced that morning, following their clash with the
Paraña Indians beyond the Xingu River. He had received another twenty soldiers to replace the three men
lost in battle—one of whom had died, the others suffering from painful wounds—and with the reinforcements came a second helicopter to provide mobility. It
was a solid vote of confidence from his superiors, despite the mixed results he had attained so far, and now
Constanzo was determined to do better, use his troops
to good advantage.

His first move had been going back to search for
stragglers from the burned-out village. Better yet, he
hoped to find the man or men who had been using
guns that morning to defend the tribe. Such traitors to
their race deserved extermination, and Constanzo
would be happy to oblige. Aside from sweet revenge,

it would be a considerable feather in his cap to bag a rebel, maybe more than one, when his superiors expected only savages.

But there was nothing to be found.

They had consumed the best part of the past two hours flying grids above the treetops, sweeping with the infrared detectors, picking up no feedback that would indicate a human presence below. Constanzo didn't know if the Paraña had been smart enough to change directions once they fled the village, swift enough to cover so much ground on foot in one short day, or if they had devised some way to beat the sensors.

No, that was impossible. He almost laughed aloud at the idea. How could a group of witless savages—or peasant rebels, for that matter—hope to outsmart dedicated trackers with the latest in technology at their disposal? It was ludicrous.

Still, he had missed them somehow, and a search at night was hopeless. He would have to start again tomorrow, bright and early, wrap it up in one more day and maybe see the last of frontier duty for a while. Obidos had big trouble back in Rio and São Paulo at the moment, and a man-hunter who proved himself would find much work to do in that arena, miles away from snakes, mosquitoes, biting flies and quicksand.

They were homing on the campsite when Constanzo's pilot got the Mayday call for help. Someone had waited for the sun to drop from sight behind the trees, then launched a raid against the camp. Not Indians, apparently, since they were using automatic weapons and explosives.

"Hurry up, for Christ's sake!" Constanzo told the pilot, leaning forward in his seat until the safety harness bit his flesh, as if the posture would allow their helicopter to achieve more speed. His soldiers were on edge, uneasy with the prospect of returning to an active war zone, but Constanzo knew they would acquit themselves with honor.

Those who failed him could expect no mercy.

He wondered who would have the nerve to raid the camp. There were guerrillas in the province, surely, but they normally operated farther to the north, around Brasília Legal or Altamira. For the most part they preferred to strike official targets. He could think of no occasion when they had bestirred themselves to bother the deforestation crews. Still, there was a first time for everything, and who could predict what crazy Communists would do?

It made more sense to kill them, in Constanzo's view, than try to read their minds.

He had thirty-three men—thirty-four if he counted himself—and that should be enough to cope with any small guerrilla band that might have lost its way and decided it was easier to hit a road crew than a troop of soldiers. They were in for a surprise, these stupid rebels. It would do them good to learn a lesson, and Constanzo, as the victor, would achieve the recognition he deserved.

The prospect made him smile. It pleased him even more than the idea of killing Communists.

They were a mile out from the camp and closing fast when Constanzo caught his first glimpse of the flames. At first he thought it was an optical illusion, some trick of the setting sun perhaps, but then he saw the smoke and knew the truth.

The camp was burning! Were they too late already?

No! The pilot still reported gunfire, meaning that the enemy was on the scene. If he could only wait a few more moments, it would be enough. Just let Constanzo's soldiers reach the battlefield, and everything would be all right.

He knew it in his heart.

Constanzo only wished his stomach didn't feel as if it was cast from solid lead.

CARL LYONS SQUEEZED OFF two rounds from the Atchisson automatic shotgun and watched the buckshot scatter bloody pieces of his target like confetti, bodies toppling over in their tracks. He had once referred to the shotgun as his "crowd killer," and it lived up to the name, capable of unloading twenty double-aught buckshot rounds as fast as he could pull the trigger. Call it 240 pellets airborne in ten seconds or less, each one the equivalent of a .33-caliber bullet, guaranteed lethal at fifty yards. He had been known to score at greater distances, but anything beyond that range was potluck for a scattergun, and Lyons seldom pushed his luck. For distance work, he had the Python, loaded with hollowpoints.

His ears were ringing from the rapid shotgun blasts, and Lyons almost missed the sound of helicopter engines closing from the north. Almost. In fact a couple of his adversaries froze and took the time to glance in that direction, giving him a chance to drop them where they stood, and there could be no doubt now about the noise, or its source.

The cavalry was coming, but this time Lyons and his friends were cast as Indians.

He had a fleeting hope the choppers might be innocent supply ships, nothing serious, but then he saw them—Huey transports, probably a surplus purchase from the U.S. military, and unless his eyes were playing tricks on him, both whirlybirds were bearing troops.

So much for wrapping up an easy score.

The Hueys thundered overhead, and Lyons cranked a round from his shotgun, more to satisfy his aggravation than from any hope of bringing down a bird. He watched the Hueys circle wide, returning to disgorge their passengers, and then he was distracted by the snap of bullets whipping past his head.

Lyons turned and saw a shooter rushing toward him, firing from the hip. The guy was fairly good, but haste had spoiled his aim. The Able Team leader swung around the Atchisson, lined up his shot and did it right the first time, opening a crater in the young man's chest with force enough to blow him backward several paces, landing in a heap.

He spun back toward the Hueys, slung the Atchisson across his shoulder and broke out the stubby

M-79. He had a live round in the chamber, high-explosive. All he had to do was cock the weapon, bring it to his shoulder and squint through the sights. There was no recoil to speak of, and a muffled *whomp!* announced the launching of the grenade.

Too late, he realized, as the last of the soldiers bailed out of his target, leaving the flight crew alone. Still, it was better than nothing. His grenade sailed in through the open loading bay, exploding on impact and ripping apart the grounded Huey. A fireball rose toward the stars, oily smoke belching out wreckage to gag the same soldiers it screened from his view.

He reloaded the M-79 and swung toward the second Huey just as it began to rise, the rotors whipping air to strive for altitude. The ship was in his sights when someone beat him to it, a projectile streaking skyward from his left. The Huey's tail was hammered out of line by the explosion, crumpling to the pilot's left as it began to spin.

The Huey's pilot almost seemed to have control for just a moment, but then he lost it. The chopper nosed down in a clumsy somersault, went over on its back, rotors chopping at tents and running stick figures like the world's biggest lawn mower out of control. A heartbeat later, when the fuel tanks blew, it almost came as a relief.

Which still left Lyons with a live round in his launcher and the weapon cocked. He sighted on the nearest piece of road equipment, slammed the shot home from a range of forty yards and watched another fireball reach up for the sky.

He knew the tide was shifting when a skirmish line of men in camouflage fatigues burst through the pall of smoke, another troop immediately on their heels. They all had automatic weapons and seemed to know their business, even if their entry to the game had been a trifle less than perfect. They were here, regardless, and they didn't need the Hueys for the kind of mopping up they had in mind.

The choice was simple: stand and die, take maybe half a dozen with him in the process, or retreat—which meant that he would have to run like hell.

Lyons ran.

He delivered a quick one-two punch from the Atchisson to slow them a bit, then he started sprinting for the nearest trees, the walkie-talkie in his hand.

"The second team's on line," he cautioned anyone who might be listening. "I make it twenty, twenty-five at least. What say we disengage?"

"Affirmative." The word came back from Striker. "Fall back on the numbers, starting now."

A part of Lyons wanted to remain and slug it out, regardless of the odds, but that was tantamount to suicide. They had already made their mark against Nazare's crew, and if they had to take another shot or two before they wrapped it up, okay. The point was to survive and see that day, instead of getting wasted on the spot.

And now the trick, Lyons thought, would be getting out alive.

THE PROBE HAD GONE all right at first for Gadgets Schwarz. He had been in position, waiting, when the others opened up, his first two targets marked and registered. The CAR-15 was light and comfortable, with the full firepower of the larger M-16, and Schwarz had dropped the sentries in their tracks with short precision bursts.

So far so good, and he was racing toward the road crew's motor pool, a line of jeeps and heavy trucks, before his adversaries realized exactly what was happening. They knew it was a raid, of course, but any sneak attack disoriented the prey to some extent, and thus provided the raider with his edge.

It might have been okay, in fact, if not for the arrival of the Hueys. Gadgets had a block of C-4 plastique in his hand, prepared to wire a jeep for doomsday, when he heard the old familiar sound of transports coming in. No way could they be friendly, in the present circumstances, so he hurried, got a second charge of C-4 placed before it hit the fan.

If he survived to ask around, he might find out who brought the choppers down. The main thing, at the moment, was that both ships had unloaded soldiers on the outskirts of the camp before they blew. Schwarz didn't have a count, not even close, but even with a light load, two ships meant another ten or fifteen guns at least.

There was no way to prepare for that contingency, no means of knowing whether the troops were assigned to guard the camp full-time or merely passing through. It made no difference, either way. The fat was in the fire, and someone would be getting fried.

Like magic, he heard Lyons speaking from the compact walkie-talkie on his belt. "The second team's on line," he said. "I make it twenty, twenty-five at least. What say we disengage?"

"Affirmative," Bolan replied without the slightest hesitation. "Fall back on the numbers, starting now."

Okay by me, Gadgets thought as he put the motor pool behind him, racing toward the tree line. Someone started firing at him after he had covered thirty yards or so, and Schwarz went down, glancing back across his shoulder for a quick fix on the gunman.

There were two of them, advancing at a steady pace. Not running, more like "walking with a purpose," as the DI's used to say in boot camp. Both guys firing from the hip and coming closer with their bullets all the time. The motor pool was just behind them, ten or fifteen paces to their right.

He keyed the detonator, beaming a deadly message back across the open ground, and winced despite himself as both jeeps blew together, taking out the one between them, bright flames spreading quickly to the other vehicles in line. The shock wave knocked his adversaries sprawling, down for good or simply stunned. It made no difference as he jumped to his feet and started to run.

CHAPTER THIRTEEN

The worst part of a forced retreat, Mack Bolan thought, was losing the initiative that came with prosecuting an attack. Retreat in haste was even worse than a defensive posture, since the troops withdrawing under fire had no defensive works to shield them, often nothing in the way of cover.

Dying was a risk in every soldier's life, but dying on the run added insult to injury.

At least the forest helped in that regard. It wasn't dense jungle, as back in Vietnam, where every yard of progress took hard work with a machete. It was possible to run and still find cover in among the giant trees, dodge bullets whispering along behind like killer bees.

His rendezvous with Able Team had been arranged before they ever hit the camp, with just such a contingency in mind. The Executioner hadn't been counting on reinforcements from the enemy, but he was old and wise enough to know that things sometimes went wrong in combat, and you had to scrap your plans if you had any hope of getting out alive.

Like now.

It was enough for Bolan, in the early moments of their flight, to see his three good comrades safe and sound. Whatever followed, they would face the test together, four good brains and eight strong hands against whatever obstacle the gods of battle threw across their path. If they were cornered, forced to make a last-ditch stand against their enemies, at least they had one another in the crunch.

For now, though, Bolan was relieved to have a clear five-minute lead. Confusion in the camp had slowed the trackers, prevented them from getting organized as quickly as they should have to effect a hot pursuit. The raiders weren't home free, by any means, but they had time to talk as they were running, make a brief pause now and then to plant grenades with loosened pins and trip wires strung across their trail. The traps were fairly obvious to anyone with field experience and two good eyes, but they were running short on time to set up more-elaborate snares, and Bolan thought the trackers might be high enough on their apparent victory to rush the chase, try going for an easy kill.

His theory was confirmed some twenty minutes from the camp, when an explosion echoed through the forest from well behind them. Bolan knew their enemies would be more careful after one hitch on the trail. In fact the other traps were never sprung, no more grenade blasts ringing through the darkness.

Fair enough. At least the extra caution would retard their progress. With the Hueys down, if they were forced to move on foot, it should be relatively simple to evade a larger party, maybe lead the enemy around in circles for a while before they disengaged.

He was about to count their blessings when the high-pitched sound of racing engines reached his ears. He hesitated for a moment, breaking stride, as did the others.

"Is that a chain saw?" Gadgets asked.

"It's more than one, whatever it is," the Politician said.

"Hard to tell with sounds in a place like this," Lyons stated. "Did I ever mention that I hate—"

"Heads up!" Pol snapped, and pointed at the bobbing specks of light, like fireflies racing toward them through the forest.

Trail bikes, damn it!

Bolan counted four of them, two on a side, and they were running well off from the estimated trail, assuming—rightly, as it happened—that the runners wouldn't zigzag, wasting time on booby traps too far afield. The bikes were gaining ground, their drivers concentrating on the ground ahead, while pillion riders swept the trees with high-beam flashlights.

They were still two hundred yards behind, but gaining fast. No way all four of them would miss their quarry, not unless the earth should open suddenly and swallow them alive.

Bolan didn't place his faith in miracles.

"We need a place to make a stand," he said, still hoping they could waste the bikers quickly and maintain at least some measure of their lead.

It was a challenge, scouting strange terrain by night, but thirty seconds brought them to a smallish glade where two great trees had fallen in the pattern of a giant X—or close enough, at any rate, to give four soldiers marginal protection if they played their cards right.

They hunkered down within the makeshift fort, two men together, back-to-back, inside the two acute angles of the X. It left them open on each side, but there was nothing they could do about it without reinforcements, and there seemed to be none handy at the moment.

"Hold your fire unless they spot us," Bolan ordered. "There's an outside chance they still might pass us by."

"Yeah, way outside," Lyons said grimly, making sure the Atchisson was locked and loaded, ready for the hellfire party to begin.

Behind him Gadgets Schwarz was following the nearest pair of bikers with his CAR-15. At Bolan's back, the Politician waited, scoping out his enemy, prepared for anything.

One of the flashlight beams swept over them, kept going, stopped, came back. Despite the whining engines, they could still make out a loud, excited stream of Portuguese.

"That's it," Pol stated. "We're toast."

"Not yet," Lyons said, grinning like a wild man in the face of death. "These sons of bitches have begun to piss me off."

CONSTANZO GOT THE WORD ten minutes after issuing his order for the trail bikes to proceed and try to overtake their fleeing enemies. The rebel pigs had gone to

ground. They were surrounded and cut off, with nowhere to run.

It wasn't hopeless yet! Constanzo had a last chance
to redeem himself.

He was determined not to let that precious opportunity slip through his fingers as the others had. He
would succeed this time or die trying.

Constanzo started barking orders to his men, directing them, demanding greater speed. It had been
some time now since they disarmed the last of several
booby traps, and he believed their quarry had decided to rely on speed for their salvation, maybe after
they ran out of hand grenades. In any case, he couldn't
let the point men steal his glory when he had so many
glaring setbacks to erase.

He still let two young troopers lead the way, of
course. A small precaution, just in case he was mistaken in his guess about the booby traps. It was no
time to risk the seasoned leader of a troop, when they
were on the verge of cornering their ruthless enemies.
Constanzo's soldiers needed him. Without him, they
were all in peril of their lives.

He didn't have a clue where they were going, hadn't
ventured more than twenty paces from the camp on
foot without an escort, and the darkened forest he
traveled through bore no resemblance to the canopy
they skimmed by daylight in the Hueys.

He wondered how much farther they would have to
run before they overtook the enemy. The bikes were
well ahead of them, but it hadn't been *that* long since

they took off to scout the forest with their lights and greater speed. Another mile, perhaps.

Constanzo stumbled on a root and almost fell, throwing out an arm to catch himself. The rough bark of a forest giant saved him, even as it scraped his palm. He cursed, would happily have kicked the tree to vent his anger, but his men were watching, slowing to see if their commander was about to stop.

"Keep on, there!" he snapped in his best authoritative tone.

He would be happy when the whole damn forest had been leveled, burned and paved like one gigantic parking lot. He hated frontier duty with a passion, from the flies and leeches to the worthless Indians who lived like animals in squalid villages that would have made a pig feel right at home.

Constanzo was in pain. The sharp stitch in his side was bad enough, but now his left knee had begun to trouble him, as well. He tried to think if he had injured it while he was scrambling around the camp to keep his men in line and save himself. It had been awkward, leaping from the helicopter at the very start.

And now his bowels were acting up, broadcasting signals that he couldn't run much farther at his present pace without one last humiliation for the evening. God in heaven, why was Nature out to make a fool of him when all he wanted was to do his job and reap his just reward?

Constanzo kept on running, though a trifle slower, letting several other troopers pass him in the darkness. If he had an accident, at least it wouldn't be so obvious, between the darkness and the fact that half his troops were out in front of him.

He tried to focus on his enemies, imagining their faces slack in death, their bodies torn by bullets. He thought of Communists and their ilk as the scum of God's creation. They were worse than Indians, in fact, because the forest tribes at least had the excuse of ignorance. These traitors to their homeland made a conscious choice to turn their backs on God and country, common decency, the very institutions that Constanzo and *his* kind had risked their lives for through the years.

That wasn't strictly true, of course. Despite eight years in military service, Constanzo had been well removed from any action until his discharge, when he promptly joined the local death squad. Even then, the actions he took part in were designed to minimize the risk for those involved. Their targets were outnumbered, often snatched from bed or shot from cars while walking down the street, outnumbered five or six to one in almost every case. Still, it was action, and with this night's work behind him, he defied all comers to deny he was a seasoned fighting man.

One of the scouts was calling back, his voice a muted whisper, but Constanzo didn't need to hear his message. He could hear the bikes, and that meant they were getting close.

A moment later he heard automatic weapons firing in the darkness, and he wondered if they might not be a bit too close. The very notion shamed him, made him stiffen with resolve. This was his night, and he had to prove himself the leader he had always known himself to be. Whatever went before was history. Fermin Constanzo had a chance to triumph now, and no one would be forgiving if he let it slip away.

His troops were slowing, a number of them stopping altogether, waiting for an order to proceed. Constanzo scowled and snapped at them like naughty children.

"Go ahead!" he ordered them, all puffed-up courage now. "What are you waiting for? I'm with you!"

If his men drew consolation from that fact, it didn't show. But they obeyed the order, slogging forward through the darkness, following the sounds of battle, dancing flashlight beams and muzzle-flashes.

Almost there, Constanzo thought. No one could stop him now.

THE BIKERS KEPT their distance, ditching their machines when they were sure they had the enemy surrounded, finding cover where they could. Without the wobbling headlights, it was dark again for several moments, then the gunners started spotting targets with their flashlights, burning white-hot tunnels through the night.

It reminded Lyons of a game, some kind of shooting gallery where you were told to aim at moving light bulbs, rather than the normal silhouettes of rabbits, ducks and bears. The problem was that every time a light blazed in his face, it left an afterimage on his retinas, distorting his perception of the moving targets.

They were good, these trackers, staying close enough for an exchange of fire without showing any flesh to their intended victims. Lyons wasted half a dozen buckshot rounds before he gave it up, unslung the 37 mm launcher, cocked it and sat back to wait. The lights were all he had to go by. When another one came on within his field of fire—

He aimed and fired in one smooth motion, sending the grenade downrange before the flashlight was extinguished. Lyons saw it wink out just before his HE round exploded several feet above the gunner's head, a deadly mix of splintered wood and shrapnel smothering his target, scoring one for Able Team.

That still left seven that he was sure of, though, and they would be more careful in the future. They had scoped out the target by now, converging streams of fire exploding from the darkness, bullets chipping at the giant trunk that shielded him or snapping overhead. Too close for comfort, and there was nothing he could do about it, short of going out to meet them in the shadows.

Forget it.

They would cut him down in seconds flat if Lyons left his awkward shelter.

His friends were giving back the best they could, but it was still a losing proposition. Lyons almost wished they had kept moving, tried to take the bikers down before they ditched their wheels and closed on foot. Too late for that now, but at least he vowed the bastards wouldn't have an easy time of mopping up. He still had four full magazines to feed the Atchisson and five or six rounds for the M-79, before he fell back on the Colt Python. And if all else failed, he still knew how to use the Ka-bar hanging pommel-downward from the left side of his combat harness.

What the hell, Lyons thought, if he had to die, the hard way was as good as any. Better than most, in fact. At least he wouldn't be remembered as a quitter, someone who threw up his hands at the first sign of a fight and got it in the back while he was running for his life.

He fed another HE round into the launcher, waiting for an enemy to forget the simple lesson he had taught them once already. Just a flash was all he needed, nothing much.

"Here's trouble," Gadgets said to no one in particular, his voice raised loud enough that Lyons heard him over the staccato sounds of automatic fire.

And damn it if he wasn't right.

The bikers had completed their assignment, pinning down their targets long enough for reinforcements to arrive. Lyons heard them coming through the darkened forest, armed men running with the rattle of equipment that betrayed an army on the move.

They really should have taped that gear to keep it quiet, Lyons thought as he swung toward the new arrivals with his launcher. They were still invisible, but it would only be another moment. He would welcome them in style, and—

What the hell was that?

A scream, sounding like some kind of jungle bird, except that birds and animals shut up when men were in the neighborhood, discharging guns. You had to give the "lower orders" credit for survival instinct, anyway, and that meant the unearthly noises he was hearing had to issue from a human throat.

No, more than one, for they were flanking his position, coming at his ears from both sides now.

There were more screams now, but of a different timbre. The initial shrieks and howls had been a warning, maybe, or a challenge. These, by contrast, were the very soul of panic, with perhaps a note of agony thrown in.

Lyons found that he was sweating, and it wasn't from the tropic heat.

THE FIRST SHRIEKS startled Bolan, but he waited, searching for their source, his senses reaching out to probe the dark before he opened fire on men he couldn't see. Whatever the ungodly noises meant, they weren't coming from the death-squad reinforcements. Rather, they appeared to issue from behind him, moving to the flanks, enveloping the small declivity where Bolan and his Able Team warriors had been forced to ground. It almost sounded like the screamers, still unseen, were closing in to meet the soldiers from the road camp, but it made no sense.

Until one of the bikers switched his flashlight on.

The beam was there and gone, two seconds at the most, but it showed Bolan everything he had to see. A naked warrior with a painted face was framed in that brief flash of light, arm cocked to hurl a spear. He made the throw, his lance drawn toward the light's source like a needle to a magnet, and the light winked out.

The Indian's appearance was a mystery to Bolan, but the sound of wailing cries, immediately followed by the screams of panicked soldiers, told him that the naked man wasn't alone. The tribal warriors clearly had some grudge against Nazare's men, and that was fine with Bolan. He would welcome any hand up from the grim predicament in which he found himself.

Unless, of course, the Indians were killing white men indiscriminately.

Who could blame them in the circumstances? Routed from their homes and hunted in the forest like game animals, they came upon two groups of soldiers dueling in the night. Which side was friendly? Why should they trust either one?

"Stay frosty," Bolan told the others. "We've got company, in case you haven't seen them. Indians. They're going for Nazare's men right now, but don't take any chances."

"Beautiful," Lyons said. "All we need now is a wagon train."

"What say we head 'em up and move 'em out?" Gadgets asked.

"Wait a little," Bolan answered. "Let's find out what's happening before we lose our cover."

Moments later the Indians clashed with Nazare's rear column, attacking from all sides at once with their lances and arrows, some running in closer with war clubs and knives when a target presented itself. The death-squad troops were firing back and scoring hits, sometimes among their own, but they were clearly not prepared for this kind of guerrilla warfare. Some of them were dying where they stood, the stragglers turning back toward camp and running for their lives with darting, shrieking demons on their heels.

And in another moment it was over. Bolan and his comrades waited under cover, fingers ready on the triggers of their weapons as the killer shadows started drifting back, surrounding them once more.

"I thought my people were supposed to be outside the Alamo," Blancanales said, sounding nervous as he sighted down the barrel of his M-16.

"Let's wait a second," Bolan said. "See what they have in mind."

The voice that answered him came from somewhere on the left and spoke in English. If his ears didn't deceive him, there was something of a Massachusetts accent to it, audible but fading fast.

"Don't fire," the voice called out. "You're in no danger now. Do you have casualties?"

Bolan glanced around him in the darkness, saw the Able Team warriors shaking heads. "Not yet," he answered, hoping they could keep it that way.

Out of nowhere, closer than he would have guessed, a tall man stepped into the open. Not just taller than the Indians, but tall and white, if deeply suntanned and disheveled, smiling humorlessly as he switched on one of the captured flashlights.

"My name is Jacob Reese. I think we need to have a talk."

CHAPTER FOURTEEN

The last thing that Luis Obidos needed was another phone call bringing him bad news. He had enough of that to last him for a dozen lifetimes as it was, and matters seemed to keep on getting worse, no matter how he tried to rectify the situation. *Hopeless* was a word he never liked to use, but things were leaning more and more that way for him.

There was no justice in this life, Obidos thought with more than passing bitterness. He devoted every waking hour to the thankless war against subversives, criminals and human garbage, trying to secure Brazil against the creeping cancer from within. His thanks, if such it could be called, consisted of ongoing slander in the left-wing press, assaults upon his person and his troops by unknown enemies and near-hysterical complaints from those he served.

Daniel Nazare, for example. The man lived for money, and to that end he had fled Brazil years earlier to live in the United States. He made a fortune there, but when he came back to his homeland after many years away, it wasn't to bestow the blessings of his wealth upon Brazil. Instead, he meant to scourge the land and make more money for himself.

Luis Obidos had no quarrel with the profit motive, but he viewed Nazare as a kind of parasite, a traitor once removed, more interested in private wealth than in his country and her people. Still, for all his faults, Nazare was extremely rich and he didn't mind spending money on his personal security—or other jobs that were designed to boost his profit margin. If Obidos saw a chance to use the parasite to build his private army, moving closer to the day when he and others like him would return to power in Brazil, what of it? At the bottom line, ends justified the means.

Still, he could do without the constant interference from a man who had no training in the military arts, no real idea of what a fighting man could do and what lay beyond his powers. On a night like this, particularly, he could be forgiven if he wished Nazare would drop dead.

"Have you found out what happened yet?"

No salutation, nothing but the snotty bastard snapping at him from the time Obidos lifted the receiver to his ear.

"I told you everything I know last time you called."

"Two hours, Luis. You could have grilled a hundred men in that time if you really tried."

"Unfortunately, as I told you, most of those who saw the enemy are not in any shape to answer questions. Most of them, in fact, are dead."

"But not all, am I right?"

"I've found one soldier who was in the thick of it. I'm having him flown in from Pôrto Nacional. He should be with me shortly."

"What? You haven't spoken to him yet?"

"You must have patience, Daniel."

"Patience? Do you realize what you are saying? Is it clear to you how much I lost tonight?"

"I understand completely, Daniel. Most of those who died were my men, after all."

"On my payroll, Luis. Remember that."

"I'm not forgetting anything."

There was a subtle menace in his tone, but Daniel Nazare seemed to miss it, bulling right ahead with his demands for action. He expected Luis to do something, do it now. He wasn't paying for a so-called army that couldn't defend his interests when he needed it the most. He paid for and expected positive results, not lame excuses for repeated failure to perform.

Obidos let him babble, didn't interrupt again. From long experience he knew the quickest way to get Nazare off the line was to be silent, let him spew out his abuse and follow up with vague assurances that everything would be all right.

In this case, while Obidos wasn't certain of the outcome, he at least had reason to expect some answers from the latest bloodbath. There was one survivor from the team he had dispatched, then reinforced that very morning to protect Nazare's road crew.

One survivor, out of close to forty men—and that didn't allow for those attached to the road crew itself, the guards in place who were among the first to die. Obidos had lost count of all his soldiers killed within the past three days, but he could feel their weight upon his shoulders, threatening to smother him.

A living witness, though, had to count for something. Not some peasant, either, but the officer in charge. Fermin Constanzo had some explaining to do—not least of all about the fact that he alone had survived when his command was ambushed in the jungle. He would never lead another unit while Obidos was in charge, but they could save that bit of information to the very last, until they milked the man dry of useful information.

A sudden lull in Daniel Nazare's strident monologue brought Obidos back to present time. He waited for another moment, listening to blessed silence on the line, before Nazare snapped at him again.

"What do you think of that?" the millionaire demanded.

Think of what? Obidos faked it. "I assure you everything will soon be taken care of, Daniel. Have no fear."

"I'm not the one who needs to be afraid, Luis. You should know that by now."

Of course. If things got too bad in Brazil, Nazare could wing off to California, New York City, Paris, London—anywhere his greedy heart desired. His business could be carried out as easily by telephone and fax machine as by the man in person. On the other hand, Luis Obidos had no foreign sanctuaries, no place to conceal himself.

He got the message, loud and clear. The risk belonged to him now, while Nazare washed his hands and walked away. It was the kind of action he expected from a rich man with no blood or sweat invested in the land. Nazare might have come from peasant stock, four generations back, but he had managed to forget his roots, the way a louse may come to think itself a man from riding on a human being's head.

"I have no fear, Daniel," Obidos told him. Maybe it was stretching things a bit, but it was good to keep a stern face with your friends, as well as enemies. "This is my home. I won't be driven out."

"See that you aren't, Luis. And earn your money while you're at it."

The humming dial tone came as a relief. Obidos cradled the receiver gently, swallowing an urge to slam it down with force enough to crack the plastic. He wouldn't allow Nazare to provoke him now, when he had need of all his faculties.

He had a witness coming from the jungle, and Obidos wanted to be sharp, alert, for that interrogation. There was time enough to let his anger show itself if the survivor didn't have the answers he required.

And that, Obidos told himself, would be a sorry night for one ex-sergeant of the guard.

CONSTANZO KNEW he was in trouble when Obidos sent a special unit out to lift him from the camp, young men who spoke in monosyllables and didn't answer questions. They had flown him back to Pôrto Nacional by helicopter, and a private plane was waiting there for the remainder of his journey back to Rio.

They were taking him to see Obidos, then, and that could only be bad news.

At first Constanzo had felt privileged to survive. It was a fluke—perhaps a miracle—that spared his life when other men were falling all around him, but he didn't like to look a cosmic gift horse in the mouth.

In fact the last grim portion of their battle in the forest was a blur. He could remember shouting orders for his soldiers to advance, men rushing toward a kind of glade where flashlight beams and muzzle-flashes served as beacons in the black of night. Before they reached their destination, though, it all went wrong. Ungodly screams and whistles erupted in the forest, as if a troop of demons were rushing to surround his men.

He had recognized the truth in seconds, once the spears and arrows started flying, but it made no difference. Indians or demons, they were still at home among the trees, while Constanzo and his men were aliens, out of their element. Superior weapons meant little or nothing when your only targets were flitting shadows, as insubstantial as ghosts.

And he had run. It was a shameful thing for any soldier to admit, but what else could he do? His men were falling all around him, bodies bristling with arrows, while the Indians closed in to bring the battle home with clubs and knives. It was a nightmare, brutal action swirling in the darkness, and his nerve broke. He could admit that to himself, if to no one else.

The confrontation with Obidos would require another explanation, something palatable. What if he was knocked unconscious in the early stages of the battle, only waking when the tribal warriors had withdrawn and left his troop in bloody ruins? Would Obidos buy it?

No.

The forest tribes were fond of mutilating corpses, sometimes taking heads as souvenirs. If they had found Constanzo lying on the battlefield, they surely would have finished him, and he wouldn't be flying back to Rio under guard to tell the tale.

Another story, then.

A variation on the theme: suppose he had been struck a glancing blow that dazed him, and he wandered in the wrong direction, somehow lost his way and managed to escape the killing ground. It made more sense, except that he bore no marks from the struggle, other than the scratches on his face and hands sustained while he was racing through the darkness, desperate to save himself at any cost.

If all else failed, Constanzo reckoned he could tell the truth, but that would mean admitting cowardice. He would be stripped of his command—an outcome that was almost certain, come what may—and it wasn't beyond the realm of possibility that Obidos might desire to punish him in other ways.

Constanzo tried to switch off his imagination, make his mind a blank, but it was difficult. The men around him, staring silently, reminded him of the position he was in. He found no cause for optimism in their eyes or in their attitude.

Another team was waiting for him at the airport when they landed. He was ushered to a limousine and driven through the teeming streets until they reached the suburb where Obidos made his home. More guards were positioned around the house, but they ignored Constanzo as he passed among them, treating him as one already dead.

He was trembling by the time a soldier led him to Obido's study, hoping that it wouldn't be too obvious. It was his first time in the leader's home, and it wasn't a treat, but rather something to be feared.

Luis Obidos sat behind a massive desk of polished teak. He didn't rise to greet Constanzo, didn't speak or even nod. His eyes were cold, unwavering. One hand came up, the index finger like a stubby pistol barrel, pointing to the empty chair directly opposite his desk.

Constanzo sat and waited, feeling silence stretch between them like a membrane, growing thinner by the heartbeat, threatening to tear around the edges. Finally it seemed as if Constanzo would go mad unless he spoke.

"I can explain," he said, and instantly felt sorry for the choice of words.

"Please do."

"We went out searching for the Indians," he said.

"And found them, I believe."

"But not at first. The village...well, there was no village anymore. We swept the forest, but our sensors picked up nothing. Finally we started back to camp, and it was only then we got a message warning us of the attack."

"Go on."

"The camp was lost before we got there. It was hopeless, the equipment burning, tents, the bodies everywhere. The raiders had some kind of rocket launchers. We were still unloading when they opened fire, destroyed both helicopters. Even so, we closed ranks and pursued them from the camp on foot."

"Into the forest."

"Yes. I sent a team of scouts ahead on dirt bikes. They were quick enough to overtake the raiding party. There was firing. We could see the muzzle-flashes through the trees. I gave the order to advance."

"And then?"

Constanzo swallowed hard and forged ahead. "The Indians came out of nowhere, screaming, shooting arrows. They were everywhere at once—behind us, all around. We were cut off, surrounded. Helpless."

"Still, *you* managed to escape."

"It was a miracle," Constanzo blurted out, immediately wishing that the floor would open up and swallow him.

"A miracle? I didn't know you were a praying man."

"Well, I—"

"You ran away. Is that not so?"

"I did my best."

"To save yourself."

"Luis—"

"What of the raiders, then?" Obidos changed the subject, seeming to relent. "You did not actually *see* them, I suppose."

"No, but…they were not Indians. Not at the camp. They must have been guerrillas."

"Ah."

"It is unusual for Communists to operate in that vicinity, I know, but sometimes—"

"Is there no chance," Obidos said, interrupting him, "that these guerrillas were Americans?"

"Americans?" Constanzo spoke the word as if it had no meaning for him. "You mean Yankees?"

"Any chance at all?"

Constanzo thought about it, wondering if it would help his case to vote in the affirmative.

"It's possible," he said at last. "I never heard them speak."

"And since you captured none of them, no weapons, there is no way to be sure."

"That's true."

"So tell me, Sergeant, is there any light that you can shed upon this incident, beyond what you've already said."

Constanzo had a sudden brainstorm, wondering if it would be enough to save him. Not his rank, perhaps, but possibly his life.

"It has occurred to me that they were working with the Indians," he said. "Perhaps employing savages as guides, on unfamiliar ground. The Indians hate us. They would gladly help our adversaries—even Yankees, I suppose—if they believed it would defeat us in the end."

Obidos thought about that for a moment, frowning. "It's something to consider," he remarked at last. "I think we're finished here."

He reached across the desk to punch a button on the intercom. Constanzo heard the door behind him and turned in time to see the last of four young men enter the room. Obidos spoke to one of them, the tall one on Constanzo's left.

"You have your orders, Lucio. Be quick about it. Leave no trace."

Constanzo's arms were seized on either side, and he was lifted from his chair before he had a chance to stand. He struggled briefly, but a solid kidney punch drained all resistance from him in a sudden wave of agony.

"Please, sir, don't do this!"

"It is nature's way," Obidos told him, smiling for the first time since Constanzo walked into his study. "Think of it as a completion of your duty. You will shortly join your men. Perhaps they'll understand your instinct to survive at their expense."

Constanzo was about to speak again, say anything that came to mind, when something heavy struck his skull and darkness blotted out all conscious thought.

He never felt the young men dragging him away.

IT WAS THE PART about the Indians that made Obidos frown. He didn't like the thought of hostile gunmen—Yankees or whatever—joining ranks with jungle tribesmen in a common cause. The sport of hunting Indians had always been a white man's game, one thing that North Americans and their Hispanic neighbors had in common. If the tables had begun to turn somehow, it could mean trouble on a scale that no one fully understood.

Obidos rose and paced his study, noting the vague aroma of fear that lingered behind his late sergeant. The man was a coward, his death no more important than the smashing of a cockroach, but his parting words had given Obidos something to think about. A new worry to prey on his mind.

Assuming that the raiders were Americans, would they join forces with a tribe of godless savages to terrorize the countryside? What had Nazare done to earn such hatred from his enemies? Was it an economic question, maybe rooted back in the United States, where Nazare did most of his business?

Obidos couldn't answer that, and it would be a waste of precious time for him to try. His job involved location, isolation and destruction of the enemy, a task that called for no more understanding of an adversary's motive than was necessary to anticipate and interdict his movements.

Victory was all that mattered in a soldier's world. Obidos was expected to deliver on the pledge that he would keep Nazare's operations safe from harm by hostile hands. If he didn't deliver soon, Nazare might well turn to other friends for aid and comfort.

Which would mean a severance of his union with the death squad and Luis Obidos. Worse, Obidos knew that it could well mean war.

And he had one war on his hands already, which was quite enough.

He also had a rough fix on his enemy's location, even if he didn't know their numbers or identity. Unless they were equipped with aircraft, they should still be somewhere in the wilds of Pará Province, near the Xingu River village where Constanzo's men had last drawn blood. It was a place to start, at least, and if the gunmen *were* allied with the Paraña tribesmen, they might be obliged to linger in the area awhile.

Obidos saw his opportunity and knew that it might be his last. If he could field another army, get his men in place without a critical delay, there was a chance that he could end his troubles in the forest, well away from Rio and São Paulo. It would be a pleasure for him to report that victory, make Nazare eat his words and keep the money flowing for at least a few more months.

And while the cash was rolling in, Obidos would be thinking of a way to get along without Nazare.

It was almost time, he told himself. The man had grown obnoxious, even for a millionaire employer. Wealth demanded certain privileges, but the demands grew burdensome at last, and any man with self-respect would have to look for some alternative arrangement.

What if Daniel Nazare was to have an accident, for instance? What would happen to his empire then? Did he have heirs in waiting, others like himself already briefed on the procedures they should follow if he came to harm? Was there some way Obidos could discover who they were, perhaps negotiate a contract satisfactory to both?

It wouldn't be the first time he had stabbed a patron in the back, but only when the target had outlived his usefulness to Obidos and the cause he served. The dream came first: a nation ruled by men who understood the dangers of a modern world and took the necessary steps to head them off, eliminating traitors, criminals and other human scum as a physician would excise necrotic tissue to preserve a patient's life. Selective amputation as preventive medicine.

Removing Daniel Nazare would require a certain measure of finesse. No simple drive-by shooting on a crowded street, for instance, but the more Obidos thought about it now, the more he wondered if the recent trouble might not be a blessing in disguise. The faceless enemy could still be useful to him, even after he had tracked them down and killed them to a man. Nazare didn't have to know that they were dead, in fact. If Obidos could move swiftly, strike a deal with one of Nazare's heirs, he could let the unknown gunmen take responsibility for anything that happened to Nazare. After the smoke cleared, Obidos would receive a hero's due for punishing the men who killed Nazare and imperiled all his great plans for the national economy.

Obidos smiled and poured himself a drink. It wasn't every day that he received a gift from God. He felt like celebrating, but he still had work to do before the brass ring came within his grasp. The plan would only work if he could corner his elusive enemies and wipe them out *before* he made the move against Nazare. It would never do to have the tricky bastards running loose, surprising him when he could least afford it.

No, it wasn't time for celebrating yet, but he could still look forward to the moment with anticipation. It was coming. He could almost taste it now. A somewhat salty flavor.

Much like blood.

CHAPTER FIFTEEN

"We were about to raid the camp," Jacob Reese said, "when you got there first."

"When you say we—"

"Myself and the Parañas," Reese elaborated. "We've had trouble with Nazare's road crews in the past."

"You know Daniel Nazare?" Blancanales asked.

"By reputation only. He's a big name in Brazil, like Trump or Iacocca in the States. Of course, he's not the only one involved in mass deforestation of the Amazon, but he has most of Pará Province in his pocket."

They were seated in the middle of a makeshift village, hastily constructed with materials at hand. Some kind of smallish pig was roasting on the open fire, complete with head and hooves, fat popping as it melted and dripped into the yellow flames. In fact it smelled delicious, but the Executioner wasn't concerned about his appetite. Instead, he focused on their host—and the three dozen Indians who ringed the campfire, totally surrounding Bolan, Reese and the men of Able Team. No effort had been made to take their weapons, but he knew it wouldn't matter if the tribesmen took it in their heads to interrupt the feast with spears and arrows.

"Have you been here long?"

"About two years," Reese told him. "I was working on my doctorate in anthropology. A perfectly detached observer, as we academics like to say—except I got involved. Diplomas don't seem all that critical when you see people being murdered in the name of progress every day."

"Nazare?" Lyons asked.

"He's not alone, of course," Reese said. "The government is his accomplice. They aren't so active as before, when there was still a military junta in Brasília. Now, instead of killing Indians themselves, the troops and politicians close their eyes while gunmen from the death squads do it for them. Rich men like Nazare pay the tab and grease the necessary palms to lock down grazing rights, oil leases, timber licenses. You have a different finger on the trigger, but the job gets done, just like before."

"You mentioned trouble with the road crews," Bolan interjected. "What exactly did you mean?"

Reese sat and stared into the fire, deciding how much he should tell these strangers, possibly debating whether he had been in error when he saved their lives.

"I live with the Parañas now," he said at last. "I don't expect you'll understand the how or why of it. At home I was another lifelong student, living in a world of dusty books. The only calluses I ever had were on my butt and elbows. When I came down here, it was to study human beings like amoebas in a test tube. I was perfectly detached, or so I thought."

Reese hesitated, found a twig and started poking at the fire. A moment lapsed before he spoke again.

"I still don't know exactly what went wrong—or right, depending on your point of view. A few months in the village, and the people weren't just specimens. I came to think of them as men, women and children. That's a grievous failing, by the way, in scientific circles. When you start to care, the faculty advisers call it 'going native.' It's the kiss of death for a respectable career."

"You don't sound too put out about it," Schwarz observed.

"You're right, of course, and that's the miracle. I mean, I don't believe in miracles, but if I did . . . well, never mind. About the tribe. These people, the Parañas, had been driven from their homes once before I ever showed my face in the vicinity. Somehow they still accepted me—with reservations, granted, but they let me in. Another miracle of sorts. Perhaps if they had chosen not to trust me, I'd be sitting in a tiny office now and grading papers, wearing tweed with leather patches on the elbows."

Reese smiled at that, a private joke, his life the punch line. Bolan had no doubt the change of plans had cost him, but the anthropologist-turned-warrior seemed to have no serious regrets.

"The road crew," Bolan prodded him.

"Of course. I'm no professor, but the mind still tends to wander. Sorry." Poking at the fire again, Reese got back to his story. "Five or six weeks after I arrived, they—we—were forced to move again. It was incredible, the way these people packed up their belongings and moved on without complaint. You may have heard about resistance from the other tribes, in Amazonas and the Mato Grosso, but I was amazed by the Parañas, their acceptance of repeated devastation in their lives.

"In any case, we moved northwest, intending to avoid the crews if possible. They found us all the same. It took eleven months, but they were back. This time I tried to reason with the foreman, talk him into deviating by a few degrees, enough to leave the village standing."

"And he wouldn't buy it," Lyons said, not asking.

"It went badly, I'm afraid. There was a scuffle. I had a machete. It was self-defense, of course, but they had several dozen witnesses against a handful of Parañas who speak neither Portuguese nor English. After that, they hunted us more openly. Accommodation was a waste of time."

"So you're a fugitive?" Pol asked.

Reese shrugged. "I don't know if they have my name. It doesn't matter. I'm not going anywhere."

"You've got some hairy odds," Schwarz said.

"We've slowed them down already," Reese replied. "Sometimes at night, we slip into the camp and sabotage the tractors, whatever they're called. I took this from the foreman's tent." He raised his shirttail to expose a .38 revolver in the waistband of his jeans. "I mean the present foreman, not the one I . . . killed."

"One pistol, with some bows and spears," Pol said. "That isn't much against the kind of hardware they were carrying tonight."

"We've never actually fought with them before," Reese said. "I didn't plan on it tonight, in fact, but you appeared to need some help."

"You got that right," Gadgets said.

"What brings you here?" Reese asked. "I mean, you're Americans."

"We want the same thing you do, more or less," Bolan said.

"You're CIA or something, right?"

"Or something."

"I'm surprised," Reese said. "Around Brasília it's an article of faith that Washington supports whatever's 'best for the economy' down here. The military and police still get their foreign aid despite clear evidence of their involvement with the death squads. All this talk about the President's devotion to the cause of human rights is like a running joke."

"We don't work for Congress," Lyons said.

"That's obvious." Reese hesitated for another moment, studying each of his unexpected guests in turn before he said, "How can I help you?"

Bolan frowned, considering his options. "There would be considerable risk involved," he said.

Reese smiled at that. "You mean, compared to the idyllic life we're leading now?"

"Be sure," Bolan said, "before you make the choice."

Reese nodded, rose from his position by the fire and huddled with a group of the Paraña warriors, speaking rapidly, then listening as they replied, each man in turn. He nodded, came back to the fire and sat.

"We're sure," he said.

NEAR MIDNIGHT Blancanales rose from where he had been dozing, several paces from the fire, and took his rifle with him as he walked through darkness to the nearby stream. The tribe had camped near water, throwing up their makeshift huts in record time, but Reese said they would make a proper village of it if they had the time.

And that, Pol thought, would be a problem.

At the moment they were five or six miles distant from the road head, well west of the crew's apparent course, but logic told him that the death squad would come hunting the Parañas with a vengeance after this night's bloody work. The men who slaughtered unarmed children on the streets of Rio and São Paulo wouldn't let an all-out challenge slide. Not when Nazare had a fortune riding on the project, in addition to the hook of injured pride.

Pol understood the macho mind-set. It had been a fixture in the barrio where he grew up, before the military taught him there were more important things to fight for than a patch of scruffy "turf" in some benighted ghetto. In Brazil, despite the changes made since 1985, there was a feeling of nostalgia for the old days on the part of many soldiers, cops and wealthy businessmen. The stampede toward democracy hadn't alleviated all the country's ills, by any means, but it had done enough that some bemoaned the loss of censorship, courts-martial and a bottomless supply of cheap labor that had been the rule when men in uniform controlled the government.

The advent of "democracy" hadn't stripped power from the ruling class, of course. It rarely did. Few nations, moving from a history of despotism into greater freedom, had gone all out like the Russians and Chinese to crush the former aristocracy. And it was just as well, perhaps, considering the record of those revolutions that supplanted one dictator with another, harsher model in the name of socialist Utopia. The Soviets had finally given up on communism, after some three-quarters of a century, and the Chinese were having problems of their own. In the Americas, Fidel alone still clung to Stalinist ideals, and even he couldn't divert the march of time. Once he was gone, Pol thought, the Western Hemisphere would have to find itself another bogeyman.

But there would always be class hatred, racial bigotry, unequal economic distribution. Anywhere that poverty and violence were allowed to flourish, there would be a breeding ground for revolution. It was part of human history and daily life, the flip side of a so-called civilized society.

He reached the stream and stood beside it, staring at the water with its sheen of moonlight filtered through the trees. For all the evidence of man's encroachment, Blancanales thought, it might have been a prehistoric forest quaking to the footsteps of the dinosaurs. If he hadn't know better, seen the evidence himself, Pol would have found it difficult to grasp that men and their machines were barely five miles distant, waiting for the crack of dawn to pick up their relentless march, destroying all life in their path.

Well, not tomorrow, anyway.

They would require some new equipment and a whole new troop of bodyguards before the project went ahead. How much delay was that? A day? A week? No more than that, he reckoned, if the crew wasn't disturbed again.

A subtle movement on his left made Blancanales turn in that direction, and he saw a short Paraña warrior watching him from twenty feet away. They didn't trust him yet—except, perhaps, for Reese—and who could blame them? Every time a white man with a gun passed through the forest, he was either stalking animals or Indians. It was a brand-new concept for the tribe, a group of soldiers fighting on *their* side, and it would take some getting used to.

They had gone for the arrangement, even so, and that had to count for something. Jacob Reese had won them over, but it still required a major leap of faith for the Parañas to allow four armed white strangers in their village, much less for them to enlist in what amounted to a personal guerrilla war against Nazare and the death squad.

Blancanales hoped the choice wasn't about to get them killed.

And if it did, what then? The tribe was dying anyway, he told himself. Their days were numbered in the forest, with the road crew and the mercenaries closing in. Before long they would wind up fighting with their backs against the Curuá River, then the Amazon, assuming any of them lived that long. It was a no-win situation for the forest dwellers. He couldn't help but admire their courage in the face of overwhelming, near hopeless odds, but part of Blancanales still felt guilty, knowing he would play a part in their destruction.

He closed his eyes, and when he opened them again, the Indian was gone. Like that. He could have been an optical illusion, something in a dream. This time next week he could be history.

Every man had choices as he moved through life. Pol himself had no guarantees that he would see the sun come up tomorrow or the next day. Every waking moment was a gamble, and the real-life bogeymen could even get you in your sleep. Some men pulled in their horns, went with the flow and hoped no predators would find them in the herd. For others, it wasn't enough to plod along and see their tracks wiped out by those who came behind, banishing all evidence of their presence.

It was a rare place in the world these days, and getting more so all the time, where people still existed in their primal state, unsullied by the sludge of "civilized" society. The Amazon, a few small pockets in the Congo basin, miles out in the Kalahari Desert, spotted here and there around New Guinea and the countless specks of Micronesia. Not so much a small world, Blancanales thought, as one that had been overwhelmed by man, his dreams and nightmares, weapons and machines.

What did it matter, in the cosmic scheme of things, if one small tribe or twenty were eradicated, slaughtered wholesale or compelled to live within the white man's sphere of influence, adopting customs that were strange beyond imagination? Would the planet miss them when the last of them were gone? Was Mother Earth aware of them right now? Would she remember they had ever been?

For Pol, right now, the fight was more important than its outcome. Effort mattered. The intent was everything. Of course, it was a treat to win one every now and then, but victory was an elusive concept. Every battle had to be refought a thousand times, on different fields, with different enemies. Because in spite of everything, the battle never really changed. Good versus evil. Man against his savage instincts. If you beat the enemy today, he would be back tomorrow with a different name, another face, with brand-new slogans to disguise the same old greed.

It was a long time, Blancanales thought, since he had first met Bolan in another jungle, half a world away from where he stood this night. The difference could be specified in terms of latitude and longitude, but it was still the same old jungle, with all the same old issues hanging in the balance.

Pol would fight this time because he could, and knowing that had given him no choice. If the Parañas joined him, fighting for their homeland, they would be marching into hell with both eyes open, knowing all their options in advance. And Jacob Reese, well, he had obviously made his choice when he gave up on academia to live among "his people," taking on their struggle for survival as his own.

So that was "going native." Pol wasn't surprised to find the notion shocking and disreputable in the eyes of Ivy League professors. He and Bolan had "gone native" back in Vietnam, to some extent, and it had helped them know the people they were fighting for.

It helped them stay alive.

Pol hoped he hadn't lost the knack, that it would see him through another bivouac in hell.

CHAPTER SIXTEEN

Lieutenant Alonso Cipriano watched his soldiers board their helicopters, fifteen to an aircraft, for a total of forty-six besides the flight crews. Each man had an automatic rifle, extra magazines and two hand grenades. Cipriano wore an Uzi submachine gun slung across his shoulder, with a Browning semiautomatic pistol on his hip.

His rank wasn't official, in the sense that these weren't real soldiers under orders from the government, but Cipriano felt like a lieutenant. Serving with Luis Obidos in the death squad was better than the regular army in most respects, from salary to the freedom of movement they enjoyed in stalking their targets. Real enlisted men were constrained by rules and regulations, limiting their effectiveness and greatly restricting their range of operations. With Obidos they were free to move against the enemies of civilized society and punish their repugnant crimes.

Of course, the death squad had its drawbacks, too. Some politicians and policemen stood up for the left-wing constitution that had stripped the army of its power in Brazil and sought to punish death-squad members for their patriotic contributions to the higher good. The press blathered on about human rights, as if Communists and criminals were actually human beings worthy of the name. There were arrests from time to time, but prosecutors rarely brought a case to trial—and when they did, it was a relatively simple matter to convince a jury that defendants in the dock were heroes, more deserving of reward than prison time.

Cipriano had no fear of being interrupted in that morning's work. He had been honored by Obidos with the chance to put things right in Pará Province, where the late Fermin Constanzo had allowed his soldiers to be overrun by Indians and rebels. It was shameful, but the shame could be expunged with fire and steel.

The lieutenant meant to do the job correctly, carry out his orders to the letter. Ruthlessly. No quarter asked or offered.

When it came to savages and socialist scum, there was no room for mercy.

All his men were loaded now, and Cipriano climbed into the lead helicopter, taking his seat behind the co-pilot and buckling his safety belt. The Huey lifted off, and he could see the others rising slowly when he glanced to left and right.

An overflight near dawn had fixed the target, several miles beyond the point of the previous night's massacre. The scouts had used a Cessna, flying high and fast enough that they didn't expect the enemy to be alerted by their passage as they swept the forest with infrared sensors until they detected a grouping of people below. There was no guarantee of identity, granted, but what other group of that size would be found in the jungle so near?

Cipriano would assume he had the proper targets until proved wrong. And if he killed a different group of Indians, it would be no loss to the world.

All of them had to go eventually to make way for towns and farms. It was a fact of life, survival of the fittest. Cipriano saw himself as one who helped maintain the natural order of things, preventing the scum of the earth from gaining the upper hand.

They flew from Altamira, following the Xingu south until it split below the Serro do Carajás, then they swung west to home in on the coordinates the scout plane had provided. It was 7:30 a.m. when they veered off from the river's course and started skimming over trackless jungle, closing on their enemies.

Surprise wouldn't be easy, Cipriano realized. The helicopters couldn't land in such dense forest; they would have to find a drop zone close enough to ground the troops without giving the enemy time to escape or mount a cohesive defense. It would be risky, going in on unfamiliar ground against a hostile force of unknown size and armament, but Cipriano had no choice. His orders were explicit.

Do or die.

He wouldn't be defeated by a ragtag group of Communists, degenerates and naked savages, no matter what the odds. His training and experience would make the difference when it counted. And with any luck at all, he just might have the enemy outnumbered.

He would hope so, anyway, as they began to close in for the kill.

THE PLANE WOKE Bolan from a restless sleep, with half an hour to go before the sun came up. He found Reese squatting by the cook fire, with a small group of Paraña warriors, roasting what appeared to be a giant rat for breakfast.

It was silent now above the treetops, but he still asked Reese, "You heard the plane?"

"I did."

"What do you think?"

Reese thought about it for a moment, finally shrugging. "It's hard to say. They favor helicopters, but this could be something new. At least it didn't circle back."

"It wouldn't have to," Bolan told him, "if they had the right equipment."

"Damn it! I suppose we'd better move again."

"Or maybe not."

"What?"

"There's two ways you can play this game," Bolan said. "One is, you keep on running every time they spot you, every time you think they're getting close. Keep on like that, and they'll run you ragged. And they'll still catch up to you in time, whoever's left."

"Or we can stay and fight," Reese told him.

"It doesn't have to be the Alamo," Bolan said. "We've got time—a little, anyway—and the advantage of familiar ground. I wouldn't be surprised if your guys knew a bit about guerrilla fighting, snares and such."

"They do indeed."

"So all we need is some idea of where the enemy will come from, if and when he comes. You said they favor helicopters."

"Lately, yes. They came in boats one time before, but that was on the Araguaia."

"So we're looking for a clear LZ—a landing zone— where choppers can unload. If we assume they've got the village marked, they'll try to come in close enough for an attack without a lot of wasted marching time. Ideas?"

Reese spoke to the Parañas, listened briefly while the tallest of the warriors answered him and pointed to the east.

"He thinks along the river," Reese told Bolan. "Otherwise, there is a kind of clearing two miles north of here and slightly to the west."

"Too far. Let's check out the river and see what we can do in terms of booby traps."

"You think they're coming, then?"

"Oh, they'll be coming," Bolan said. "It might not be this morning, and the plane we heard could just as well have been a tourist flight from Rio, but they're not about to let this go. Your people are an obstacle, and worse than that, you kicked the death squad's butt last night. There's definitely payback coming, and my guess would be sooner rather than later."

"You're right, of course. We should get started right away."

And so they did.

The traps were ready now: grenades with trip wires strung between the trees at ankle height, with ferns for

cover; springy saplings bent and tied back, bristling
with sharpened branches, ready to whip forward when
released; a heavy deadfall rigged a few yards farther up
the trail. There was no way to open up a perfect field
of fire, but they would work with what they had,
dodge in and out among the trees if necessary, sniping at the soldiers as they came.

And there was no doubt they were coming, none at
all in Bolan's mind. He knew the men they would be
facing—not their names or faces, but the way they
thought, their need to punish even minimal resistance
with a crushing show of force. They would be eager to
avenge their fallen comrades, reaffirm their own machismo with a ruthless massacre.

He knew the type, and he was ready long before he
heard the helicopters coming from the east.

CIPRIANO JUMPED from the helicopter and almost lost
his footing on the grassy riverbank. He saved it with a
minimum of wobbling on unsteady legs and fell in step
behind his point men, moving toward the tree line.
There was no time to be lost here at the landing zone,
when he was sure the noise of their arrival had to have
put his targets on alert. The local Indians weren't in-
telligent, as Cipriano understood the term, but they
were crafty, smart enough to stay away from men who
sought to kill them, and they had a technical advantage in that they were fighting on familiar ground.

Still, Cipriano had no reason to believe his troops
couldn't deal with the savages, avenge the recent loss
of comrades who would be recalled as martyrs to the

cause. Their weapons, training and experience would compensate for anything they lost in terms of absolute surprise.

The trail was barely visible, a narrow track for animals that forced his soldiers to move in single file. That didn't bother Cipriano, either, since he wanted several men in front of him if anything went wrong. It wasn't cowardice, he told himself, but simple common sense. Without a leader, how could he expect his soldiers to survive?

The trail was cool and shady once they left the riverbank behind, deep shadows mocking daylight in this forest where the sun would never truly shine. All that was changing, though, and Cipriano was proud of his contribution to Brazil's progress. When the next history books were written, he might even rate a footnote for his role in helping pacify the savages. Stranger things had happened.

There was a thrashing in the undergrowth to Cipriano's left, as if a heavy body was plunging through the ferns. He spun in that direction, leveling his Uzi, flushing with relief as a stunted pig broke cover for a moment, swiftly dodging out of sight once more among the trees.

Strained laughter came from the troops behind him, and he turned to face them, glaring, with a finger lifted to his lips, reminding them to keep their mouths shut. Even granting that the enemy had to have been wakened by the helicopters, there was no point in announcing their approach with careless chatter, treating deadly business like a children's game.

Cipriano's hands were sweating where they clasped the Uzi, and he spent a moment wiping each in turn, nothing obvious to make his men think he was nervous. It was the humidity, he told himself, and it was fortunate they hadn't landed in the middle of a rainfall, when they would be soaked before they reached their destination.

They were making decent time, and Cipriano had begun to calculate the distance to their target, working from the readout on the pilot's tracking unit, when it happened. Some thirty yards ahead of him, a scream raised his hackles, much as if an ice cube had been slipped inside his shirt.

He froze, craned forward, peering through the murk, and saw his point man die. The soldier was impaled somehow—it seemed to be a spear of sharpened sapling, thrust completely through his torso, but he didn't fall, as if the shaft were anchored at the other end, to hold him upright. Cipriano couldn't bring the soldier's name to mind, but he could hear the young man screaming, still alive despite the piercing wound and all that blood.

The other point men stood like statues on the trail, uncertain whether they should dive for cover, move to help their comrade, maybe open fire despite the dearth of targets. Cipriano's mind was racing, thinking that a spear or simple mantrap meant they would be facing Indians alone, without the more sophisticated help of Communist guerrillas. Rebels would have opened up with guns, but there was still an eerie silence in the forest, if you didn't count the dying soldier's screams.

"Get off the trail!" he shouted, finally recovering his voice. "Find cover!"

Suiting words to action, Cipriano took a few steps to his left and knelt behind a giant tree that towered some two hundred feet above him. He felt like an insect, crouching there, but it was cover, and about the best he could expect to find. His palms were slick with sweat again, but he didn't take time to wipe them, clinging to his Uzi like a sacred talisman.

If only he could find a target!

Someone up ahead was firing, the familiar echo of an FN FAL, and he could only hope his men wouldn't go wild, waste all their ammunition on elusive shadows. As for Cipriano, there was little he could do, in terms of leadership, unless he worked his way up to the point.

He was gathering his nerve to make the run when an explosion echoed through the trees.

IT WAS A DIFFERENT GAME this time, different than any of their other raids, and Reese was trembling as he lay behind a fallen tree with the revolver in his hand. Whatever happened, he had promised not to fire until the trap was sprung, and that was happening right now as he lay watching through a screen of ferns and lanky grass.

The first man in the death-squad column had been fifty feet in front of Reese and closing when he tripped the snare and took a sharpened six-foot sapling through his upper body, puncturing a lung and coming out the back below his shoulder blade. The screams began a heartbeat later, fraying Reese's nerves like fingernails across a chalkboard, but he waited, fought the urge to fire one of his precious rounds and finish it.

Not yet.

The other mercenaries froze in place, four visible from where Reese lay, with untold others straggling out behind them on the game trail. Was it possible that they would turn around, retreat with only one man wounded? If the forest shadows frightened them, perhaps—

But no.

Reese heard the leader snapping at them, in Portuguese. "Get off the trail! Find cover!" They responded instantly, well trained and not as frightened as he might have hoped under the circumstances. Breaking left and right, they dropped from sight among the trees.

Exactly as Belasko and his friends had planned.

How long before one of them found a trip wire and the battle joined in earnest? Reese ducked back behind his log as bullets started flying overhead. A couple of the forward soldiers fired aimlessly. No way they could have spotted him while dodging phantom enemies.

He waited, counting down the seconds in his head.

The first grenade went off somewhere between *thirteen* and *fourteen*, spraying shrapnel from a cloud of smoke and dust. A second voice was screaming now, the first one growing weaker by the moment, several other automatic weapons laying down a screen of fire on both sides of the trail.

Reese poked his head above the log and started looking for a target. He could jump in any time now, with the others firing, no more risk that he would give the set away by acting prematurely. He was squinting through a pall of smoke and looking for an enemy to sight on when the second blast went off, immediately followed by a third.

A flitting shadow on his right resolved itself into a young Paraña warrior, there and gone before Reese had a chance to focus and identify the man. There would be others closing in around the soldiers, armed with bows, spears and knives, prepared to sacrifice themselves if that was what it took to save the tribe. How different they were from "modern" men and women, always busy looking out for number one.

They shamed Reese with their simple courage, but he stayed exactly where he was, his .38 revolver pointed in the general direction of the enemy, still looking for a target. He was no great marksman, certainly no soldier, but he had it in his heart to kill if it would help his people. He had proved that once and would again before this day was done.

The mercenary seemed to come from nowhere, bolting in the wrong direction, frightened and disoriented in the midst of chaos. Reese could see an arrow dangling from the young man's buttocks, like the tail of some peculiar costume, but it didn't slow him. Infused with panic, he was sprinting through the forest, breaking from the column, running with his automatic rifle clutched against his chest.

Reese had no way of knowing if the young man ever saw him as he rose from behind the fallen tree like some hallucination, the revolver clutched in both hands as he aimed. His first shot struck the mercenary's shoulder, staggered him, but it wasn't enough to bring him down. The second was a better effort, drilling through his chest with force enough to put the young man on his knees.

But he wasn't dead yet. His automatic rifle swung outward in slow motion, with a dying finger curled around the trigger. Reese fired twice more, the last shot wasted on the trees, his adversary slumping over backward in a boneless sprawl.

And they were right, whoever said that spilling human blood was easier the second time. Reese hardly felt a thing.

Reese scuttled out to claim the dead man's automatic rifle, grabbed it, then hurried back to hide behind his log. At least two dozen guns were firing now, the bullets swarming overhead like fierce, blood-hungry insects. Reese suppressed an urge to run and hide, continuing to scan the forest for another target. They were out there. All he had to do was find them, take advantage of the new skill he was learning through experience.

His first had been an accident, but number two was easier.

Reese clenched his teeth and focused on the search for number three.

CARL LYONS WAITED for the second hand grenade to detonate before he raised the Atchisson and sighted on a soldier hiding thirty feet away and slightly to his left. The guy had lots to learn about concealment in the forest, but he should have learned it on a training exercise instead of waiting until his life was on the line.

Too late.

The shotgun bucked against his shoulder, and Lyons saw his target splatter, going over in a blur of crimson as the buckshot nearly vaporized his head and upper torso.

Easy.

In the general confusion of the firefight, no one seemed to mark his muzzle-flash or the report of an unusual weapon. Lyons took advantage of the moment, shifting his position slightly, scoping out the ground in front of him to find another mark. There had been two or three big choppers coming in, which meant somewhere from two dozen to forty hostile guns. Five or six of them were out of it by now, and while he knew what the Paraña warriors were capable of with their primitive weapons, there was still a lot of lead in the air.

He spied a second adversary, crawling on his stomach from the game trail, toward a shallow gully cut by runoff during heavy rains. The ditch was choked with ferns that would provide a screen of sorts, but nothing in the way of solid cover from incoming fire.

He waited, leading with the Atchisson, and let his man reach "safety," letting down his guard a fraction. Seconds later, when the guy reached up to nudge the ferns apart and peer out in search of targets, the shotgun slammed against Lyons's shoulder, reaching out to close the young man's eyes forever with a dozen buckshot pellets.

Lyons found another target breaking from the group and running in a zigzag pattern from the trail, unleashing short bursts from his FN FAL without a target, as if he thought a stream of slugs would somehow clear the way and keep him safe. The Able Team leader had him spotted by the second burst, and when he stroked the Atchisson's trigger it was just like shooting turkeys on the wing.

It had been years since Lyons used a gun for sport, his taste for idle killing ruined by exposure to the real thing when his life was on the line. Some people slaughtered rabbits, birds and other animals for relaxation, but Lyons couldn't see it. There were still too many predators of the two-legged kind around for a man of conscience to waste time on creatures that had never harmed a soul.

Grenades were going off in rapid fire now, some on trip wires, others clearly launched from Bolan's AUG or Pol's M-203. The blasts began to merge, like giant fireworks or the echoes of the biggest machine gun anyone had ever conjured up in martial nightmares. Here and there, the blasts were trailed by screams, the sound of small trees going down, but it would take a concentrated C-4 charge to drop the larger forest giants. They were here to stay—at least until some road crew came along with dynamite and chain saws to destroy another piece of paradise.

But not this day.

The shoe was on the other foot, and it was kicking ass.

If anyone had asked him, Lyons would have said he thought that Mother Nature would approve.

CHAPTER SEVENTEEN

Bolan slammed a 40 mm MECAR rifle grenade downrange and watched it detonate against a fallen log. The wood was rotten, termite riddled, and it went up in a cloud of splinters. Someone screamed in the background, cries of anguish fading as the echo of the blast was dissipated, lost.

It was another kill—or at least, a wounding. Bolan didn't think his adversaries were professional enough to fake that kind of a reaction as a ruse to dupe their unseen enemies. In any case, he wasn't falling for it, had no time or inclination to pursue the fate of one maimed soldier when he had so many able-bodied targets yet to choose from.

Counting them had been impossible. The point man had gone down before a dozen of the enemy were visible, and they had fanned out seconds later, blundering into the trip wires planted by himself and Able Team. Between explosions and the crack of rifle fire, he heard a rushing sound as someone tripped the deadfall and the log swept down to crush its target, piercing flesh with jagged stumps of branches like a great spiked rolling pin.

He shifted to his left, stayed under cover as he moved, the forest hiding him, a blithe accomplice to his plan. While some unhappy souls described the jungle as an enemy, a hostile place, he knew that such was not the case. The jungle didn't give a damn who won or lost a skirmish in the endless game of kill-or-be-killed. Whether it was insects eating one another, or a group of men intent on proving that the "higher" species was the most destructive of them all, the forest was a neutral, totally dispassionate observer to the war games that had been played out, in one form or another, since the dawn of time.

He used the forest as an animal might use it, blending with the shadows, following the contours of the land and seeking cover where it was available, instead of crashing through the undergrowth and seeing how much racket he could make for every yard of ground he covered. Bolan was a master at the killing game, and while a twist of luck or fate could stop him in his tracks, he didn't plan on letting any gang of city boys dressed up like soldiers put him in his place.

A pair of shooters broke from cover ten or fifteen yards ahead of Bolan, to his right. He spun in that direction, bringing up the AUG to meet them, taking up the trigger slack before they glimpsed death coming for them through the trees. He fired a 3-round burst that dropped the taller of his targets, and swiveled for a second burst to take down his sidekick. The second man was turning when the bullets hit him, opening his chest and slamming him against a nearby tree trunk, pinned there for a heartbeat until gravity took over and he toppled forward on his face.

The trees and ferns, the spongy ground beneath his feet, all acted to absorb the sounds of combat, muffling gunshots, muting cries of pain and smothering the echo of explosions as grenades kept going off along the trail. It wasn't quite like fighting in a vacuum, but the battle had a sense of unreality about it, even with the crimson splashes visible around the killing field and dead bodies littering the ground.

He kept on moving, cloaked by shadows, listening to bullets whisper in the humid air around him. Some drilled into trees or grazed the trunks, white scars displayed in passing, but if anyone was sighting on the Executioner, his aim was poor indeed.

He moved on, hunting, like a forest predator intent on finding prey.

ALONSO CIPRIANO HUDDLED in the shadow of a tree that had collapsed but never made it to the ground. Instead of falling to the forest floor, it leaned against a giant neighbor, with its topmost branches tangled in the giant's lower limbs. Between the two trees, Cipriano found a kind of makeshift cave where ferns and weeds had taken over, giving him a place to hide.

He felt like a pathetic coward, hiding in the shadows while his men were dying, but the grim alternative was worse. He couldn't see the enemy, much less direct a charge against them, and he hadn't even fired his Uzi yet, because there were no visible targets.

That didn't stop his men from firing, left and right along the trail, but Cipriano reckoned they were wasting ammunition. Worse, they would reveal themselves to any adversaries lurking in the forest, looking for an easy target. Chasing shadows with a bullet was the quickest way that Cipriano knew to give yourself away.

One thing he knew, and that was that their enemies weren't just Indians. The first trap, which impaled his point man, might have been a native snare, but they were also under fire from automatic weapons and dodging shrapnel from grenades. That meant a well-armed, organized response by someone with a greater knowledge of munitions than the average forest dweller would possess.

Who were they?

Cringing in his cave, Cipriano ran the short list in his mind and came up empty. Communists or smugglers, peasant rebels with some ancient grudge against the government—it hardly mattered now. The fact was they were winning, and the last thing Cipriano needed at the moment was to wind up as Fermin Constanzo had, an officer who lost his men and paid for the mistake in blood.

Of course, the way things looked right now, reporting back to Rio was the least of Cipriano's problems. He could think about Luis Obidos later, if he lived that long. Meanwhile, survival was the first priority, and the lieutenant knew that he couldn't survive without his men. He needed guns around him to protect him on the run back to the waiting helicopters.

He had given orders to the pilot in advance, before they left the airfield back at Altamira. The helicopters were to wait, remain in place, until Cipriano and his men returned from their engagement with the enemy. If that meant setting down and switching off the engines, fine, but he didn't intend to find himself on foot, a hundred miles from nowhere, if the mission went awry.

The trick now would be getting to the helicopters in one piece. He knew that several of his men were dead or wounded, but a head count was impossible with all this shooting, the explosions, voices shouting back and forth in fear or anger. Calling to them was an option, but they might not hear him, and the truth was that he feared to give himself away. For all he knew, a savage could be creeping up behind him even now, a flint knife in his hand, red lips drawn back from sharpened teeth.

The mental image made him check around behind him, coming up with nothing. It would be a joke to say that he was safe, but Cipriano knew that he was better off than many of his men. At least the enemy didn't appear to have him spotted yet. He clutched the Uzi tighter, index finger curled around the trigger, wishing he had something—anything at all—on which to vent his fear and anger.

Cipriano knew which way he had to run if he was looking for the trail, and that in turn would lead him to the river, where the helicopters waited. There was just a chance—not much, but some—that he could make it on his own, without the others, but he caught himself before the traitorous idea took hold. If he wasn't concerned with loyalty to his men, self-preservation made him hesitate. He thought once more about Constanzo, coming back alone from an engagement with the Indians, and what Obidos had in store for him.

No, Cipriano thought, if death was certain, then he might as well die fighting with his men. Conversely, if he wanted to withdraw, his best bet was to take at least some of his soldiers with him, maybe leave a rear guard to delay the enemy while he was racing back along the trail.

Communication was the key, but he was on his own now, separated somehow from his radio operator when they scrambled clear of the game trail. He couldn't alert the helicopter crews to danger, nor could he reach out to the survivors, spread out along the trail. If he was going to collect a bodyguard, present some semblance of an organized retreat, he would be forced to leave his hiding place and crawl from man to man, delivering his orders one by one.

And he would have to do it in the middle of a cross fire, where his own men were as dangerous to Cipriano as the enemy.

At once he saw the opportunity behind the risk. It would be a heroic move, in fact, the kind of thing they decorated soldiers for in wartime. If he pulled it off and saved some of his soldiers in addition to himself, Obidos couldn't help but be impressed. It was embarrassing to be defeated by the enemy, but a commander who thought first about his men and tried to save their lives was someone to be valued, possibly promoted to a more responsible position.

A position where he wouldn't have to face the terrors of the bush a second time.

Cipriano swallowed hard and double-checked the safety on his Uzi before he left his shady sanctuary, crawling on his belly through the grass and ferns. He had his eyes fixed on the game trail more or less, though it wasn't exactly visible from his position on the ground. Still, Cipriano knew his men were there, the ones who still survived, in need of leadership. His leadership.

He was about to save them *and* himself.

Provided no one shot him dead before he had the chance.

JACOB REESE CHECKED the safety on his captured assault rifle, making sure the weapon was ready to fire. He fumbled with another catch, withdrew the magazine and tried to guess how many rounds were left. He couldn't tell—how many did it hold when full?—but several rounds were visible, a staggered row of deadly polished brass.

Some twenty feet away from Reese, almost invisible from where he stood, a young Paraña archer drew his bow and sighted quickly, sending his arrow skimming toward a target Reese couldn't make out. He wished the bowman luck, had no idea if it was possible to choose and strike a target under these conditions, but if anyone could do it, the Parañas—veteran jungle hunters that they were—would pull it off.

Reese started moving toward the game trail and his enemies, in search of someone he could kill. The urge didn't surprise him as much as the ease with which he had accepted it, incorporated the desire to murder as a part of who he was. He had three bodies to his credit now, a second since his first kill in the present battle, and he still had many cartridges to spend before he was effectively disarmed.

A subtle movement in the shadows up ahead froze Reese in his tracks. It was a man—that much was certain—and the figure seemed too large for a Paraña. Still, it wouldn't do for him to fire without a clear view of his target, risking injury or death to Belasko or his friends.

Reese took his time, creeping forward like a man afraid each step may be his last. The shadow-shape in front of him acquired more human features as he closed the gap, became a man in jungle camouflage, his face in profile, with some kind of floppy hat atop his head.

It wasn't one of Belasko's soldiers, then, for none of them wore headgear.

Reese stopped, knelt slowly, trying not to rouse the man before he had a chance to strike. The rifle's weight surprised him, a physical manifestation of its deadly latent power. He wedged the butt between his cheek and shoulder, sighting on his adversary's profile.

This time he managed not to jerk the trigger. Squeezing gently, he was ready for the recoil when the weapon bucked against his shoulder. There was no smoke to speak of, not like in the movies he remembered from his last days in the States, and even with the sounds of gunfire ringing in his ears, Reese heard the bullet strike its target, drilling through the soldier's cheek to whip his head around and punch him over on his side.

He scuttled forward, hurrying, in case the man was only wounded and had strength enough to raise his weapon. Crashing through the ferns to stand above the body, Reese saw instantly that such was not the case. It was a solid hit, the left side of his target's skull obliterated, leaking from a fist-size exit wound.

And that made four. Reese wondered what his former friends would think if they could see him now. Astonishment would soon give way to horror, he had no doubt.

Reese knew there could be no turning back. His course was set, and while it seemed unlikely he would live to witness victory, at least he knew that he wouldn't have lived in vain, a hollow man who went through all the motions, signifying nothing.

He was standing tall above his latest conquest when a bullet whispered past his ear and burrowed deep into a nearby tree trunk. Reese dropped to hands and knees, aware that he was kneeling in the soldier's blood, uncaring. There was blood enough to go around. The next spilled could be his unless he watched his back and took precautions to defend himself.

He waited for another bullet, but it didn't come. At last Reese told himself the slug had been a stray. His adversaries didn't have him spotted, after all.

His luck was holding.

Thinking of survival, Reese spent a moment grappling with the corpse to free its bandolier and drape the bloodstained ammo belt around his own neck. He was covered now, in case his captured rifle should run out of bullets. He could hold the pistol in reserve, for grave emergencies, a last-ditch option.

Reese crept toward the game trail, putting the corpse behind him. Death was everywhere, and he had no need of reminders that he might soon join the others in oblivion. At least, in that case he would know that he had gone down fighting for his people and a cause that he believed in, rather than wasting his days in a classroom that smelled of tobacco and chalk dust.

It was time to kill, perhaps to die.

Reese spied another target up ahead, and started working toward it, closing for the kill.

HERMANN SCHWARZ squeezed off a short burst from his CAR-15 and watched two gunmen sprawl back in the undergrowth, unmoving where they fell. It was a bad idea for soldiers to bunch up that way in combat, even though it offered the illusion of security when you had someone there to watch your back. Without a trench or foxhole, two men simply made a target twice as large, inviting trouble with a capital *T.*

Schwarz moved as soon as he had fired, a wriggle to his left, just far enough to spoil the aim of any gunmen who might have him spotted by his muzzle blast. It was unlikely, in the circumstances, with so much confusion all around, but you could never be too careful in a kill zone.

Up ahead, some thirty yards in front of him, he detected vague movement in the shadows. Several men were in motion, from the look of it, but they weren't advancing. Pulling out? It would be tricky, under fire, but Gadgets did a double take and verified that they were working back along the game trail, in the general direction of the river.

Had the others seen it? Should he risk a radio transmission that could just as easily betray one of his comrades with a word or wisp of static?

No.

He trusted Bolan and the others to remain alert, pursue the enemy wherever they might go. As for himself, Schwarz started following the drift of soldiers, moving parallel, not sniping at them yet. It would be better, he decided, if he let the early bug-outs pick up more along the way, provide a greater wealth of targets as they broke from cover to move back along the trail or through the trees.

He tried a head count, lost it in the shifting, dappled shadows, but he guessed that there were roughly a dozen soldiers in the group now, pulling back. It didn't qualify as a full-scale rout, but they were getting there. Perhaps, if he could spook them, get them running...

Gadgets palmed a frag grenade and pulled the safety pin. He had to watch the angle of the pitch, avoid some kind of daffy ricochet among the trees, and still miss taking out the men he hoped to panic. If he dropped them now, before the bug-out had a chance to gather steam, his effort would have been in vain.

He made the pitch, stood fast instead of ducking under cover as the HE canister arced briefly out of

sight, then tumbled back to earth a few yards west of
where the death-squad troops were pulling back. Its
detonation raised a cloud of dirt and leaves, sent
shrapnel zinging through the trees, but no one fell on
the receiving end.

Instead, they bolted, running for their lives.

Schwarz followed, giving chase, alert to the inher-
ent risk of stumbling into booby traps the Indians or
members of his own team had arranged to greet the
mercenaries. He was gaining on the column's rear
guard, closing fast, when sudden movement in the
corner of his left eye warned him of impending danger.

And it figured, sure. In any action, much less one
concocted by a few men in the heat of battle, there was
always someone left out in the cold, who never got the
word. It never entered Schwarz's mind that this man
had been left behind deliberately to cover the retreat,
since there had been no time for a cohesive plan. The
young man was a soldier on his own, keyed up and
anxious for a clear shot at his enemy, which made him
every bit as dangerous.

The one thing Gadgets couldn't figure out, no matter how he thought about it afterward, was why the
shooter rushed him, closing for a hand-to-hand
showdown, instead of simply lying back and sniping
him from twenty feet away. It was a risky business,
charging through the trees like that, despite the edge
provided for him by surprise.

Schwarz had a chance to pivot on his heel and bring
around the CAR-15 to block a roundhouse swing that

would have crushed his skull had it connected. As it was, his weapon shivered with the impact of the young man's heavy FN FAL assault rifle, but he struck back quickly, lashing out with a kick to the groin and following through with a buttstroke from the carbine, aiming for his adversary's jaw.

It was a fact that neither move connected perfectly, but the combined effect was still enough to drive his young opponent backward, throwing him off-balance. When the gunner recognized his error, tried to use the FN FAL for its intended purpose rather than an awkward cudgel, Gadgets got there first and shot him in the face. The soldier vaulted backward, dying on his feet without a sound, and went down in the shadow of an ancient, looming tree.

Schwarz didn't need to check his pulse. It was a mortal wound, and it would make no difference to the outcome of the battle if he died at once or half an hour hence.

The other troops were running, and they had the Able Team warrior's full attention now. If necessary, he would chase them all the way to hell.

CIPRIANO RECKONED he was dead no less than half a dozen times on the retreat from where they had been ambushed to the helicopter landing zone. One time a soldier moving just beside him had gone down, blood spouting from a bullet hole between his shoulder blades, and Cipriano braced himself for the explosive impact of a second round—but nothing happened. Slugs were whistling all around him, sometimes drop-

ping soldiers in their tracks, while others chipped the
bark from trees, trail blazing with a vengeance.

Any kind of orderly retreat was hopeless, Cipriano
realized, and he made no attempt to place his men in
columns, where their ranks would make it easier for
snipers to destroy them. Cipriano guessed that he had
lost one-third of his command already, and there
would be more dead on the trail before they reached
the helicopters and were lifted out to safety.

If they reached the helicopters, that was, and the
pilots could evacuate the landing zone before their
enemies cut loose with armor-piercing rounds and
more grenades.

Mortality had never preyed on Cipriano's mind before, and now that he was likely to be killed at any
moment, the lieutenant found he was preoccupied
with the minutia of combat. Fear was ever present, but
he had no time to contemplate what it would feel like
being shot or blown to smithereens. Instead, his mind
was full of time and distance, how fast he could run in
battle dress and the escape velocity of loaded helicopters.

They wouldn't be fully loaded, Cipriano thought,
and while it pained him to admit it, there was something of relief in how he felt. With fewer men to load
and less weight, the choppers would be quicker lifting
off.

And every second counted; there was no mistake on
that score.

Even knowing that, he broke stride long enough to
turn and fire a short burst from the Uzi, back in the

direction he had come from. The lieutenant knew he didn't have a hope of scoring with the aimless fire, much less of doing any major damage to his enemies, but it would look bad to the brass in Rio if he never even fired a shot. So what if it was wasted effort? He was fighting for his own life and the lives of soldiers under his command.

The riverbank was getting closer. He could smell it now, the scent of rotting vegetation at the water's edge that had a different tang from mulch decaying on the forest floor. He wondered if the helicopters would be waiting, whether they had gone aloft for safety's sake and how long it would take between his signal and the time their loaded transports lifted off.

The open bank wasn't defensible, per se, but they could always wade into the river if it came to that. Cipriano would prefer to take his chances with the caimans and piranha, rather than with Communists and godless savages.

His lungs were burning, even though the run hadn't been long, his flat-out speed no challenge to the great Olympic stars. He blamed the forest's brooding heat, humidity that sapped a man's strength after moments of exposure. If he lived to talk about it, it would be one more argument in favor of the current plan to raze the jungle that devoured and dominated so much of Brazil.

A blast behind Cipriano sent him reeling, buffeted by the concussion and superheated air that singed his nape. He kept his balance with an effort, slogging through the undergrowth, high-stepping over hummocks, fallen trees and stones that blocked his path. He kept the game trail on his left, but didn't follow it precisely, worried that the extra bit of visibility would give his enemies an edge.

A cry behind him marked the downfall of another soldier, but he kept on going, never looking back to see if the commando was alive or dead. They had no time for stragglers, walking wounded and the like. Those men who couldn't make the pace were out of luck and out of time.

He spied the river up ahead, a glint of sunlight on the water that was brown and sluggish, armpit deep in places, with a layer of mud and shifting stones beneath that would make any crossing treacherous.

No helicopters waited on the riverbank.

Cipriano ran down from the tree line to the water and raised a hand to shield his eyes as he gazed skyward, looking for the choppers. There they were, at treetop level, hovering. He waved an arm in their direction and was about to fire a short burst from his Uzi in the hope of gaining their attention, when his field communications officer appeared from nowhere, thrusting out the walkie-talkie in one hand. A shouted order brought the pilots lower, spiraling like giant vultures on the scent of carrion.

The lieutenant turned to face the jungle, standing with the Uzi braced against his hip. The only thing he had to do from that point on was stay alive until the choppers landed and received his men.

It was a relatively simple task, all things considered.

Cipriano wondered whether he could pull it off.

WHEN BOLAN SAW the soldiers pulling out, he knew their time was limited. A clean sweep meant that they would have to cut off the retreat somehow, prevent Nazare's men from slipping through the net. If they escaped, though...

Bolan aimed another MECAR round downrange and let it fly, the 40 mm missile wobbling slightly as it dropped toward impact. It went off with a smoky flash among the trees, and cast the rear guard of the mercenary column into disarray. He followed, stepping over corpses, milking short bursts from the AUG, but his opponents held their lead, returning fire in wild, erratic bursts.

Some of the bodies on the ground had arrows sticking out of them, and one had been impaled, a long spear pinning him against a tree as if he were an insect in some giant entomologist's collection. Others had been dropped by automatic fire and shrapnel, but he wasted no time counting them, intent on finishing the job before their comrades slipped away.

Helicopters were somewhere ahead of him, still hidden from his view by trees. The sound of their engines told him that he might already be too late.

More speed, then. Bolan started jogging, firing short bursts from the hip when there was anything to shoot at. He dropped one man and then another when they stopped and turned back to defend the column's rear. Another blast, away somewhere to Bolan's right, told him the Able Team warriors were in hot pursuit and following the death squad on its run back to the riverbank LZ.

One of the Hueys was already airborne when he got there, with another lifting off, the third still boarding stragglers. The Executioner fired a short burst at the grounded chopper, then took time to load another 40 mm round before he raised the AUG, took aim between the pilot and his sidekick and let it fly.

The grounded Huey shuddered, rearing back on a roiling ball of flame, and came apart before his very eyes. The fuel tanks detonated almost instantly, the rotors flying off in jagged sections, raising water spouts and thunking into trees like giant ax blades. Bolan ducked as smoking shrapnel sang above his head, but kept his gaze fixed on the airborne helicopters, looking for a way to bring them down.

Too late.

Around him the men of Able Team and Paraña tribesmen were emerging from the trees, unloading on the whirlybirds with everything they had, but all in vain. It took only a moment for the Hueys to ascend beyond effective range, and Bolan stood beside the brackish river, watched them dwindle out of sight.

And they were gone.

"What now?" Reese asked, appearing at his elbow with an FN FAL assault rifle in his hands.

"Some of them got away," Bolan said, "and they know exactly where to find us. We can run away, sit here and wait for them to gather reinforcements, or..."

He hesitated, not much liking any of the options, letting Reese inquire about the final option.

"Or?" the anthropologist demanded.

"We can go for the initiative," he said. "Attack."

"The road crew?"

"That would be my guess. If they fall back to any kind of settlement, we'd never catch them anyway."

Reese hesitated, staring at the sky above, now vacant but for circling birds. Another moment passed before he said, "I'm with you."

"And the others?" Bolan asked.

"I'll ask," Reese said, "but I expect they'll come along. What real choice do they have?"

CHAPTER EIGHTEEN

Alonso Cipriano didn't take his soldiers back to Altamira from the battle zone. Instead, he flew his twenty-two survivors back to what was left of the Nazare road crew's campsite. Charred machines and frightened men were waiting for them, with a few tents still intact. The workers were relieved to see the troops arrive, at least before they got a look at Cipriano's walking wounded and the shaken soldiers who were physically unscathed.

The detour to the camp hadn't been Cipriano's choice. He had been headed back to Altamira with the two surviving choppers when Luis Obidos reached him on the radio and ordered the diversion. There was no point arguing; it simply would have made things worse. This way, at least, his soldiers had a chance.

His adversaries in the forest had enjoyed a run of luck so far, but Cipriano didn't think they would be fools enough to raid the camp a second time. If they were wise—a proposition that, admittedly, didn't apply to savages across the board—they would regroup and try to cut their losses, run for cover while they had a chance.

If they were wise.

But what if they were reckless and emboldened by their recent victories? What then?

He would be forced to post a guard, at least. It would be better if his whole force, save for those who had been seriously wounded, could remain alert throughout the night and watch for any sign of an impending raid. Cipriano wished he had a larger force, but it had done him little good that morning, when he tried to take the native village by surprise.

If nothing else, at least some of his questions had been answered, doubts laid to rest. Cipriano knew, for instance, that some of his men had been killed with modern weapons, while he had seen other corpses pierced by spears and arrows. That confirmed the merger of two enemies, a band of Communist guerrillas with the forest savages he had been sent from Rio to eradicate. The confirmation didn't help him, though, in that he still had no way to defeat his enemies as yet.

He had requested reinforcements, but Obidos promised nothing. There was trouble in the cities, Cipriano realized, with the attacks that had occurred in recent days, but it infuriated him to think that he would be abandoned, with the small force that remained to him, when they were facing mortal danger in the wilderness.

It came down to a waiting game, and wondering how long his men could last without support. They still had ammunition, though a good deal less than they had started with, and food should be no problem for the next few days. The camp had adequate supplies, despite some losses in the raid that had destroyed Fermin Constanzo's troop, and he could always send a hunting party out in search of game if things got tight.

His major problems at the moment were morale and preparation for another strike by those who were determined to prevent the road crew from proceeding with its work. His soldiers needed time to lick their wounds, regain their confidence, and Cipriano knew the surest method of recapturing their fighting spirit would be through a swift, decisive victory against their enemy. Unfortunately, they weren't in any shape to risk another head-on confrontation at the moment, and he feared that an immediate renewal of hostilities might well result in the annihilation of his troops.

It was a weird, uncomfortable feeling, knowing that his men had come off second best. Not merely losing an engagement—that was possible for any fighting force—but losing to an enemy that should have been so easy to destroy.

Cipriano was accustomed to the easy victories that were a rule of thumb in Rio and Recife. There the death squad would select a target on the basis of behavior or political ideas and plan the execution in advance, make sure the odds were in their favor—five or six to one was best—before they ever made a move. If anything went wrong, it was a simple matter to escape in stolen cars, regroup and lay new plans to get it right the next time, with a minimum of fuss.

It was a whole new world out here, where civilization was a theoretical concept and man was simply a part of the food chain. Nothing could be taken for granted in the jungle, as demonstrated by his own hu-

miliation in the recent firefight. If a force like his—
well armed, well trained—could be embarrassed by a
tribe of aborigines, then anything was possible.

His reputation would be damaged by the loss, no
question there, but Cipriano was determined to reverse the situation, salvage something from the
wreckage. If Obidos would agree to reinforcements, he
could launch a new offensive, count on overwhelming force to do the job. If not, then he would take a
different tack, pursue his enemies with the remainder
of his force, but on their own terms, as guerrillas,
taking full advantage of the land to stalk them, wear
them down.

Cipriano had no special training in guerrilla warfare, but how difficult could it be if illiterate peasants
and Indians mastered the craft? He was a military
man, of sorts, with knowledge of strategic operations, and his reading had included several texts on the
suppression of insurgency. Instinct would do the rest,
and he had all the motivation any man could want.
His reputation was at stake, perhaps his very life, and
Cipriano wouldn't rest until he cleared his name.

That was not literally true, of course. He was ex-
hausted at the moment, from the predawn muster,
grueling flight, the battle and precipitate retreat. Despite the thoughts that clamored for attention in his
head, his eyelids drooped, and Cipriano knew that he
had to rest soon, gather strength, in order to remain
effective as a leader to his men.

He commandeered a small, undamaged tent, and
didn't feel foolish in the least when posting guards

outside. The sentries had their orders: four straight hours, undisturbed, unless there was some critical emergency demanding his attention.

Safe at last, the lieutenant lay on his cot and went to sleep, perchance to dream.

"WE HAVE DISCUSSED IT," Reese told Bolan, "and I couldn't force my will on the Parañas if I wanted to. They're tired of running."

"And they understand the risks?"

Reese smiled at that. "You've seen the way they live, the way they fight. Between the military government and death squads fielded from the private sector, they've been hunted down like animals for fifty years. There were eleven thousand members of the tribe in 1947. Those you see around you are what's left."

"My point," Bolan said, "is that the plan we have in mind could hasten things along. They're not exactly well equipped for going up against a paramilitary force."

"They did all right this morning," Reese reminded him.

"Okay." Bolan shrugged, exchanging glances with his three companions. "No more arguments from me."

"So, what's the plan?" Reese asked.

"We go back for the road crew, finish what we started yesterday. I'm guessing that the remnants of the force we met this morning will be sent to guard the camp, since they're already in the neighborhood. If not, we're points ahead. The road crew can't have many soldiers left.''

"They're all expendable, you know," Reese said. "Nazare can replace the crew in nothing flat. He'll take the cost of new equipment out of petty cash.''

"We're buying time," Bolan stated. "I want to stall the clearance program long enough that we can get back to Nazare, maybe reason with him.''

Lyons laughed. "I'll reason with the bastard," he said. "Make him an offer he can't refuse.''

"You'd kill Nazare?"

Bolan shrugged again, but Reese could read the answer to that question in his eyes. "We have a job to do," he said, "by any means available.''

"He's not alone in this, you understand. Remove Daniel Nazare, and you've got a hundred others lining up to take his place. Brazilians—some of them, at least—are more concerned with fattening their bank accounts than making sure their country has a future.''

"Changing human nature's not our province," Bolan told him. "We do what we can with what we have. If that means working one-on-one, we try to set a positive example for the people we can't reach directly.''

"Use Nazare as an object lesson?"

"Or a warning. Granted, taking out one robber baron—or a hundred—won't stop certain greedy men from going for the gold. It might dissuade a few, though.''

"It'll damn sure stop Nazare," Lyons said. "I've never seen a thief rise from the grave."

"Anyway," Bolan went on, "when we hit the camp tonight, your people should be ready for some concentrated fire. We obviously don't have guns enough to go around."

Reese glanced at the Paraña warriors standing to one side, a group of four detailed to join in the discussion and decide what role was best for them to play in the attack. Reese spent a moment translating the gist of it so far, and watched them nod in understanding.

"Warfare is a way of life for forest tribes," he told Bolan and the others. "Nothing on this scale, of course, but they fight constantly among themselves. The Jivaro are probably the best example, with their raids for trophy heads. They may not have the latest hardware, but they're far from helpless."

"Granted," Bolan said. "I'm just telling you there may be losses. Probably, in fact. I'd count on it."

"I understand. *They* understand."

"Okay. Then all we need's a plan that won't backfire and get us killed."

"Is that all?" Lyons asked. "You had me worried for a minute there. I thought there was a problem."

"Not unless you count the march," the Executioner stated, "together with the fact that we're outnumbered and outgunned."

"That's not a problem," said the oldest of his three companions. "It's a challenge."

"Right." Bolan smiled, picked up a stick and started scratching in the dirt. "Here's what I had in mind. Jump in if you see any problems."

AFTERWARD, WHEN THEY HAD all agreed upon the plan, Bolan stood apart and waited for his little army to get ready for the march. There really wasn't much to do in terms of preparation. The Parañas were already "dressed" for battle, with their spears and bows, requiring only dabs of warpaint to complete their outfits. Able Team was busily reloading magazines and cleaning weapons, making sure that every piece of gear would function properly upon demand.

As for the Executioner, he still had two concerns. The march was part of it, a trek of seven miles or so through jungle where the enemy, if he was thinking, could prepare an ambush anywhere along the way. In fact the notion of a trap was no great worry now that he had seen the death-squad troops in action. They were clearly unfamiliar with the forest and would probably equate an open camp with safety, mounting stationary guards instead of sending out patrols or ambush teams to execute preemptive strikes.

Was he correct in guessing that survivors of the hit team would be detailed to protect Nazare's road crew? And if so, would they be reinforced by nightfall, lengthening the odds against his own small crew's survival?

Bolan was prepared for any risk, and he would trust the men of Able Team to do their part, but he was still concerned for Jacob Reese and the Paraña tribesmen.

Reese was still a novice when it came to combat, even granting his experience with the Parañas and their recent efforts to harass the road crew. At the moment he was fired up with the urge to save "his" people, and he hadn't dropped the ball so far. But there was all the difference in the world between defensive action and a swift, proactive raid conducted in the dead of night.

He thought about the last time, Reese and the Parañas coming out of nowhere, driving back the soldiers who had cornered Bolan and his comrades. Luck was part of it, he realized, their adversaries taken by surprise on dark and unfamiliar ground. As for the strategy involved, he had to credit most of that to the Paraña hunters who had grown up in the forest, stalking wildlife and their neighbors in a struggle to survive from day to day.

The Indians would fight—he had no doubts on that score—but the question of their motivation troubled him. If they were desperate, resigned to death, they might take chances that imperiled Bolan and his Able Team, risking life and limb in the equivalent of a demented kamikaze charge. It would be their choice ultimately, but he didn't relish shouldering responsibility for the annihilation of a race. Nor, when he thought about it, would a band of suicidal allies be the best insurance for his own survival on the killing field.

A problem, then, but one that he could try to work around. Beyond that night, the bloodshed that was coming, Bolan thought about Luis Obidos and his patron, Daniel Nazare. Both of them were safe in Rio de Janeiro, doubtless heartened by the fact that there had been no recent strikes against their urban fronts and friends. Obidos would be working overtime with his connections in the army and police force, trying to discover the identity of Bolan and his crew. It was a hopeless task, but it would keep the death squad's leader busy for a while, perhaps divert some measure of his focus from the bloody drama being acted out in Pará Province.

Bolan hoped so, anyway. He didn't want Obidos and Nazare heading for the hills before he had a chance to finish his business in the hinterland and drop by for a final call in Rio. Everything that he had done so far was setting up the main event—elimination of the men responsible for so much of the daily violence in Brazil.

He didn't count on any lasting change, of course, but sometimes it could be enough to change the players, shake up the whole production a bit and see what happened next. Nazare's fall wouldn't prevent some other highway crew from picking up where he left off—and there were other crews at work right now, in fact, throughout Brazil—but he was still among the largest, richest backers of destructive "progress." His removal from the scene, when publicized, would give the others food for thought, if nothing else.

And some of them would find the prospect difficult to swallow.

Small victories. Sometimes they were the only kind available.

His motley troops were nearly finished with their preparations now, the Indians receiving a last-minute

pep talk from Reese, while Able Team packed up their
freshly loaded magazines, checked hand grenades,
then stood ready to depart. For just a moment he was
back in Vietnam, the highlands, where his penetra-
tion team—including Schwarz and Blancanales—had
enlisted native Meo tribesmen to harass the Vietcong.

But that was ancient history. His war lay in the here
and now, where living men were on the way to risk—
and maybe sacrifice—their lives for something they
believed in. They had varied motives, but it all came
out the same in their commitment to a struggle that
could change the course of life for some of them...or
end it altogether.

War was like that: all or nothing, one of the few remaining human activities that called for ultimate sacrifice. All other blood sports paled in comparison,
their motivations frivolous, sometimes obscene. It was
only in warfare, and in some of the nonviolent pro-
fessions devoted to serving mankind, that a practi-
tioner could leave his mark and know, whatever might
become of him, that heroism counted. It wasn't a part
of ancient history, confined to dusty texts on World
War II or the Crusades.

His heroes had closed ranks, and they were waiting
for him now. Five minutes later Bolan followed two
Paraña scouts into the jungle, marching south and
west to meet his fate.

CHAPTER NINETEEN

Alonso Cipriano's sentry woke him right on time, but the way he felt, the lieutenant may as well have had no sleep at all. Instead of resting and recuperating from his ordeal, he had tossed and turned, a dervish on the small, uncomfortable cot, pursued by demons in his dreams. He wasn't a religious man, nor were these "ordinary" demons. Rather, some of them were dressed in camouflage fatigues, while others were entirely naked, save for breechcloths and some gaudy feathers. They pursued him with a vengeance, through an endless jungle, shrieking after him with voices out of hell.

It didn't take a psychoanalyst to tell where those dreams came from, after all that he had been through since the morning. Cipriano didn't view the nightmares as a sign of weakness necessarily, nor did he think of them as omens. He was educated to a point, and knew enough of dreams and the subconscious mind to understand their function. Everyone had nightmares now and then, but he would keep these to himself, in case someone should misinterpret them and take him for a weakling.

There had been no message from Obidos while he slept, no offer of support. It was another thirty minutes until sundown, but the forest floor was black as night already, shadows reaching outward from the nearby tree line to enfold the camp.

He had considered pulling back a quarter-mile or so to put a larger field of fire between his soldiers and the forest, but he finally decided they could put the time to better use by digging in on the perimeter. Not trenches, which would block the new machines when they arrived, but some strategic foxholes for his riflemen to give them cover and increase their confidence.

The work was nearly finished when Cipriano left his tent. His wounded were together in a makeshift tent consisting of a tarp stretched taut between four wooden poles. While there was no doctor in the camp, first aid had been applied, and five of them were resting comfortably. The other two were comatose, one with a bullet lodged somewhere behind his eye, the other with a deep wound from an arrow in his chest, and Cipriano doubted whether they would last the night.

So many dead, and he had no idea if they had killed a single enemy. Of course, he would make up a body count when he reported to Obidos with the details—who could prove him wrong?—but it was still embarrassing. He almost wished the enemy would follow them, give him another chance to prove himself. No, that was crazy. Why invite another beating when his men were weary, drained of energy?

For just a moment he was nervous, thinking back to the teachings of his childhood, when his mother told him you could sometimes make a thing come true by wishing for it. That was foolishness, of course. It ranked along with UFOs and Father Christmas on the list of childish fables. Still, he almost crossed himself, resisting with an effort in the knowledge that his men would lose respect for him—whatever they had left— if he should let himself seem weak.

The first grenade came in from somewhere on the northwest front, a long shot from the tree line. Cipriano didn't see it coming, couldn't even swear he heard the launcher's muffled echo when it fired. He heard the blast, though. The shock wave knocked him sprawling in the dirt, one of his bodyguards laid out beside him.

He scrambled to his feet and started shouting for his soldiers, telling them to watch on the perimeter, prepare for anything, as if they needed any further warnings. Half of them were firing by the time Cipriano raised his voice, though he would bet his life that none of them had solid targets.

God in heaven, it was happening again! The enemy *had* followed him somehow, and launched another raid against the camp.

Around him members of the road crew were already scrambling for the nearest cover, terrified that the previous night's massacre would be repeated. Cipriano stood his ground, but ducked involuntarily when bullets started swarming overhead.

He had been looking for a chance to prove himself, and here it was. Lieutenant Cipriano only hoped the effort wouldn't cost his life.

BOLAN HAD FIRED the opening gun for the mission himself, aiming downrange with the second-to-last of his MECAR grenades, letting fly when his sights had the cook fire locked in. At the sound of the blast he was moving, a shadow of death that belonged in the darkness, his face and hands darkened with warpaint. Around him he heard the Paraña advancing, unleashing the first of their arrows as guns opened up from the camp.

They had marched seven hours through the forest, one hour per mile, their pace slowed by terrain and the need to be watchful of traps. With an hour to go before sundown, they stood in the trees and looked out at the camp, counting heads, memorizing defenses, revising their plan on the spot.

Fifteen soldiers that Bolan could see, and he reckoned there might be a few more in tents, resting from the earlier fight prior to standing their watch. From the road crew itself, there were fifty-odd men, with a dozen or so visibly armed. Call it thirty men packing for sure, with the rest of them fit to resist if they chose, using any odd weapons at hand.

With Jacob Reese and the Paraña warriors, that made decent odds, no more than three or four to one by Bolan's final count. Still, the Paraña would be going in with Stone Age bows and spears, against a group of men with automatic weapons who had clearly spent the daylight hours digging foxholes for themselves.

A challenge and then some.

He had stationed Reese and most of the Parañas—twelve of the nineteen—around the southwest quadrant of the camp to slam the back door on their enemies if any started bailing out. The rest were spread out on the northwest front, where Bolan placed himself. The men of Able Team were spotted to the east and west to box the camp as best they could.

All things considered, Bolan thought it was a decent plan, but you could never really tell before the battle, when idyllic theory ran head-on into reality. From that point on, anything could happen, and he knew that they would have to be prepared, take nothing for granted on the killing ground.

There were no barriers per se on the perimeter in front of him, but Bolan saw three soldiers crouched in foxholes, two more frozen where they had been walking post before the MECAR charge exploded. None of them could see him yet, but they were firing blind into the forest, hoping for a lucky hit on someone, anyone.

He sidestepped, ducking under cover in the shadow of a giant tree that would be quick to fall if Daniel Nazare's crew resumed their work. A swift glance out and back let Bolan fix the hostile muzzle-flashes in his mind, note where the foxholes were located in relation to himself.

It would be difficult to root out the buried soldiers with rifle grenades, and he had only one in his waist pack. But a hand grenade could do the job if he was accurate enough, and he had two of those.

Five soldiers, three foxholes and two hand grenades. No matter how he tried to break it down, rewriting the equation, Bolan's enemies still had the edge.

Okay. He would press on and do the best he could with what he had.

They hadn't seen him yet, and he decided he should take the standing gunners first, get rid of them before they slipped away or found some decent cover for themselves. Another peek around the tree trunk, and he had them spotted. He brought up the Steyr AUG, its fire selector set for 3-round bursts.

He caught the first man as he grappled with an empty magazine, reloading, 5.56 mm tumblers opening the gunner's chest and dropping him without a sound of protest. Number two had glimpsed the muzzle-flash and was pivoting to fire in that direction when a second burst reached out to pummel him. He went down kicking, thrashing, firing off a last wild burst in the direction of the moon.

That left the foxhole gunners, all three of them firing now, though one of them, at least, still hadn't spotted Bolan. Ducking back as bullets raked the tree, he palmed a frag grenade and yanked the pin, held down the safety spoon as he began to count, the doomsday numbers running in his head.

It would be dangerous, but so was living.

Bolan broke from cover on his left, gambling that his adversaries would be looking for him on the same side of the tree where he had shown himself to kill their comrades. Darkness helped to cover him, and it

was no great trick to make the pitch, some forty feet
downrange, and drop his lethal egg into the middle
foxhole.

The blast kicked up a spout of dirt and mutilated
flesh, a minigeyser that inspired the flanking gunmen
to duck under cover for a moment, dodging shrapnel.

It was all the break that Bolan needed.

Sprinting forward, he unpinned the last grenade and
lobbed it toward the foxhole on his left, while firing
short bursts from his automatic rifle at the other pit.
For just an instant Bolan thought his pitch had
missed, falling short, but the grenade wobbled for a
moment on the lip of the foxhole, then dropped out of
sight as it blew.

And that left one.

The second blast brought Bolan's adversary bobbing to the surface like a prairie dog erupting from its
burrow, bent on sniffing out the scent of danger. They
were close enough to look each other in the eyes, his
opposition grappling with an FN FAL assault rifle,
longer than he needed in the confines of his hole. The
Steyr got there first, three rounds exploding through
the gunner's face and scalp, his nearly headless body
slumping back and out of sight.

The way was open, bloody chaos reigning in the
camp.

AT FIRST it seemed to Jacob Reese that he was being
given easy duty on the south perimeter. He knew that
Belasko and the others didn't care for the idea of
risking more Parañas in another battle, and he won-

dered if their being stationed at the rear was just a clever way to keep them from the fighting.

Moments after it had started, though, Reese knew he was mistaken. They would soon have all the action they could handle, and a good deal more.

The unarmed members of the road crew bolted first, a handful at the start, becoming a stampede in seconds flat. Nazare's men had seen enough of killing, and they were running for their lives—or driving, in the case of half a dozen who had found a working jeep.

The driver switched on his headlights, a pair of giant, glowing eyes aimed back along the road in the general direction of Pôrto Nacional. Of course, the town was something like two hundred miles away, but it was still a goal to shoot for, something to inspire their mad dash from the camp.

Reese aimed his captured rifle at a point between the headlights, elevated by perhaps three feet. He had the weapon set for automatic fire and held the trigger down, the muzzle flashing, weaving back and forth along a narrow arc. He didn't hear the windshield shatter, but he saw the headlights swerve, the driver hit or terrified. The jeep hit something, rolled, went over on its side, disgorging men like rag dolls in the dark.

They were alive, most of them, but they didn't have a chance with the Parañas, arrows whistling through the air before the jeep had even come to rest. One member of the road crew took an arrow in the throat and went down to his knees, blood spurting from his open mouth. Reese saw another take three hits, all in the torso, as he struggled to his feet. A third was running back in the direction of the camp when two Parañas fired together, scoring silent bull's-eyes as they brought him down.

It took the others by surprise to see the jeep roll out that way, some of them breaking stride while others veered off to the left or right and sought a new path to the cover of the trees. There were too many of them for the bowmen, dodging silhouettes with firelight at their backs, but Reese supposed it didn't matter if a few slipped by. Where would they go? What made them think they could survive the long trek back to Pôrto Nacional—two hundred miles of jungle, rivers, quicksand, snakes, jaguars, ants, mosquitoes, biting flies. A few of them would make it—someone nearly always managed to survive a grueling challenge—but it would be days or maybe weeks before they reached civilization on their own. By that time, he imagined, search teams would be hunting for survivors near the camp, but there was no way they could cover half the province, well back into Goiás.

Reese emptied the rifle's magazine on moving silhouettes, reloaded, fired again. He told himself that he was doing them a favor, making it a quick kill, rather than the long death of the forest. Drop them in their tracks instead of letting them escape to wander through the trackless wilderness until they starved or stumbled on some hungry predator. He was rationalizing, of course, but it helped him do the job.

Reese didn't know how many men he shot that night, how many of them died. The wounded who couldn't escape were finished off by the Parañas in their turn, a ruthless mop-up in which Reese took no part. He didn't try to stop them, either, as he would have twelve months earlier. Too much had changed inside him. There could be no turning back.

He listened to the screams of dying men, the racket of the guns, and understood why some men fell in love with war. There was a rush that came with fighting for your life, a giddy sense of triumph when your enemies were down and out but you were still alive. He understood at once why some police were trigger-happy, why some soldiers left the peacetime army to fight on as mercenaries, scouring the globe for other people's wars.

Reese hated knowing that about himself, but there was no way to forget the lesson once it had been learned.

He was a warrior now. His fate was sealed.

CARL LYONS FRAMED the runner in his shotgun sights and squeezed the trigger, buckshot pellets reaching out to punch his target through an awkward somersault that ended with the soldier stretched out on his back, unmoving.

Away to Lyons's left, a sniper in a foxhole sighted on his muzzle-flash and sent a short burst crackling inches overhead. Poor aim, but you could write that off to the excitement of the moment, and he dared not give the guy a second chance. Two quick rounds from the shotgun kept his adversary's head down while

Lyons broke for cover, sliding underneath a burned-out grader, so that he was covered on three sides.

The soldier missed him when he dared to raise his head again, spent frantic seconds searching for the stranger he had tried and failed to kill. Lyons waited for the perfect shot, convinced the guy would lean out of his hole to scan the battlefield, and he'd be ready when he did.

There! Stretching up on tiptoes, with his elbows braced against the muddy ground. The Atchisson barked once and nearly took the sniper's head off from a range of forty feet. His body toppled back into the hole and disappeared from view.

Lyons wriggled out from underneath the grader, rising to a combat crouch. His shotgun's magazine was still half-full, no purpose in reloading yet. The trick was finding worthy targets, now that most of them had scattered, seeking cover to prolong the duel with unseen enemies.

There was a stampede going on behind him, in the southern quadrant of the camp, where Jacob Reese and his Parañas were supposed to have the back door covered. Lyons chose a pair of runners twenty yards away and sighted on the narrow empty space between them, squeezing off another buckshot round. The heavy pellets spread enough to drop both men, though he wouldn't have guaranteed that either one was dead on impact with the ground. It would require a closer look to finish them, and Lyons was distracted at the moment as another spray of bullets whispered past his face.

The shooter had no pit to hide in this time. He was moving toward the Able Team leader more or less, and firing as he came. The guy wasn't wearing camouflage fatigues, so he had to have been a member of the road crew who had found himself a gun and knew enough to use it.

Lyons ducked as one round struck the blackened steel behind him, ricocheted and nearly took his ear off on the rebound. Cursing, he was lined up with the Atchisson before his enemy could fire again, the shotgun bucking twice against his shoulder, dishing out some overkill.

The first blast punched his target over backward, airborne, then the second struck and spun him to his left, like an Olympic diver trying out some new routine. The dead man's head and shoulders hit the ground before his heels touched down, and there was no bounce to him, no attempt to rise again.

How many hostiles left? It was impossible to say from where Lyons stood, since he could see only a portion of the battleground, and that was cast in shadows that deceived the eye. He had a fair idea how many of the opposition *he* had killed so far, but there was no way to account for Bolan or the others, much less for the tribesmen with their silent spears and arrows.

A victory, in realistic terms, was almost any battle where you walked away with fewer losses than the other side. In that event, Lyons told himself, they may have "won" already, but they couldn't proclaim a victory while Daniel Nazare's crew was still in any kind of shape to push ahead, to continue felling trees as they had been assigned to do.

This time around, the victory required annihilation, or the next-best thing. If they could rout the crew, disperse them in a hostile forest and leave them fighting for their lives against the elements, *then* maybe it would be enough.

Until the next crew was dispatched from Rio or Recife to resume the job.

Sometimes it felt as if he was bailing with a teacup in the cargo hold of the *Titanic,* but it wasn't in Lyons's nature to surrender. He would do this job right now, without regard to what came afterward or whether he would have to do it all again—with brand-new enemies—in six months' time. In combat there was only living for the moment, finding out what worked and rolling with the punches, hitting back with everything you had.

Like now.

Two gunners were rushing him—or were they simply trying to escape the bloody chaos of the camp? No matter. They were running on a hard collision course with Lyons, weapons held across their chests, and there was no way he could let them slide. The Atchisson came up instinctively, his finger on the trigger, and he cranked off two quick rounds almost before he had a chance to aim.

The gunner on his right appeared to stumble, took a header in the dirt with arms outflung and didn't rise again. His sidekick caught the buckshot in his chest, but sheer momentum kept him upright for another moment, staggering, before his legs turned into rubber and he fell.

The stench of death and cordite wafted over Lyons as he checked his weapon's load, deciding it was adequate. Spare magazines were heavy in the bandolier across his chest, and if he used them all, there was the Python slung beneath his arm. By that time, Lyons told himself, the issue should have been decided. He would be victorious or dead.

And it could still go either way, within a heartbeat.

Lyons focused on the kill and went in search of prey.

Before they came to him.

POL BLANCANALES FED his last grenade into the M-203 launcher, scanning for a target that was worthy of his final HE round. Fifty yards in front of him and a little to his left, a small group of Nazare's men had gone to ground behind a truck that sat on four flat tires, its canvas cover burned away, the windows in its cab reduced to jagged stubble in the frames. Pol didn't have an angle at the human targets with his M-16 A-2, but that didn't mean he would have to let them go.

It was a tricky shot but not impossible. He had to lob the round through the open windshield, past the steering wheel and dashboard, to explode against the inside of the driver's door. If he was accurate enough and timed it properly, he thought the blast would open up the port side of the cab and scourge the gunmen hiding there with shrapnel.

It was worth a try in any case.

He spent another moment lining up the shot, did everything within his power to make sure he got it right. A gentle squeeze, and Blancanales counted off the seconds in his head until a fireball suddenly erupted in the truck's cab, blowing off both doors. A couple of the gunners hiding there were toasted where they sat, but several others bolted, one in flames, all anxious to put ground between themselves and the inferno. Two broke to his right, another pair sprinting to his left, the long way.

Blancanales sighted on the nearest gunmen first and raked them with a burst of 5.56 mm manglers, punching both of them a few strides closer to a destination that would never do them any good. As they collapsed together, Pol was swinging to his left and picking up the other two, the sprinters doing fairly well, all things considered.

But they never had a chance.

No man alive could win a race with bullets. These runners obviously weren't familiar with the ground. They jerked and stumbled, almost falling in a heap while Blancanales tracked them, sighting down into the kill.

He stroked the trigger of his rifle lightly, sending half a dozen bullets off in hot pursuit. Despite the darkness, Pol could see them hit, his targets lurching forward, arms thrown out as if to catch themselves, with no strength left to pull it off. They went down hard, and he waited long enough to satisfy himself that both were dead before he started looking for another mark.

It was that kind of party, counting on attrition to defeat the other side. Pol saw a couple of Paraña warriors dart from cover, launch their spears and scuttle back again. Downrange both lances found their marks, and two members of Nazare's road crew dropped in their tracks.

No mercy.

The open ground was filling up with bodies, not all of them hostiles. From his vantage point, beside what used to be the mess tent, Blancanales saw a dead Paraña warrior lying on his back, his bow still clutched in one hand. A burst of automatic fire had opened up his chest, and Pol knew it was doubtful that he ever knew what hit him.

One less member of the tribe, Blancanales thought, and how many losses could they stand before the race was doomed, no matter what? Reese said the birth rate had declined already, with a corresponding jump for deaths in childbirth, so the tribe was losing out both ways. Each time another member fell, the loss was nearly irreplaceable.

Then again, what option did they have? How long could you expect a man to run and hide before he turned around and stood his ground to fight?

Whatever happened in the next few hours, someone somewhere would remember the Parañas as a tribe that stood its ground, refusing to be humbled by its enemies. It mightn't count for much in academic circles, but it meant a lot where Blancanales came from, and he knew that helping them—whatever the result—had to count for something, too.

He only wondered, scoping out another target for his automatic rifle, whether it would be too little and too late.

CHAPTER TWENTY

Someone had set the night on fire. It would have seemed impossible to Bolan after the previous night's raid, but there were still combustibles around the camp. A jeep, for instance, had capsized on the southern outskirts of the camp and was burning. A heap of rubbish was in flames. Tents were engulfed.

He had one MECAR round remaining, and he hoped to use it well, but there was nothing in the camp that merited another HE punch. The transport helicopters had withdrawn in search of safety, once their human cargoes were disgorged, which left Nazare's men on foot.

That hardly seemed to matter at the moment, since the troops in Bolan's view were bent on standing firm, defending their unsightly patch of turf. While unarmed members of the road crew were attempting to evacuate en masse, their watchdogs were committed to a brutal holding action. Brutal not because of any tools or tactics, but because the very nature of the conflict mitigated strongly against taking prisoners. Where would he put them, anyway? And how long would it be, if they were freed, before the goons were back at work on this or yet another forest crew?

A chunky man in khaki slacks, no shirt or shoes, was moving toward the Executioner. He had a shotgun, muzzle pointed skyward, and as Bolan watched, he braced the scattergun against his hip and fired a charge of shots across the camp.

There was no point in trying to find out what he had seen or whether any of the pellets found their mark. Instead, a 3-round burst from Bolan's AUG toppled Mr. Big as if he were a tree with rotten roots, upended by a sudden gale. The shocked expression on his face showed more surprise than pain.

The Steyr's see-through plastic magazine was almost empty, and he switched it for a full one, wanting to be ready in the crunch. Another HE round exploded somewhere to his left—that would be Pol's M-203—and Bolan took advantage of the brief distraction, knowing it was natural for any soldier not already occupied with a specific target to glance briefly toward the blast site, checking up on friends and enemies.

The spotty fires helped Bolan navigate across the camp, avoiding ditches, stumps and craters as he searched for targets. Just in front of him, two soldiers rose from what appeared to be a slit trench. The aroma radiating from their camouflage fatigues told Bolan they were hiding out in what had been a latrine.

One of them spotted the Executioner and shouted something to his friend in Portuguese. The first gunner had his dripping rifle shouldered when a burst of 5.56 mm tumblers raked his chest and blew him over backward, out of sight. His companion started firing from the hip before he had a target spotted, wasting precious rounds on empty air, but it was all that he could manage in the face of sudden death.

The wild rounds came in high and wide, no threat to Bolan as he squeezed the Steyr's trigger, slamming half a dozen rounds into his standing target from a range of twenty feet. The guy jerked through a twitchy little dance, then folded, slumping back into the sewage with a muffled splash. The stench was nothing to him now, his mouth and eyes wide open as he sank below the scummy surface.

A sudden revving-engine sound from Bolan's left brought him around in time to see a chunky adversary coming at him with a chain saw, angling for a swing that would have taken the Stony Man warrior's head off had he stood and waited for it. Backing up three paces, Bolan let the Steyr rip at point-blank range. There was no time to aim before the guy was on him, closing for the kill. His slugs ripped through the logger's chest and staggered him, the chain saw dropping with its trigger mechanism still engaged, a spray of crimson mixed with khaki as it ripped into the dying hacker's leg.

The guy collapsed, facedown, his saw still growling underneath him for another moment, finally stalling out. The muddy ground received his offering of blood and drank it down.

He moved back toward the sounds of battle, hunting. They weren't done yet, as long as Daniel Nazare and the death squad had a living soldier in the area.

Scorched earth.

It was the only way he knew to play the game.

THE SHOT THAT ALMOST finished Gadgets Schwarz came at him from his left, low down. It would have drilled his hip if he hadn't been wearing a canteen suspended from his web belt. As it was, the bullet's impact knocked him off his stride and dropped him to all fours. His hip stung where the canteen had absorbed the impact and recoiled against his flesh. The left leg of his camou pants was soaked with water sloshing from the twin holes that the bullet left in passing.

Schwarz scanned the killing ground in search of his assailant, wondering if the shot had been a stray or a deliberate effort. Either way, it had been too damn close for comfort, and he took no chances, dropping prone and tracking with his CAR-15.

A gunner rose in front of him, seemed almost to emerge from earth itself. A foxhole, maybe, not that it made any difference at the moment. He was carrying an FN FAL and stared right at Schwarz, the rifle coming to his shoulder in a rush.

The Able Team warrior hit him with a rising burst that seemed to lift him off his feet, dark crimson spurting from his wounds as he went over backward, squeezing off a long burst toward the sky. The soldier's boots drummed briefly on the ground before he finally lay still.

Schwarz rose, ignored the sodden trousers clinging to his leg. He had been lucky that time, but he couldn't count on luck to see him through the battle if he let his guard down. Vigilance was critical in any killing con-

frontation, and his aching hip was all it took to rein-
force that old, familiar lesson.

He was up and moving when he heard the raspy
sound of motorcycle engines and saw two dirt bikes
racing for the tree line with their lights off, drivers
hunching low across the handlebars. It brought back
memories of their pursuit the previous night, but this
time Schwarz's enemies were running, fleeing for their
lives.

He chased the bikers with a long burst from the
CAR-15 and saw the lead bike waver, lose momentum, wobbling over broken ground. Another moment and the driver lost it altogether, stood the cycle
on its nose and vaulted clear across the handlebars.
The bike came down on top of him with crushing
force, the second driver swerving wide to clear the
wreckage, miss his friend.

Schwarz had the fleeing biker in his sights when
suddenly a spear flashed in the firelight, pierced the
soldier's chest and slammed him backward off the
motorcycle seat. The bike went on without him for
another twenty yards or so, then struck a tree and
toppled over on its side, the engine stalling out.

Gadgets glimpsed the young Paraña warrior who
had made that toss, imagined he was smiling, but it
was impossible to say with any certainty. One moment he was there; the next he had evaporated into
darkness, like a wisp of smoke dispersed on the night
air.

Some soldiers, he thought. They might not have the
latest in technology or military hardware, but they

knew guerrilla warfare inside out, and they were
fighting on familiar ground. No wonder that the death
squads found it hard to pin them down, resorting to
the kind of random terrorism that included drops of
poisoned food. It had to be humiliating, getting
bogged down in pursuit of Stone Age enemies who
couldn't read a map or even write their names. Machismo would demand a swift response, but it was
hard to mount effective strategy when you were dueling with the wind.

Schwarz saw more shadows closing from the forest, launching spears and arrows at the soldiers they
could see. He worried for a moment that the tribesmen might mistake him for a member of Nazare's
team, but there appeared to be no risk of that. Their
excellent night vision gave them another small but
crucial edge against their "civilized" opponents.

The group of five or six Parañas had advanced for
all of thirty yards before they met resistance, several
death-squad riflemen unloading from the cover of a
charred bulldozer. Gadgets saw one Indian go down,
and then another, the remainder starting to retreat, as
if outrunning bullets was an option.

Cursing, Gadgets ran around the near end of the
earth mover, coming in behind the soldiers, waiting for
a clear shot at their flank before he cut loose with the
CAR-15. The unexpected stream of 5.56 mm rounds
cut through them like a hot knife slicing butter,
dumping them together in a lifeless heap.

He stepped around their bodies, looked for the
Paraña warriors, but they had already disappeared,

their wounded likewise vanished into darkness. Like
the Vietcong, he thought, except that these guerrillas
weren't fighting for a twisted ideology that called for
domination of a country or the world at large. They
simply wanted to be left alone, allowed to live in
peace.

It was a losing battle, Gadgets realized, but they
wouldn't go down without a fight.

He knelt to frisk the dead men for grenades, found
several and immediately clipped them to his own web
belt. No point in letting hardware go to waste when it
could serve a better cause.

THE RAPID-FIRE EXPLOSIONS shook Cipriano, jarring
him out of the daze that had him nearly paralyzed. It
seemed impossible that this could happen twice, his
soldiers being overrun by savages and peasants, but he
couldn't doubt the evidence presented by his ears and
eyes.

His men were losing. There were no more than a
handful of them left, and soon there would be none.
The certain knowledge of his own mortality made
Cipriano tremble, even with his hands clenched tight
around his Uzi.

So far, he hadn't found a single target. He cringed
in the darkness while a desperate battle raged around
him, men on both sides dying close at hand. The foxhole Cipriano occupied was muddy and claustro-
phobic, but at least it gave him an illusion of security...until a new round of explosions rocked the
camp.

He didn't know where they were coming from, which side was lobbing the grenades, but they were getting closer. Far too close for comfort, as he huddled in his hole and felt panic on the verge of taking over.

Any second now the marching blasts might bury him alive. Nobody knew where Cipriano was, and they wouldn't have time to look for him if they were busy fighting for their lives. He could imagine squirming underneath a mound of dirt, arms pinned against his side, no oxygen available for straining, dying lungs.

He bolted from the hole, relieved and frightened all at once as he lay clutching at the open ground. The night around him was alive with screams and gunfire, bullets swarming overhead. It would be suicide to stand erect, worse yet to lie immobile, waiting for the enemy to find him.

Cipriano started to crawl, digging with his boots and elbows, tasting mud and mouthing silent curses. Anything was preferable to doing nothing, yet he had the sense that there was no right choice, no safe direction he could travel in the midst of so much death.

He thought about Luis Obidos, safe in Rio, wishing he could reach across the miles and smash that smug face. Obidos didn't give a damn about his officers and men, as long as they performed on cue and kept the money flowing in from men like Daniel Nazare. Where was loyalty when it mattered most of all? What had become of a commander's personal devotion to his men?

All lies, Cipriano realized. He had been used, deceived with all the patriotic bull that convinced him he was helping hold the line against subversives, clearing the frontier for settlers and a free economy. In fact, unless he missed his guess, he was about to die for nothing, lying facedown in the mud, surrounded by a band of naked savages.

As if on cue, Cipriano saw an Indian advancing toward him, armed with what appeared to be a homemade ax or hatchet constructed out of flint and wood, the head secured to the shaft with something that resembled twine. It was a crude tool, but he had no doubt it would be capable of opening his skull and spilling out his brains.

The grisly mental picture of his own demise provided Cipriano with the jolt he needed. Rolling on his side, he thrust the Uzi in front of him and held down the trigger, sent ten or fifteen parabellum manglers streaking toward his adversary. The Paraña took most of them in his chest and stomach, one round drilling through a painted cheek before he toppled over backward, dead.

A victory, by God! Cipriano felt like cheering for himself, but he restrained the impulse, knowing that the less attention focused on him now, the safer he would be. He scanned a quick 360, saw no other adversaries close enough to strike, and let himself relax for just a moment, savoring the warm rush of adrenaline.

The Indian wasn't the first man he had killed, but all the others had been setups: drive-by shootings, simple executions where the victim's arms and legs were bound, one instance where the target was unconscious by the time Cipriano shot him in the head. This painted savage was the first man he had ever killed in self-defense, his own life hanging in the balance, and it was a very different feeling from the rest.

For the first time since he had donned a uniform, Cipriano knew what it felt like to be a soldier rather than a simple bodyguard or executioner.

And it made all the difference in the world.

He scrambled to his feet, no longer cowed by fear of bullets flying overhead. He was an officer, a leader, and his soldiers needed him. It might already be too late to save the camp, but maybe there was still a chance. If nothing else, he could collect the remnants of his decimated force and organize a counterstrike against the enemy.

With courage, anything was possible.

Cipriano stood erect and went to find whichever of his men were still alive.

THE RUSH WAS OVER, bodies scattered everywhere in front of Jacob Reese and his Paraña archers. They had stopped Nazare's men from fleeing—most of them, at any rate—and if a few escaped into the forest, it made no great difference. They were city boys, most of them, and Reese doubted whether they would last a weekend in the jungle on their own.

If necessary, in the morning he could organize another hunting party, track them down and finish it.

Reese hoped that it wouldn't be necessary after all the killing he had done and seen these past two days. He felt the thrill of hot-and-heavy combat passing from him, leaving a fatigue and vague depression in its wake. The Indians didn't appear to share his feelings, but he understood that they had been conditioned over centuries, with countless generations raised to hunt their tribal enemies the same way they were taught to stalk wild game.

Instinctively Reese pulled his rifle's empty magazine and snapped a fresh one into place. He had one more, then he would have to scrounge around the battlefield for ammunition. It wasn't a cheery thought, but looting corpses had to be at least a marginal improvement over making them.

Two more of his Paraña allies had been killed before the rush was broken, one shot down, the other bludgeoned with a pickax seconds after he had thrown his spear. They lay together now, arms at their sides, eyes closed in death.

How many more had fallen in the attack? Was Reese to blame? Could he have talked them out of it somehow, instead of leading them to their destruction? Would they come to blame him later for the losses they had suffered here?

No matter.

It was done, and there was nothing he could do to change it now, no turning back the clock to try another course of action. Without complaint he would bear whatever blame accrued to him for this night's work, and know that he had done his best to help the tribe defend itself against the men who would eradicate all traces of the jungle's aboriginal inhabitants if they were able.

The battle wasn't over yet, as Reese could tell from the explosions and reports of gunfire emanating from the nearby camp. Belasko and his men were still engaged in mopping up the death squad—or were *they* about to be mopped up?

Reese told himself that he had done enough, risked everything he and his chosen people had to come this far. There would be no shame if they simply faded back into the forest, left the trained professionals to cut down one another and so decide the outcome of the contest.

But, he asked himself, suppose Belasko and his comrades failed? What then? Would there be any consolation in the knowledge that Nazare's gunmen could have been defeated with a bit of extra effort? When the tribe was hunted to extinction, would he look back on this moment as the turning point and know that he had let his people down?

Reese stood and gripped the heavy rifle in both hands. He faced the waiting tribesmen, reading expectation in their faces, knowing they were ready. Still, he dreaded the idea of asking them to fight when it could cost them everything.

"I am not finished yet," he told them, slipping easily into their dialect. "It may be better if you wait back in the trees."

A brief exchange of glances, and the warriors shook their heads in unison. The tallest of them, Noitu, spoke for all when he replied, "We still have enemies to kill."

"Let's get on with it, then," Reese said, "before they're gone."

THE WORST PART of a critical mistake, Mack Bolan thought, was having time to recognize your error, with no means to put it right. It was the kind of feeling he imagined that a mountain climber had to experience when pitons lost their grip and sent him plunging to his death because he didn't swing the hammer hard enough to seat them properly.

The ultimate regret, with no escape.

In Bolan's case, he had been suckered by a couple of Nazare's soldiers. Running for their lives in the direction of the tree line, they had fairly begged him to follow them and take them down. The sounds of combat had been trailing off a bit, and Bolan took the opportunity to score an easy doubleheader, falling in behind them, jogging through the darkness as he fed a fresh mag to his AUG.

He overlooked the foxholes somehow, missed the four men crouching and waiting for an easy target to present itself. The blunder was apparent when they popped erect like jumping jacks, with rifles braced against their shoulders, rattling off convergent streams of fire.

He should have been cut down immediately, but his instinct saved him, took him low and to the left behind a burned-out piece of road equipment. Two rounds grazed him—one across the shoulder, one inside his thigh—but he was otherwise intact.

And he was also trapped, with no retreat in sight.

They had him boxed, emerging from their holes to cover both ends of the charred machine, the runners coming back to make it six on one. The odds weren't insurmountable, but he was covered left and right, with no way for him to make an end run and surprise his enemies.

They hadn't started to lob hand grenades, but if they had some it would be a simple job to kill him where he sat or flush him for the waiting guns. One pitch to find the range, perhaps, and then a couple for effect. He would have no defense, no place to hide.

He couldn't see the Able Team warriors, but imagined they had to have their hands full, mopping up. He could have called for help, but let it go. Distractions from a squawking radio would be no favor to his friends when they were fighting for their lives. This mess was Bolan's, and he reckoned he would have to clean it up himself.

Assuming that was possible.

One of his adversaries had a submachine gun, probably 9 mm, while the others all used automatic rifles. Did the smaller weapon indicate an officer, or simple preference for lighter arms? It hardly mattered at the moment, as he racked his brain for some way to defeat the trap, reverse the situation, give himself the upper hand.

But nothing came to mind.

Escaping from a trap like this required assistance, ample cover or at least a suitable diversion. He was on his own, with open ground on every side, and there was nothing he could think of at the moment to distract his opposition while he made a break for safety.

He had no hand grenades remaining, and the AUG—while excellent for its intended purpose—was a single weapon, facing six of equal range and power. Even if he charged the enemy, got lucky with an early hit or two, it seemed impossible the other four would miss him, blow their chance to nail him when he came out in the open.

No, there had to be a better way.

The firing grew more concentrated, and it took a heartbeat for the Executioner to understand his enemies were aiming somewhere else. Their guns were hammering away, but no slugs were coming anywhere near him.

Now what?

He risked a glance around the gray hulk to his left and found the soldiers grappling hand-to-hand with eight or nine Paraña tribesmen. Guns were fired at skin-touch range, while naked warriors fought with knives, clubs, spears. The soldier with the SMG dropped one Paraña in his tracks before a second launched his spear and nailed the soldier.

Bolan went to join the fight. Closing on the death squad's flank, he struck with his rifle butt in lieu of firing through his enemies and thereby endangering the warriors who had saved his life. It was a brief and brutal confrontation, blades and brute force carrying the day. When it was over, and the last few scattered shots had trailed off into echoes on the far side of the camp, he knew their work was done.

This portion of it, anyway.

The main event was yet to come, when they got back to Rio and started hunting Daniel Nazare and his stooge, Luis Obidos. Figure one day wasted traveling, but they were getting there.

The Executioner could hardly wait.

CHAPTER TWENTY-ONE

Captain Emilio Barbosa wore his full dress uniform, complete with decorations, when he went to see Daniel Nazare. He had been commanded to appear, and while his errand would undoubtedly involve some sort of criminal behavior, even a corrupt policeman had to realize the need to demonstrate authority when dealing with civilians. Thus, Barbosa wore his uniform *and* side arm, traveling as always with a team of half a dozen bodyguards.

One couldn't be too careful in Brazil these days.

Nazare's butler met them at the door, bowed stiffly and proceeded to the library, where they would leave Barbosa's guards while he was talking to Nazare. The man's study was several paces farther than the spacious corridor. Once inside, Barbosa saw Luis Obidos seated on the sidelines, rising from his chair with hand outstretched in greeting to the man who once had been his aide and gofer on the force.

"Emilio, you're looking well," Obidos said.

"And you, Luis."

It was a lie, of course. Obidos looked like death warmed over, tired and rumpled, heavy bags beneath his eyes that testified to lack of sleep.

Daniel Nazare came around the massive desk to shake his hand in turn. "I'm happy you could come on such short notice. Please, sit down."

"You mentioned an emergency," Barbosa said when he was settled in his chair.

"That's right. You've heard what happened to my road crew out in Pará Province?"

"The attack?" Barbosa nodded. "Yes."

"There have been two attacks," Nazare told him, frowning. "Once again last night. The crew has nearly been wiped out, from what I understand. Luis lost several men, as well."

"More than a few," Obidos interjected. "Over fifty men."

Barbosa hesitated, wondering what he should say. He thought he saw a way of wriggling off the hook. "You understand, my jurisdiction—"

"Yes, of course," Nazare interrupted him. "The army will be helping us in Pará. But we think the men responsible are coming back to Rio soon."

It was Barbosa's turn to frown. "I understood your crew had been attacked by Indians."

"By Indians and rebels," Nazare said. "They're connected somehow. I don't have the details yet. It's not important. What I need from you is guaranteed protection."

"The police will do their best to—"

"No, no, *no!*" Nazare's voice had risen almost to a shout. "That isn't good enough, Emilio. I need personal protection."

"You have bodyguards already," Barbosa argued. "With Luis's men, you have an army."

"But Luis's men haven't been so effective lately," Nazare said, all but sneering at Obidos. "They keep getting killed instead of dealing with their enemies."

"What is it you expect from me?"

"A team of twenty men around the clock should be enough," Nazare said. "Supported by my own, of course. The rebels may think twice about attacking uniformed police."

Barbosa nearly laughed out loud. "That's sixty men for three eight-hour shifts," he said. "A force that size to guard one man would never be approved."

"It has been," Nazare told him, smiling without warmth. "Call Major Escalante if you doubt me."

Instantly the captain lost his smile. "Well, then, if you already cleared the project, what has this to do with me?"

"You'll be in charge," Nazare said. "I asked for you specifically. An officer I trust to do his best."

"I see. And when does this protection start?" Barbosa asked.

"Immediately. Twenty officers are on their way to this location as we speak. You'll take command when they arrive, make certain everything is as it should be for the best results."

"And this assignment is supposed to last how long?"

Nazare shrugged. "A few days, I suspect. Our enemies will find a few surprises waiting for them when they get back to the city. They've been lucky so far, but their luck is due to change.''

"And if they don't come back?" Barbosa asked.

"They will," Obidos said with perfect certainty. "I know these men—their type, at least, the way they think. They haven't finished yet, while Daniel is alive."

Nazare smiled again. "And don't forget about yourself, Luis. Another tempting target, even if your modesty gets in the way."

"You really think these strangers mean to kill you, then," Barbosa said.

"I'm counting on it," Nazare replied, sounding weary. "It's the only hope we have."

"YOU'RE GOING, then," Jacob Reese said.

"We still have work to do in Rio," Bolan told him.

"Sure, I understand." Reese felt a little foolish, standing there like some pathetic teenager afraid to say goodbye to friends at summer's end.

"What will you do?" Bolan asked him, nodding in the general direction of the tribesmen who stood watching them.

"The best we can," Reese said. "First thing, we need to put some space between ourselves and the scene of the crime, so to speak. The army will be coming this time, probably this afternoon or evening. They'll inspect the damage before they mount a search. We should have time."

"Where will you go?" Bolan asked.

"I'm thinking west," Reese replied, "toward Amazonas. We can skirt Manaus, if we get that far, and parallel the Rio Negro. If we have to, we can always try Colombia or Venezuela."

That was fantasy, Reese knew. A thousand miles or more on foot, through territory occupied by hostile tribes, guerrilla armies, drug cartels. They would be lucky if they made it to the boundary of Pará Province, much less into Amazonas and beyond. Still, there was nothing to be gained by standing still and waiting for the soldiers to arrive with their machine guns, bent on wiping out the remnants of his shrunken tribe.

Four dead in the previous night's battle, and another three with wounds that would inevitably slow them. Still, no one in the village seemed to think the loss exorbitant, considering the damages they had inflicted on their enemies. It was a major victory by tribal standards, possibly the greatest in Paraña history.

The elders had been generous in praising Reese, but he could barely face them, thinking of the young men who had sacrificed their lives to stall a project that would certainly, inevitably move ahead no matter what they did, no matter how they fought to stop it. He felt more like a Judas than a savior of the tribe, but there was no way to explain his feelings without sounding like a fool.

"You're going for Nazare," Reese said.

"We're taking care of business," Bolan stated. "If you leave the brain intact, an octopus can grow new arms."

"You realize it's hopeless?" Sudden bitterness welled up inside of Reese. "It doesn't matter if you wipe out half the government. The people of Brazil don't care what happens here, away from all the stores and traffic."

"Some do."

"Not the ones who matter. Money talks, you know? And it talks louder in Brazil than in the States, if you can fathom that. Back home the money men can change laws if they want to, get a special waiver for some business that would otherwise have trouble with the law, pay off police to look the other way if all else fails. Out here, those same men *are* the law. You understand the difference? When they want a village moved, they send out a private army to kill the people and destroy their homes. The military and police 'investigate' and either blame the whole thing on guerrillas or else announce there's been no crime committed in the first place."

"Systems change," Bolan said.

"Of course, in time. It took only two decades for the army to surrender its control and give democracy a try, for what it's worth. There's been no change out here, you realize. Eradication of the forest tribes is still a top priority with everyone from cattle ranchers to the legislature, and the killing still goes on. The gunmen just wear different uniforms."

"You're not alone. There is a movement in the cities, growing stronger every day."

"In Rio or São Paulo, maybe. Five, six hundred miles away. They haven't been out here, and by the time they get around to coming, there'll be nothing left to see."

"This isn't finished," Bolan said. "Don't give up. You have friends in the States, as well. You just don't know it yet. They're working overtime to save the forest and its people. When the word of what Nazare's done gets out back home—"

"We'll be a hundred miles away from here, with any luck. My people haven't got the kind of time it takes for Congress to debate a pay raise, much less any changes in the state of foreign policy."

"You may be pleasantly surprised."

Reese smiled. "You know," he said, "the one advantage of our present situation is that any old surprise is pleasant. We expect the bad news every day. It never takes us by surprise. I'll tell you, we could use a few surprises, but we're working on a deadline here."

"How do we reach you, just in case?" Bolan asked.

"Don't even try. I haven't had a letter in two years, and there's no Western Union office where we're going."

"But—"

"We'll know there's been a change if they stop hunting us. Meanwhile, I'm not about to hold my breath."

Bolan nodded toward the rifle slung on Reese's shoulder. "You have ammo for that thing?"

"As much as I can carry. There was quite a bit of surplus in the camp last night."

"In case we don't meet up again—"

"We won't," Reese interrupted him, "but thanks for everything you've done, or tried to do. For what it's worth, my people won't forget you."

"I'd say it was worth a lot."

"You never know," Reese said. "Sometimes remembering is all we have."

"I'd wish you luck, if it would help."

"You'll need it more than we do," Reese replied. "They have to find us before they kill us off. You won't have anywhere to hide in Rio."

"Hiding's not the plan."

"I gathered that. Good luck, in any case."

They shook hands like two men who realize they'll never meet again, a little something extra in it, from the heart. When Bolan turned away to join his waiting comrades, Reese stood watching, raised a hand in parting as they struck off toward the river.

THEY FOUND THE LONG CANOE where Reese had promised it would be. Handcrafted from a single log, with space enough for all four men and their equipment, it would get them down the river if they didn't lose it in the rapids twenty miles due south. Beyond the river terminus, they had a hike of fifteen miles to reach a trading post complete with airstrip, where a bush plane could be chartered for the flight to Rio.

Simple.

It would take the best part of a day to reach the trading post, of course, and more time to negotiate the pilot's fee. Since money was no object, Bolan counted on a swift departure from the trading post. With any luck, they should be back in Rio de Janeiro by the time dawn broke tomorrow, ready to begin their final blitz.

He thought of Jacob Reese as they were pushing off, with Lyons in the bow, Pol second, Bolan third and Gadgets at the stern. Despite the differences in background and training, the anthropologist-turned-jungle-warrior was a kindred soul. He knew what it was like to burn your bridges, focus on the road ahead to the exclusion of all else, because you simply had no other way to go.

His words came back to Bolan as the current grabbed them, sweeping them downstream: *The bad news never takes us by surprise.*

And Bolan knew the feeling. He had been living with the bad news for longer than he cared to think about. Sometimes he couldn't recognize the good news when it came, since it was all mixed up in blood and suffering, disguised as one more dispatch from the battlefront. There had been days when Bolan would have given anything to make his mind a blank, forget the war and all its trappings for a while.

Sometimes remembering is all we have.

Okay.

But there was also looking forward, planning the destruction of your enemies. It had to count for something, when you stopped them in their tracks and kept them from defiling one more innocent. If anyone was keeping score, it damn well *had* to matter.

"That's a funny guy," Gadgets said, leaning forward, speaking loud enough for Bolan to make out his words above the background noises of the river and the forest.

"Who?" As if he didn't know.

"That Reese. You figure he's for real?"

"What else?" Bolan asked.

"I don't know. It just seems weird, you follow? Here's an Ivy Leaguer with diplomas up the butt—you know he had to have some kind of teaching job lined up back home—and he just chucks it all for nothing. Now he lives a thousand miles from anywhere, he's got the army and the death squad on his ass—I mean, for what?"

"You have to ask?"

"It seems peculiar, don't you think?"

"Like you and Pol, for instance."

Gadgets shook his head. "It's not the same," he said. "I mean, we had the training and experience. We knew what we were getting into, and it sounded better than a humdrum nine-to-five. This guy's no soldier. He came down here working on a research paper, and he winds up playing Jungle Jim. It doesn't scan."

"We could all use a surprise from time to time," Bolan said, quoting Jacob Reese.

"I guess, but there's a limit, don't you think?"

"Each man decides the limit for himself."

"You think he's got it all together, then? I mean, he's not some kind of flake?"

"He's doing what he has to, and he's picking up the tab."

"I guess." But Gadgets didn't sound convinced. He changed the subject. "What's the plan for Rio?"

"Have to wait and see," the Executioner replied. "With any luck, Nazare may think we're still tied up in the forest. If he lets his guard down, that's the time to move."

"And if he doesn't?" Blancanales asked, half turning as he dipped his paddle in the river.

"We move anyway. It's a tighter game, that's all."

"Tight's right," Gadgets said. "I can hear it squeaking all the way from here."

"It won't just be the death squad, after all the hell we raised in town before we left," Blancanales added.

"No."

He had been mulling that one over, knew that Daniel Nazare had the pull in Rio to demand police protection, possibly military involvement if he felt the need. The odds were that they would have to face police, along with vigilante gunmen, when they made their move.

"You've got a problem with the cops," Schwarz said, not asking.

"We'll work it out."

"The way I look at things, they sell their badges to protect an asshole like Nazare, so they can take their chances. Course, that's only my opinion."

"We'll work something out," he said again.

"Okay, suits me."

The river swept them on in silence for a while, beneath an arching canopy of trees that opened up enough to let the golden sunlight through. It felt like coasting through an endless placid garden, if you didn't stop and think about the predators that might be watching from the trees on either side, prepared to pounce and feed at the first opportunity.

They were proceeding from one jungle to another, but the predators would still be waiting for them, taking on a different form, but every bit as ravenous. More dangerous, in fact, for their intelligence and malice, traits that had no counterpart among four-footed hunters in the wild.

Nazare and his breed were used to feeding as they liked, on weaker members of the species, confident that no one could oppose them. They were in for a surprise, though, when the Executioner and Able Team came back to settle up the tab.

It would be judgment day in Rio when they hit the streets again, and Daniel Nazare would be standing in the dock. His sentence had already been decreed.

It only waited for an Executioner to carry out the judgment of the court and settle up Nazare's debt.

In blood.

CHAPTER TWENTY-TWO

"The troops are searching," Barbosa said, "but it may take time. You know the territory that's involved. It's possible they won't find anything at all."

Nazare felt his anger building like a head of steam. If there had been a pressure valve attached to his skull, the needle would have redlined as he paced the floor, hands clasped behind his back.

"They *will* find something," he retorted, "if they have to search that godforsaken jungle for the next two months! You understand, Emilio?"

"I hear you, Daniel, but I don't command the army, as you know."

"That's right," Nazare told him, raging. "*I* command the army! For the money I have paid the secretary of defense and his generals, I should have a set of stars myself!"

Barbosa and Luis Obidos sat and listened to him, neither one responding to the outburst. They knew better than to challenge him when he was in a mood like this, both of them knowing all too well which side their bread was buttered on—and whose hand held the knife.

"I don't see how a bunch of savages can disappear like that," Nazare said, still pacing. "Has the army used its helicopters? Infrared devices?"

"Everything is being done that can be done," Barbosa told him. "I've been assured they have three hundred soldiers on the job."

"Then use six hundred," Nazare snapped. "Use whatever number is required to get the job done!"

Barbosa stiffened in his chair. "You'll have to pass that message on yourself," he said. "As I've explained—"

"You don't control the military," Nazare finished. "So I've heard. You *do* have some authority with the police, though, do you not?"

Barbosa bit his lip to keep from snapping back at this man who could have him broken to patrolman with a single phone call. "Twenty men around the clock, as you requested."

"Will it be enough?" Nazare asked.

There was bewilderment behind Barbosa's smile. "How can I answer that? So far, there's been no indication of—"

"So far!" Nazare turned upon him, fairly snarling. "By the time I'm threatened, it may be too late for all of us."

"I understand," Barbosa said, "and I believe that twenty men are adequate, considering the force Luis has detailed to protect you. That makes close to seventy in all."

"I want a hundred," Nazare said.

"Ah." Barbosa glanced at his companion in distress. "Luis?"

"A hundred? Well, that means another thirty-five around the clock. Still, I suppose—"

The sound of the explosion cut him off before Nazare could find out what he supposed. The businessman stood rooted to the carpet in the middle of his study, fists balled at his sides. His face was crimson, with a hint of purple, threatening a stroke if he didn't explode.

"You see?" Nazare shouted. "It's too late, you bastards! Get out there and earn your money, damn you, or I'll have you shot myself!"

They left him, without a backward glance, and Nazare walked around behind the bar that occupied the north wall of his study, reaching for the hidden catch that opened a secret panel. Inside, a rack of guns stood waiting for him, every weapon oiled and loaded. Ready.

He selected one and cocked it, conscious that his hands were trembling, hating any sign of weakness in himself.

"Someone will pay for this," he told the empty room, and started toward the door.

MACK BOLAN WENT across the eight-foot wall in darkness, having first determined that Nazare had no sensors mounted at the top. For all his futuristic plans, the wheeler-dealer still relied on men and guns to keep him safe at home.

The Executioner had plans to disappoint him in a major way.

Some lighting on the grounds would have been helpful to the home team, but Nazare had them working in the dark, except for floodlights around the house. It put experienced intruders on an almost equal footing with the guards—perhaps a little better, if you factored the advantage of surprise.

Not much surprise, though, from the look of things. There was a squad of uniformed police out front, and men in olive drab or faded denim had the grounds staked out, some walking post, while others stayed in place and tried to blend in with the scenery. Bolan spotted seven guns before he had a clear view of the house.

More cops, inside and out, the former visible through downstairs windows where the draperies were open, bright light spilling onto the lawn. He gave up counting, knew that he would have to do his best without direct impact on the police, leave that to other members of the team if they were so inclined.

But how to start?

He had the answer in another instant, lifting a grenade from his waist pack and mounting it onto the Steyr's built-in launcher. The house was a two-story structure, and no lights were on upstairs. He would just have to gamble that none of the guards would be sleeping tonight.

Bolan lined up his shot, aiming for the northwest corner. A bedroom, most likely, but what did it matter? He needed the noise, smoke and fire, a distraction for those down below, while he tried to get closer.

There was always some noise from the launcher, but one shot would be hard to place in the dark. No guards were close enough to be clear on the source at the moment. He had to work swiftly, with no time for mistakes.

Bolan fired, then heard the window implode from a distance, the blast coming next, with an orange tongue of flame licking up toward the roof. Sentries raced around shouting in Portuguese, no doubt calling for help, shouting questions and orders.

All right.

It was clear, more or less. There were still several men in his way, but they looked like civilians, more goons from the death squad, and all of them had their eyes fixed on the house. It was sloppy, a product of substandard training. Bolan had no qualms about attacking from their blind side, closing the gap to a bare thirty feet before opening up with the Steyr.

Bodies jerked and fell, a few turning in time to look death in the face. They were too slow to nail him, too awkward to run. Bolan dropped them like tin silhouettes on a target range, using up most of a clip in the process but getting it done.

Fifty feet remained to the door he had picked for his entrance, and Bolan was gaining when bodies came spilling out into the night.

Uniforms.

The police.

Bolan veered to his right, seeking cover, and squeezed off a burst toward the floodlights above him. Cool darkness descended, but someone had seen him, unloading with small arms, not stopping to aim.

A barbecue constructed out of bricks loomed ahead of him. He threw himself behind it, buying time. The

Executioner palmed a stun grenade and waited, counting down the doomsday numbers in his head. There was one chance to get it right, and that was all.

He offered up a silent prayer to the Universe, and pulled the pin.

CARL LYONS DIDN'T SHARE his colleague's soft spot for police who sold their badges to the highest bidder. In his view, they rated special punishment, along with rapists, child pornographers and dealers pushing drugs in elementary schools. If possible, he would have vaporized them all and started fresh, a brand-new crop.

This was the real world, though, and Lyons had to take it one step at a time.

He knifed a pair of sentries near the outer wall, then did his best at creeping past the others, working toward the house. They were supposed to wait for Bolan's signal or the next-best thing—some indication that the probe was blown—and Lyons took his station at the southeast corner of Nazare's house. Some thirty yards of open ground lay between his cover and the mansion, with a scraggly skirmish line of uniforms thrown up across the lawn.

He counted seven cops, all spit and polish, but a trifle short on combat discipline, their automatic weapons dangling casually while they smoked cigarettes or conversed back and forth. He braced the Atchisson against his shoulder, sighting on the far end of the line and waiting.

There was no specific arranged signal, but Lyons knew the blast was Bolan's work before the cops reacted, seven heads swiveling in that direction, two men already running off to join the party when their leader called them back. It was enough of a diversion for Lyons's purposes. There was no point in stalling when he had a perfect field of fire.

The Atchisson held twenty rounds in its detachable box magazine, the rate of fire restricted only by a shooter's skill. Lyons started on his left and worked his way along the line without a break, one blast for each of seven uniforms in turn. He had three on the ground before the others knew exactly what was happening, and by the time they started to react, it was too late.

The fourth in line—and leader of the pack, from all appearances—was pivoting toward Lyons with a submachine gun when the charge of buckshot struck him in the chest and knocked him sprawling. Number five had that much extra time to aim and fire, but he was clumsy off the mark, still fumbling with his weapon's safety when the Atchisson pronounced its final word on his career in law enforcement.

That left two—the eager beavers who had broken the formation—and it seemed that they were having second thoughts about returning to the fold. One turned and bolted for the house in panic, while his sidekick froze, and that was all it took for Lyons to complete his sweep. An easy touch for number six, and he was down, the runner covering a few more yards before a seventh charge of buckshot overtook him, striking like a giant fist between his shoulder blades and slamming him facedown into the grass.

Lyons broke from cover, jogging toward the house, alert to any ambush that the opposition might have waiting for him on the way. He covered half the distance in a rush, before he heard a shout behind him and turned in time to see four gunners round the corner, trying to catch up.

He spun to face them, firing from the hip, and watched the shooter on his right go down, blood spraying from the scarlet ruin of his chest. The others dodged, one dropping prone, his partner jumping to the left and crouching, leveling an automatic rifle for the kill.

And Lyons took the only option left to him. He charged, unloading with the Atchisson in rapid fire, a storm of buckshot pellets reaching out to find his enemies. It was a winner-take-all situation, and the Able Team leader didn't plan on losing if he had a choice.

Ten seconds later Lyons was reloading on the move, backtracking toward the patio and sliding doors. He meant to have a few words with the master of the house, but anyone could play.

As long as they showed up prepared to bet their lives.

POL BLANCANALES SLAMMED a 40 mm high-explosive round into the first door of a customized five-car garage and followed with a short burst from his M-16 A-2. The combination seemed to work, one of Nazare's vehicles exploding, spilling fuel and flames across the concrete floor. More explosions followed, like a string of giant firecrackers. The roof flew back as if on hinges, smoke and flame erupting skyward, shrapnel from the minifleet of classic cars compelling Pol to duck for cover as the whole thing went up.

So far so good.

A handful of disoriented gunners came in through the drifting pall of smoke, some of them clearly looking for a target, others gaping at the ruin of their boss's motor pool.

Pol didn't give them time to work out the priorities among themselves. Instead, he raked them with a string of 5.56 mm tumblers, working left to right along the line, and scattered them in little piles of flesh and bone before they understood exactly what was happening. One of them managed to return fire, more or less, but he was more adept at trimming trees than spotting human targets, as he toppled over backward and collapsed.

All done.

Reloading as he rose, the Politician jogged around Nazare's tennis court and met another pair of gunners by the swimming pool. These two were almost ready for him. They did their best and came up short, one sprawling facedown on the deck, his buddy whipping through a crude half gainer, adding color to the deep end as he sank.

The house was still his prime objective, but he had to get there in one piece or he would be no good to anyone. Pol could see smoke pouring from the second story now, and as he watched, a new blast rocked the house, this one downstairs. Nazare's men were catching hell, but they still had the numbers on their side, if they could pull together, make it work.

It was the "ifs" that got them every time.

Pol fed another HE round into his launcher, moving toward his target through the smoke screen that combined fumes from the mansion and garage. It made for decent cover, and he was within a dozen paces of the house when a hardman with a machine gun opened up and sent him diving for the turf.

THE FIRST THREE KILLS were easy, soldiers standing with their guns at their sides, when Gadgets shot them in the back. He could have had them turn around, but that was bullshit out of Hollywood, where bad guys always got the first shot free and clear. In real life any soldier with an interest in survival took the shots that came his way and felt no qualms about an easy tag.

It was the stand-up, face-to-face engagements that were killers every time.

It got a little hairy after that, once the defenders realized that first explosion was a bomb and not some leaky gas line going off. Predictable confusion helped him out from there, but everyone was jumpy, squeezing off at shadows, adding to the general chaos of the scene.

Schwarz tried to take advantage of the situation, moving swiftly toward the house as if he were a member of the team, no matter that his camouflage fatigues bore no resemblance to the other uniforms in evidence. When someone stopped to challenge him, he shot him, then kept on going, covering approximately half the fifty yards that separated him from Daniel Nazare's house before he hit a major snag.

Six cops and three hardmen dressed in olive drab emerged from the house no more than thirty feet in front of him. The leader of the bluesuits was some kind of officer, brass winking on his collar in the floodlight's glare. He aimed a bony hand at Gadgets, reaching for his pistol with the other as he barked an order to his men. Schwarz didn't need a Berlitz course in Portuguese to know his ass was in a sling.

Without a second thought, he gave them everything he had. The HE round went first, and he was sweeping with the M-16 A-2 before it detonated in the middle of the pack. He had a brief glimpse of the leader, airborne, trailing what appeared to be a severed leg behind him, like the booster stage of an unsteady rocket, then his full attention focused on the task of nailing anything that moved.

The combination of swift reflexes and sheer audacity saved Gadgets in the crunch. A number of his adversaries managed scattered shots, but they were thrown off-balance by the HE blast and heavy fire from Schwarz's automatic rifle, ducking, dodging for their lives when courage might have saved them. By the time his magazine ran dry, the lawn in front of him was strewn with bodies, one or two still twitching in their death throes, none of them in any shape to challenge his advance.

He ditched the empty magazine and replaced it, moving past the twisted corpses as he passed on toward the house. The officer in charge lay just in front of him, a mangled rag doll with a dazed expression on his face, eyes open, staring at infinity.

Schwarz wondered what he saw there, then let it go before the thought was fully recognized. There would be time enough to scope that view when it was his turn. At the moment, though, he still had work to do, and Gadgets planned on walking off this battlefield alive.

The house was burning brightly, flames dancing on the roofline, licking at the eaves. The men inside would be evacuating soon if they had any sense at all, and Schwarz was moved to reconsider his approach. The best that he could hope for going in was smoke and heat, with desperate soldiers fighting to get out. A better way, all things considered, seemed to be for him to wait for them outside.

He doubled back to find a vantage point that let him watch the nearest doorway. He stretched out on the grass among the dead and settled in to wait.

NAZARE MET OBIDOS coming to fetch him with a pair of bodyguards. The death squad's leader was disheveled, with a strange look in his eyes. He blinked twice, staring at the rifle in Nazare's hands before he spoke.

"We have to go," Obidos said. "The house appears to be surrounded."

"What? Go where?"

"It doesn't matter, Daniel. Out. Away."

It made Nazare furious to think of being driven from his home, but he appeared to have no choice. The house was burning—he could smell it now—and by the time a fire brigade arrived, they could be dead. Police were on the scene already, with Emilio Barbosa in command, but there would still be questions when the smoke cleared, some of them no doubt embarrassing.

"Let's go, then," Nazare said, swallowing his anger in the interest of survival. "Lead the way."

Obidos nodded, glancing once more at Nazare's rifle, turning back along the corridor in the direction he had come from. At his order, the two bodyguards moved out in front, prepared to intercept all comers and defend the men who paid their salaries.

"They've blown up the garage," Obidos told him, lowering his voice, "but there are still some vehicles out front. Police cars, and my own."

Obidos was fond of riding in an armored Lincoln Town Car to protect himself from would-be killers and to simultaneously dazzle women with his style.

"We'll take your car," Nazare said.

"Of course."

There was the slightest echo of reluctance in his tone, but nothing like sincere resistance. In the present circumstance, Obidos had to know there was no way Nazare meant to let him leave alone.

The smoke got thicker as they went along, until Nazare's eyes were watering and he was short of breath. He nearly tripped on someone lying in the middle of the hallway, then kicked the body viciously without attempting to discover who it was or whether he was still alive. To hell with stragglers when the man in charge was trying to escape.

He could feel the heat now, getting worse as they approached the parlor and found the north wall of the room engulfed in hungry flames. More bodies littered the floor, some of them moving, but he wasted no time counting, much less helping the survivors. These men had been paid to risk their lives, so let them earn their money.

"Here," Obidos said, directing his employer toward the tall twin doors. "We're almost there."

Indeed they were, but stepping out onto the porch was no relief. The cloying smoke came after them, clung to them like a shroud, and there was worse in store outside.

The Lincoln was burning brightly, with its tires already melted flat.

"My car!" Obidos wailed, disconsolate.

"The next one, then!" Nazare shoved him toward the nearest squad car, still untouched by shot or flames. "Get in!"

Nazare suited words to action, crawling in the back, Obidos close behind him, while the gunner sat in front, another at the wheel. The driver found keys in the ignition and fired the engine. The door had closed behind him by the time Nazare realized there was a cage between himself and the front seat, no handles on the insides of the doors. He was a prisoner, unless he smashed the windows out and freed himself that way.

Given the situation, it didn't matter.

They were rolling now, along the driveway, cutting corners over grass, tires slipping for an instant, finally digging in.

In front of them, a tall man dressed in camouflage fatigues arose to bar the way. He had some kind of automatic weapon raised as if to fire, the muzzle heavy with a strange attachment that Nazare didn't recognize.

"Run over him, for Christ's sake!" he roared, beating on the wire mesh with his fist and shouting at the driver. "Hurry! Run him down!"

THE STUN GRENADE WORKED well enough, although it was designed for use indoors. The shock wave flattened Bolan's adversaries, left them writhing on the grass as he broke free of cover, putting them behind him, racing toward the front porch and the surest way to get inside the house.

Too late.

The place was burning now, flames leaping everywhere, and by the time he reached the front, it was apparent that a probe inside the house would mean unnecessary risk for minimal reward. The rats were bailing out, and anyone who made it through the fire would probably evacuate the house through one of four specific exits. Bolan and his Able Team warriors had been working from a floor plan of the mansion when they chose their angles of attack, one soldier homing on each doorway to complete the box. It all came down to watching now, and dealing with the remnants of Nazare's army that were still outside, in shape to fight.

He found two gunners crouching in the shadow of a Lincoln Town Car, near the wide front porch, both squeezing off reflexive shots in Bolan's general direction. Dropping to a crouch, he slammed a grenade into the Lincoln's grille and blew the hood off, flames erupting from the engine block and racing back along the fuel line, setting off the gas tank. He was ready when a pair of dancing human torches broke from cover and staggered across the lawn, treating them to mercy rounds that dropped them in their smoking tracks.

He was maneuvering for an improved position when a group of men charged through the double doors, paused briefly on the porch, then bolted for the first of several squad cars lined up in the drive. There were no uniforms among them, but he recognized Nazare's profile, thought the chunky guy behind him bore a strong resemblance to Luis Obidos.

They were in the squad car by the time he palmed another grenade and got it mounted on the AUG. It would have been a chancy shot to hit them from the flank when they were moving, so he risked it all and ran out to the middle of the driveway, blocking them. The driver had him spotted, hunched behind the wheel and aiming like a kamikaze pilot.

Bolan stood there, waiting, with the rifle at his shoulder. He aimed at a point between the grille and windshield, squeezing off when he was ready, no point rushing even when the odds were shaved this thin.

The high-explosive round was dead on target, swatting the patrol car with a fist of smoke and flame. He saw the burning hulk swerve to his right, the driver's left, momentum trailing off. The men up front were obviously dead, but that left two in back.

Inside the cage.

They had to be stunned, he calculated, or they could have used their weapons on the windows, tried to liberate themselves. He was prepared for that, the Steyr primed and ready, but it never happened. Whether they were dazed or dying, maybe hit by shrapnel, Daniel Nazare and his chief enforcer grappled weakly with their doors, one of them clawing at the wire mesh of the cage.

Too late.

The gas tank blew a moment later, swallowing the squad car in a roiling sheet of fire. There might have been a man's voice, screaming in the midst of that inferno, but the Executioner couldn't have said for sure.

He found the walkie-talkie on his belt and thumbed the button down. "We're finished," Bolan told his warriors. "Disengage ASAP."

"Affirmative," Blancanales said, sounding small and far away.

"Roger that," Gadgets stated.

"I was running out of targets, anyway," Lyons added, heading for the trees. He would find darkness there, and shelter.

With the fire behind him, Bolan felt as if the worst of it was over.

For the moment, anyway.

Tomorrow was another day, and it would take care of itself.

"I'm glad to be home," Juliana Alegrete said.

Bolan smiled. "I'm betting home feels the same about you."

They were driving back from the airport to Alegrete's apartment in Rio, with a tail from Able Team, three car lengths back. There was no reason to believe that anyone was stalking the woman, with Nazare and Obidos gone, but Bolan liked to play it safe.

"You settled everything," she said with something like amazement in her voice.

"I wouldn't go that far."

"Nazare and Obidos," she continued. "I confess I didn't think it would be possible."

"You've still got opposition," Bolan told her, slowing for the intersection, signaling a turn. "Remember, we were looking at a limited objective from the start."

"Of course, I understand. It's something, though, you must admit. This time last week, Nazare and Obidos were like gods. Today they're nothing."

"That leaves room for other would-be gods," Bolan declared. "You'll need help to weed them out, some kind of grass-roots movement. Nothing's ever quite as easy as it seems."

"I've learned that. Lorenzo taught me something, after all. And you avenged him."

"It's a start," Bolan said, leery of the overconfidence that often followed partial victories. "I wouldn't count on too much help from the establishment, right off. In fact I wouldn't be surprised if you were questioned by police."

"No problem. My alibi is—how you say it in America?—airtight."

"That's what we say. Be careful, all the same."

"I will. And you may be surprised at some of those in 'the establishment' before we're through. Not everyone supports the so-called justice of the death squads."

"All the same, you need to use some caution when you're picking friends."

She placed a hand on Bolan's arm and smiled into his eyes. "Don't worry. I've become a better judge of character. You'll see."

"I wouldn't be surprised."

They were approaching her apartment building now, already slowing. When Bolan brought the compact to the curb, Alegrete lingered, visibly reluctant to break contact.

"You are leaving now?" she asked.

"A few more hours," Bolan said.

"I don't suppose..." She let it trail away, unwilling or unable to complete the question.

"Hey, you never know. I get around."

The words rang hollow, and she knew it. "Even so," the woman told him, "I won't hold my breath, as you Yankees say."

"That wouldn't be the best idea."

She leaned across the seat and kissed him softly on the corner of his mouth, then pulled back before the parting kiss could turn to something else.

"I won't embarrass you," she said, a quick glance toward the car nosed in behind them, "with your friends."

"It's not a problem," Bolan told her.

"Not for you, perhaps." Her door was open now, and she was stepping out. "But it will take some time, I think, before I can forget."

She closed the door behind her and turned away. He watched her disappear inside the building, then put his rental car in gear and pulled out into traffic, with the Able Team warriors following.

Sometimes remembering is all we have.

That last day in the jungle, Jacob Reese had said it all.

A flare-up of hatred and violence threatens to engulf America

BLACK OPS #2

ARMAGEDDON NOW

created by MICHAEL KASNER

The Black Ops team goes where the law can't—to avenge acts of terror directed against Americans around the world. But now the carnage is the bloody handiwork of Americans as Los Angeles turns into a powder keg in a sweeping interracial war. Deployed to infiltrate the gangs, the Black Ops commandos uncover a trail of diabolical horror leading to a gruesome vision of social engineering....

Take
4 explosive books
plus a
mystery bonus
FREE

Mail to: Gold Eagle Reader Service
3010 Walden Ave.
P.O. Box 1394
Buffalo, NY 14240-1394

YEAH! Rush me 4 FREE Gold Eagle novels and my FREE mystery gift. Then send me 4 brand-new novels every other month as they come off the presses. Bill me at the low price of just $14.80* for each shipment—a saving of 12% off the cover prices for all four books! There is NO extra charge for postage and handling! There is no minimum number of books I must buy. I can always cancel at any time simply by returning a shipment at your cost or by returning any shipping statement marked "cancel." Even if I never buy another book from Gold Eagle, the 4 free books and surprise gift are mine to keep forever.

164 BPM ANQY

Name	(PLEASE PRINT)	

Address		Apt. No.

City	State	Zip

Signature (if under 18, parent or guardian must sign)

* Terms and prices subject to change without notice. Sales tax applicable in NY. This offer is limited to one order per household and not valid to present subscribers. Offer not available in Canada.

AC-94

Don't miss out on the action in these titles featuring
THE EXECUTIONER®, ABLE TEAM® and PHOENIX FORCE®!

SuperBolan

#61444	SHOCK TACTIC	$4.99 U.S.	☐
		$5.50 CAN.	☐
#61445	SHOWDOWN	$4.99 U.S.	☐
		$5.50 CAN.	☐
#61446	PRECISSION KILL	$4.99 U.S.	☐
		$5.50 CAN.	☐
#61447	JUNGLE LAW	$4.99 U.S.	☐
		$5.50 CAN.	☐

Stony Man™

#61901	VORTEX	$4.99 U.S.	☐
		$5.50 CAN.	☐
#61903	NUCLEAR NIGHTMAR	$4.99 U.S.	☐
		$5.50 CAN.	☐
#61904	TERMS OF SURVIVAL	$4.99 U.S.	☐
		$5.50 CAN.	☐
#61905	SATAN'S THRUST	$4.99 U.S.	☐
		$5.50 CAN.	☐

(limited quantities available on certain titles)

TOTAL AMOUNT	$
POSTAGE & HANDLING	$
($1.00 for one book, 50¢ for each additional)	
APPLICABLE TAXES*	$_____
TOTAL PAYABLE	$_____
(check or money order—please do not send cash)	

To order, complete this form and send it, along with a check or money order for
the total above, payable to Gold Eagle Books, to: **In the U.S.:** 3010 Walden Avenue,
P.O. Box 9077, Buffalo, NY 14269-9077; **In Canada:** P.O. Box 636, Fort Erie, Ontario,
L2A 5X3.

Name:_____

Address:_____ City:_____

State/Prov.:_____ Zip/Postal Code:_____

*New York residents remit applicable sales taxes.
 Canadian residents remit applicable GST and provincial taxes.

GEBACK14A